THE WEDDING NIGHT BEFORE
CHRISTMAS

THE WEDDING NIGHT
BEFORE CHRISTMAS

When an opportunity to take everything from the powerful family who destroyed his mother's life falls into Caleb Moore's lap, he needs help from the one person with more power and money than they have—business mogul, Audrey Clarke. The trick is getting her attention. So he approaches the infamous ice queen with an unusual proposition: marriage.

The odds of a snowball surviving in hell are better than the chances of a rich, classy lady like Audrey Clarke marrying a mechanic from the wrong side of the tracks. He only hopes that she might consider a business partnership when she's finished laughing at his marriage proposal.

He never expects her to say yes—or that the ice queen could burn so hot. Because Audrey Clarke isn't cold at all. And if Caleb's not careful, the only thing he'll give her on their wedding night…is a broken heart.

KATI WILDE

THE WEDDING NIGHT BEFORE
CHRISTMAS

THE WEDDING NIGHT BEFORE CHRISTMAS

Also by Kati Wilde

The Hellfire Riders MC Romance
(Discreet Cover Editions)
SAXON
BLOWBACK
GUNNER
BULL & DUKE
STONE
(Original Covers & Ebooks)
THE HELLFIRE RIDERS: SAXON & JENNY
THE HELLFIRE RIDERS: JACK & LILY
BREAKING IT ALL
GIVING IT ALL
CRAVING IT ALL
FAKING IT ALL
LOSING IT ALL

Contemporary Holiday Romances
(Discreet Cover Editions)
SECRET SANTA & ALL HE WANTS FOR CHRISTMAS
THE WEDDING NIGHT BEFORE CHRISTMAS
(Original Covers & Ebooks)
SECRET SANTA
ALL HE WANTS FOR CHRISTMAS
THE WEDDING NIGHT

The Dead Lands

(Discreet Cover Editions)

THE MIDWINTER BRIDE

(MORE DISCREET COVERS COMING SOON)

(Original Covers & Ebooks)

THE MIDWINTER MAIL-ORDER BRIDE

THE MIDNIGHT BRIDE

PRETTY BRIDE

THE MIDSUMMER BRIDE

(COMING SOON)

Wolfkin & Berserkers

BEAUTY IN SPRING

HIGH MOON

TEACHER'S PET WOLF

SHERIFF'S BAD BEAR

(COMING SOON)

Contemporary Romance

GOING NOWHERE FAST[1]

THE KING'S HORRIBLE BRIDE

Fantasy Romance

EVIL TWIN[2]

---

[1] Includes cameos by the Hellfire Riders

[2] Set in the same world as the Dead Lands

THE WEDDING NIGHT BEFORE
CHRISTMAS

AUDREY

H ERE IS WHAT'S SUPPOSED TO HAPPEN: The elevator doors open to Clarke, Incorporated's executive level, and I walk through them, trading the noisy disorder of the outside world for the calm efficiency of my private offices.

Here's what really happens: I stride out of the elevator and stop dead, because everything's off-kilter. A man is taking up too much space in the reception area. And he's standing in the wrong place.

He unbalances *everything*.

Visitors have a clearly designated waiting area opposite the reception desk. Yet he eschewed the comfortable chairs, instead choosing to stand in front of the plate glass window overlooking the lake. And even that's all wrong. Because with his immense height and broad shoulders, his proportions overwhelm the window frame and the enormous body of water that lies beyond it.

It's unsettling. In the place where I most need to be settled.

Damn him. The incongruity of it all is *bothering* me. So much. And I can't look away. His presence seems to tilt the entire room in his direction, as if he's not just tall and broad, but massive enough to create a perceptible gravity well.

A familiar voice comes from the opposite direction. "Miss Clarke?"

With effort, I tear my gaze from the man's back and give the rubber band around my wrist a sharp tug before releasing it.

Snap.

The sting against my inner wrist helps yank my focus away from the man and the mess he made of my equilibrium. Now I have to be careful not to look that way again.

My boot heels click over bamboo flooring as I approach the sleek reception desk. Jessica currently mans the station, her dark curls and lively eyes giving her a girlish appearance that seems at odds with the seductive, buttery voice that emerges every time she speaks. I once told her that she could have made a fortune as a phone sex worker, but Jessica only laughed for a few minutes before stating that she'd rather work for Clarke, Inc. I don't know why she didn't take my advice—I pay her very well, yet it's hardly a fortune—but I'm not sorry she stayed. Personal assistants who are smart, efficient, and who don't make me want to hurl rocks at their heads are hard to come by.

Fortunately, I've found two. Jeremy was in the elevator with me and I assume he's following close behind. Judging by the way Jessica's gaze settles on him and her eyes widen, she's silently asking what distracted me for those few seconds, and he's wildly gesturing his answer.

Which must have been "I don't know," because Jessica asks me, "Are the holiday decorations okay?"

I don't even notice the white lights and pine boughs hanging along the edge of the reception desk until she mentions them. And I'm not going to look around at the rest of the decorations now, because I might get stuck on *him* again.

The fact that I didn't already notice the decorations, though, means that I don't need to look. "They're fine."

"And everything went okay at the rezoning hearing?"

That was also directed to me, but Jeremy jumps in. "Approved, seven to zero," he tells her with a triumphant grin. "So now there's just the two-week comment period, followed by the city council vote. Then, bam! We're good to go."

That isn't quite accurate, but I let it slide and pass a manila folder to Jessica. "The planning commission gave me these forms to fill out and submit to the city council. Please re-staple them properly so that I can look at them."

Because I can *still* see them. Even hidden safely away in their folder. Two documents, exactly the same—except one was stapled on the diagonal, and the other stapled vertically.

Who *does* that? Only a monster.

"Oh no," Jessica breathes, accepting the folder. She glances at Jeremy, who shakes his head.

"It wasn't too bad," he says easily. "I didn't even notice that she'd spaced out until she started snapping her band. That was when Commissioner Melbourne began speaking."

"I only missed Jamison's comments," I inform them. "And that's no loss, because he never says anything worth listening to. Did you already show John Holtzmann into my office, or is he running late for our appointment?"

Because it's just a few minutes before four o'clock, but Holtzmann isn't in the waiting area. Only the gravity well of a man is.

"Oh! He had to reschedule. A weather delay at the airport," Jessica explains with a slight grimace. "It happened after lunch, so you probably didn't see the updates to your calendar yet."

Obviously I haven't, or I wouldn't have assumed he'd be here. "Very well, then. I'll take my tea and—"

"But," Jessica continues in a lower voice and indicates

the waiting area with a subtle lift of her chin. "Mr. Caleb Moore called earlier this morning to set up an appointment with you. He claimed to have an urgent matter to discuss and was disappointed when I told him that you had nothing available until February. So when Holtzmann cancelled, I asked Mr. Moore if he could be here at four. And he could."

So the big man upsetting the balance of my waiting area is named Caleb Moore. And he probably isn't looking out of the window now, but facing this direction—it would be the logical response of anyone anticipating someone else's arrival. Turn and greet them.

But I dare not turn yet. I can easily gloss over the back of a head and a pair of shoulders—they're almost featureless in themselves. It was only his proportions within the waiting area that disturbed me. But a face isn't featureless, and not as easy to look away from. And if his features are as unsettling as his proportions, I might become severely distracted.

Oh, I'm already distracted, standing here and pondering the effect he might have on me. Unless his face is as bland as the back of his head. Is it?

I want to look. I want to look so badly.

Snap.

But not here. Better to be somewhere his proportions won't combine with his face—whatever form it takes—and completely distract me. "Very well. Please bring my tea and Mr. Moore to my office at four," I tell

Jessica. "Jeremy, please take over the desk."

He flicks a salute while Jessica quickly gathers up her electronic tablet. She catches up with me on the wide spiral staircase leading to my offices.

I keep my gaze firmly fixed ahead instead of letting it stray down to where the man waits. "What is Mr. Moore's urgent matter?"

"He said it's regarding the Wyndham estate," Jessica responds immediately. "So I looked him up. Eleanor Wyndham left him everything."

Which would include all the property that I approached Eleanor about less than a year ago, hoping to buy it. The woman refused to sell, claiming that she intended to leave everything to her grandson. I assumed that meant Christopher Wyndham, not a man called Caleb Moore. But whatever his name, it's easy to deduce his reason for coming: to liquify the estate's assets as quickly as possible.

Before veering off toward the kitchen, Jessica adds, "I didn't tell him that you already purchased a different property for your camp project."

Good. I don't need the Wyndham mansion or the surrounding land, but real estate is often a good investment. If Caleb Moore is eager to get rid of it, he'll likely accept a lowball offer. He'll get cash and I'll get an estate that I can unload later for a hefty profit. A win-win.

I like a win-win. But then, I also like a win-lose. Especially when I'm on the winning side.

I usually am.

In my office, I hang up my wool trench and let my gaze skim the room. The decorators were in here as well, but there's nothing distracting, nothing out of place. No blinking fairy lights or uneven garlands.

Jessica has already prepared the office to receive a single visitor, removing the second chair that usually faces my desk, so there can be no *wrong* place for my guest to sit. The desk itself is sleek and seamless, the surface uncluttered. Behind it, sheer glass forms the fourth wall of my office and offers a stunning view of the lake. Today the water is slate gray, darkened by a leaden sky. Even as I cross over to my desk, tiny splatters against the window mark the first snowflakes.

I watch the falling specks of snow, delighting in the wonderful random eddies and swirls of wind that move through them, and all the while breathing deeply, evenly—trying to will away the last of the tension that lingers from the planning commission hearing. Rooms filled with people are among my least favorite things. Even when meetings are governed by supposed rules of order, people still speak over each other, or cough or shuffle papers or whisper, and in the background doors open and close while phones buzz and chime. And even when people follow the rules of order, speaking one at a time, so many talk without saying anything relevant. Or they repeat what others have already said. Simply sitting through the hearing had been exhausting.

Now I'd rather have an hour to myself than speak to yet another person—especially since an enquiry of this nature could be sent via email. But people always want a face-to-face, as if the personal interaction might sway me in their favor. All too often, it does the opposite, and people that I could have easily interacted with through email are almost impossible for me to deal with in person.

But that's why I have assistants to interact for me, when I need them to. At precisely four, Jessica sweeps through the door carrying the tea tray.

Caleb Moore follows. Better prepared this time, I meet him at the center of my office, carefully not focusing on his face but on an invisible spot just behind his head. His features are a blur framed by short dark hair as I shake his hand and invite him to sit. He's no smaller than he was in the reception area—I judge him at about six inches taller than my five-ten in these heels—but my office is so large that even he can't overwhelm the negative space and throw everything off-balance. Grateful for that, I take the seat behind my desk and, as Jessica arranges the tea service, finally allow myself to study him.

It's a good thing that I didn't really look earlier, because his features are absolutely fascinating, an arresting mix of symmetrical and irregular. His nose must have been broken once. Sporting a faint bump, it sits just off-center between perfectly matched cheekbones that rise like cliffs above the hollowed planes of his cheeks. A scar bisects one of his eyebrows, which form heavy slashes over the narrowed brown eyes that are scrutinizing me in return. Each side of his firm lips are almost exactly mirrored to each other from left to right, yet his bottom teeth are slightly crooked, the incisors overlapping each other the barest amount.

Jessica softly clears her throat. "Will that be all, Miss Clarke?"

Snap. "Yes. Thank you. I'll let you know if Mr. Moore and I require anything further," I say, which tells Jessica that I won't need her to stay as my go-between. Instead I want to interact with a man who's already proven to be incredibly distracting.

It's not a logical decision but…well. Even I have my moments.

Neither tea nor coffee sits in front of him, though I assume Jessica offered him refreshment while I was lost in my perusal of his face. So he must have declined. Usually that means my visitor hopes this meeting won't last long, or is nervous and doesn't want to risk a spill.

Caleb Moore doesn't appear nervous. So he likely just wants to get this over with. "Thank you for agreeing to meet with me, Miss Clarke."

Another fascinating incongruity—such smooth words from such a rough voice. And the words don't seem to emerge easily, as if he's unused to deferring to another person. Yet now he needs something from me…

and I don't think he likes being in this position.

He might like it less by the time we're done.

"You have nothing to thank me for yet," I reply bluntly, then remember there are social niceties to convey first. "Please accept my condolences regarding your grandmother's death." And now I need to say something nice about the deceased, but I can only think of one thing I liked about the woman. "I appreciated that Eleanor always spoke her mind."

So few people do. Though, in Eleanor's case, I might have liked her better if I also appreciated what came out of the woman's mouth.

His jaw clenches for an instant before a wry smile quirks those symmetrical lips. "Did she?"

I wouldn't have said so if she didn't. But since I can't interpret his tone, I move on. "I assume you heard that I once approached Eleanor with an offer for her lakeside property."

"That's right," he confirms brusquely, apparently as ready to move on from the topic of his grandmother as I am. "And that your offer was for more than the property's worth—which suggests to me that the project you had in mind is important to you."

"It is," I admit, but won't give him anything else until I see what he's brought me.

"Then I believe we can be of use to each other. I have a proposal for you here."

The briefcase that he sets on the desk between us

appears new, the bottom free of scuff marks. His suit also appears new, and a little too small—though if he's uncomfortable, he doesn't let that discomfort show. As he opens the case, black wool pulls tight around each of his biceps. The sleeves are too short, exposing his wrists and a hint of sinewy forearms. The seams strain at the points of his shoulders, and I'd wager that he can't properly button the blazer across his massive chest, though he might manage the buttons at his waist. He hasn't fastened the shirt's topmost button around the muscular column of his neck, though his neatly knotted tie almost conceals that. His hard jaw is incredibly smooth, as if freshly shaved, instead of shadowed by the whiskers that other men with similarly thick and dark hair tend to sport this time of day. Dark flecks on his snowy white collar suggest that his haircut is also new, and that the barber was either careless or hurried, and didn't completely brush away the trimmed hairs.

A jagged swirl of black ink peeks up from the left side of Caleb's collar. Hardly enough of the tattoo is visible to even begin to guess at the design, yet I can't stop myself from trying to picture what would complete that artwork. How far down the length of his neck does it extend? Just to his shoulder? Down over his chest? Or was the rest of the tattoo decorating his back?

Oh no.

Snap.

I jerk my focus away as he withdraws a presentation

folder from the case. His hands and his long, blunt fingers are roughened by labor—I can still feel the scrape of his thick calluses from when we shook hands.

How can I make sense of him? "What is your profession, Mr. Moore?"

His dark gaze clashes with mine as he holds out the presentation folder for me to take. His voice contains a steely note of challenge. "I'm a mechanic."

"Ah." Satisfaction fills me as the pieces slide into place. So he was invited at the last minute to a four o'clock appointment and hastily prepared for this meeting. But he didn't have time to find a suit that fit his big frame, instead grabbing the nearest size to his own off the rack. Yes, that makes perfect sense. And the ill-fitting suit might have been adorable on someone else. On him, the knowledge of how and why he wore it simply makes him more compelling.

I take the folder, extrapolating from what his answer told me. He's the Wyndham heir, yet isn't named Wyndham. And unlike a Wyndham, he works a blue-collar job. He also doesn't own a properly fitted suit, which suggests that he doesn't socialize with the Wyndhams, either. Now he's here to sell the property Eleanor left him.

Given what I know of the Wyndhams, though, it's hard to believe that he *can* sell it. "The family didn't contest Eleanor's will?"

"They did. They are." Caleb Moore snaps the briefcase

closed and sets it aside. "Which is why I've come to you with that."

He indicates the presentation folder—which is surprisingly neat, the included papers perfectly aligned. Given how quickly he threw together his own appearance, I expected something messy. But this is an incredibly pleasing package.

Yet Caleb Moore is far more interesting, so I return my focus to him. "What do you propose?"

In that rough voice, he tells me, "I don't have a hope in hell of fighting the Wyndham lawyers alone."

"I imagine not," I reply, and see where he's going with this. "So you want me to take on the cost of the legal battle to secure your inheritance…after which you would sell the property to me, minus the legal fees I incur?"

"What I'm proposing is more complicated."

The quirk of his lips is fascinating, as is the interplay of that tiny smile with the unyielding hardness of his brown eyes.

Snap. "How complicated?"

"I've outlined it there."

He gestures to the folder again. Reluctantly, I drag my gaze from his face and read the title page through the translucent cover.

A PROPOSAL OF MARRIAGE

TO SECURE THE WYNDHAM ESTATE FOR

AUDREY CLARKE AND CALEB MOORE

In a gruff voice, he says, "I want to marry you."

CALEB

S*NAP.*
Snap.
Snap.

If the woman facing me wasn't repeatedly plucking that damn rubber band around her wrist, I'd have thought shock had frozen her solid. Or that she'd stroked out. But she isn't looking *through* me now, as she did when I was shown into her ridiculous office. Her attitude then was dismissive and vague, and she obviously hoped to get rid of me as quickly as possible. And her smug little "Ah" after I told her my occupation was followed by a clear reluctance to even glance at the proposal I spent two goddamn weeks typing up and poring over, as if nothing I do could possibly be worth a minute of her precious time.

But I've got her attention now.

I have no clue what's going through her gorgeous head, though. Her narrowed gaze is locked onto my face but she might as well be a sculpture made of ice, because she doesn't give a damn thing away. I expected laughter, maybe. Or outrage. She's pure class, and I'm a grease monkey who just aimed way above my station.

I'm not the first Moore to do so, though. And the Wyndhams ground my mother into the dirt for it. So I'll do anything—*any goddamn thing*—to take everything from them. Even marry a woman who looks straight through me.

Though I know it won't come to that. In a second, she'll be laughing. Or she'll put me in my place. Hell, maybe that's what this silence is—the way that classy, elegant people tell someone to get the fuck out. Maybe I'm supposed to be collecting my proposal and slinking away.

Snap.

Fuck. The ball is in her court now. So why isn't she lobbing it back?

If she's still playing at all. If so, I know what offer she'll send my way. She already said it—her lawyers fight the Wyndhams' lawyers, and she'll buy the property from me at a reduced price. She would be assuming some risk, though. If the Wyndhams won, she'd be out a fortune in legal fees.

I have a pretty damn good idea of what those fees will amount to. Because I've already tried to go that route. But the law firm I approached wouldn't even take me on as a client, claiming the chances of beating the Wyndhams weren't solid enough—and if I didn't win, they'd never recoup their costs from me. So my next stop was at a bank, hoping to secure a loan for a legal retainer. But they basically told me the same damn thing: no one would bet against the Wyndhams. The bank manager gave me something on my way out the door, though.

"My advice?" he called after me. "Find yourself a rich wife!"

I don't want a wife. But the idea ate at me. Not finding a wife, but a business partner. Because there had to be someone out there who would bet against the Wyndhams.

That someone might be Audrey Clarke. But I didn't even know who she was until a few weeks ago, drunk as fuck and hanging out at my friend Patrick's house after Thanksgiving dinner. That was when Patrick's younger brother, Mike—who is currently studying for his MBA—told me that Audrey Clarke had once tried to buy the Wyndham property, and then slurred his way through all the reasons why the CEO of Clarke, Incorporated would be the ideal candidate.

Not for marriage. If she only offers to pay legal fees in exchange for the property, I'd be fucking thrilled. The proposal is simply about making sure she really stops to look at me. That was Mike's advice, too.

"Dozens of people ask Audrey Clarke for money every damn day. So you've got to stand out, make her notice you. Then you've got to ask for a whole damn pie. Because although you only want a single slice of that pie, if you only *ask* for a slice, most companies like Clarke's only give a tiny bite. But if you ask for the whole thing… well, maybe you'll get the slice you want."

Like I asked for a slice from the law firm and the bank. But they didn't even give a bite. Maybe Audrey Clarke won't, either. But I won't lose a thing by trying.

So the day after Thanksgiving, I looked her up. And found damn little. There's almost nothing about her on the company website or in the press, except that she's always listed near the top in articles like "The Wealthiest Women in the World"—and *is* at the top when the lists don't include women who inherited their money. But I still don't even know what Clarke, Incorporated *does*. Spends money to make more money, it seems like. The tagline on her website only reads, "Investing today in a better tomorrow." Which sounds like some bullshit.

More helpful were the online forums where entrepreneurs talk about their interactions with her. There I discovered that anyone who comes into a meeting with Audrey Clarke without a solid business plan might as well not even set up an appointment. And a single factual error or typo in a proposal can be a kiss of death.

So I put my proposal together as carefully as possible.

Yet she's barely looked at it. She just stares at me. And now I'm thinking some of the other comments I read on those forums aren't so far off. There was a whole lot of *ice queens*, *rich bitch*es, and *conceited cunt*s tossed in there. Most of that, I dismissed as the disgruntled bull- shit some men sling around after they've been rejected by a woman, even if it's just a business rejection. But the ice? The snobbery? Yeah. I can see that.

And Christ, this place. The Clarke building is a pre- tentious lakeside palace made up of steel and glass. And she doesn't mingle with the rabble of her own company, as far as I can see. She's up here in an executive suite all by herself—a suite that takes up at least four levels. I could fit two of my apartments in her office alone. No, six of my apartments, because I'd have to stack them up just to fill the space up to the ceiling. Yet the only shit she even has in here is a desk and a chair. She sits in front of thirty-foot-tall windows like a queen laying claim to everything around her.

But even though her manner is as cold and as empty as this office, she's as gorgeous as everything outside that window. Goddamn fucking beautiful. Her pale blonde hair is scraped back in a ponytail that falls halfway down her back. Her face is like some kind of fairy princess's, with finely arched eyebrows, a delicate nose, and lush pink lips.

But her eyes. Her goddamn eyes. They are glittering

chips of ice, pale blue and freezing cold. The kind of eyes that can flay a man alive.

Snap.

Teeth gritting, I glance at the rubber band. Just a cheap yellow one. She's snapped that damn thing so many times, the skin of her inner wrist is bright pink.

I clench my fists, barely stifling my impulse to reach out and stop her from snapping it again. What she does to herself is none of my business.

But I can't stand the idea of her doing it again. And although I was waiting for her to respond, impatience grips me now.

With frustration roughening my voice, I tell her, "I'm not talking permanently, of course. I know marriage isn't a conventional business arrangement, but—"

"It's perfectly conventional," she cuts in smoothly, as if she didn't just spend the past three minutes staring at me in complete fucking silence, like a woman stunned by my oh-so-conventional proposal. "Though perhaps not as commonplace as it once was, securing property through marriage is a tradition as old as the vows themselves. So, go ahead. Let me hear your pitch."

My pitch. She wants to hear *my pitch?* Isn't that why I wrote that damn business plan? But she hasn't even looked past the cover page.

Shit. Okay. I've read that business plan a billion fucking times in the past few weeks. So I dredge up what I can recall from the "Executive Summary" section.

"I propose a marriage contract that would lock me into selling the Wyndham mansion and surrounding estate to you for thirty million dollars, in exchange for Clarke, Incorporated handling all legal fees incurred while fighting the Wyndhams—and those fees would be reimbursed from the monetary inheritance I'll receive if we win. The marriage itself would be dissolved after all challenges to Eleanor Wyndham's will are settled and probate is granted. I believe this arrangement would be mutually beneficial to all parties involved."

Christ. That last bit looked great on paper, but sounds really fucking stupid said aloud. But she doesn't look amused. Instead she nods once…as if considering it.

"Thirty million for the property?" she asks after a moment. "Including all of the mansion's furnishings and artwork?"

"Yeah."

Her eyes narrow again. "It's worth five times that amount. Even if we have to fight the Wyndhams for ten years, the legal fees still won't make up the hundred-and-twenty million dollars' difference. Why sell so cheap?"

"Because I want to get rid of it."

"And the Wyndham fortune?"

"I'll get rid of most of that, too." I'll look for a charity that helps women like my mother. "Except maybe hold enough back to start up a recycling company and name it Wyndham Trash."

Her lips twitch and she leans back in her chair, her icy gaze still on my face. "Why propose marriage when simply asking me to take over the legal battle would suffice?"

I prepared a bullshit answer for this, too. "Because if something happens to me, chances are the estate would go to them anyway, even if I leave a will. They'd probably contest that, too. But if I'm married—and if that woman has your resources—it won't matter. It will all go to you, instead."

She seemed still before, but now her stillness seems preternatural. "Do you expect something to happen to you, Mr. Moore?"

I shrug. "Not especially. But we're talking about a whole lot of money. Fuck knows what'll happen if the Wyndhams get desperate. I wouldn't put anything past them."

Not after what they did to my mother. And I shouldn't have said 'fuck' in this elegant office. But Audrey Clarke doesn't react in any way, except to subject me to another of those scrutinizing looks.

"So you inherit a fortune, but your only plan is to sell the property and start a trash company to besmirch the family name. Do you intend to do nothing for yourself with that money?"

"Not really. I don't give a shit about the money."

"Why pursue it, then?"

Because I'll settle for a slice of pie, if I have to. But

what I really want is the whole goddamn thing.

Or rather, I don't want the Wyndhams to get any of it. Not even a bite.

"Revenge," I say bluntly. For all the good it will do. My mother is dead. She'll never see any of the Wyndham money, never know the comfort it could have brought, never know the satisfaction of seeing justice done. "Or just out of spite."

Her brows arch. "Spite?"

"Yeah." And some rage, a little more hatred. "Spite."

"Spite," she echoes softly, then laughs—a sound so full and rich and amused, so damn unexpected, it almost knocks me out of my chair. "Oh, I like that."

That reply is unexpected, too. And I can't stop my own grin in response.

Her gaze drops to my mouth. A hard *snap!* follows, then she elegantly rises from her seat, arms folded beneath her breasts. Half turning away from me, she moves to the window and looks out over that million-dollar view.

My view is worth a hell of a lot more. Audrey Clarke is a statuesque column of ivory and gold from head to toe. Her cream-colored sweater clings to every curve and looks soft and touchable. Just like her pants. When I first saw her, I thought she was wearing a long skirt until I watched her walk away and realized they were wide-legged trousers. High-waisted, too, cinching around her middle in a wide band. But all that ivory material doesn't conceal the round shape of her ass or the long lengths of those legs, as if her pants were tailored specifically for her. Hell, I bet they were. I bet her entire outfit costs more than my monthly rent. Yet she doesn't wear any jewelry with it. No rings, no necklace—though by rights, she should be dripping with rocks and ice. But no. Just soft, flowing clothing—and that rubber band.

Snap. "How do you propose to handle sleeping"—*snap*—"and living arrangements?"

"It's all laid out in the business plan." Which she apparently still has no intention of reading, because she simply looks over her shoulder at me until I continue, "Nothing would change. I'd stay in my apartment, you'd stay in your place. I'd keep my head down for the duration of our marriage, keeping to myself and focusing on work. I wouldn't do anything to embarrass you or your company."

She tilts her head slightly. "Do you think I'm easily embarrassed, Mr. Moore?"

I have no fucking idea what she is. I can't make any sense of her. "I suppose you'd have to care about what others think of you, first."

She smiles again. "Yes. I would. And what about consummation?"

"Consummation?"

"Intercourse, Mr. Moore. Sex traditionally seals a marriage contract."

Christ. Instantly I picture her beneath me, staring up

with those icy eyes and lying absolutely still and silent except for the jiggle of her tits and the soft gasp escaping those plush lips every time I slam my cock into her. Giving it to her hard and rough. Trying to crack that ice, to make her pussy melt around me. She'd probably be so goddamn tight—

"Mr. Moore?"

"Yeah. Sorry." I shift in the seat, pulling at the edge of my jacket to cover the brainless, aching bulge of my cock. Goddamn it. These new pants were already a bit too small and now they are *really* too fucking small. "Some stupid shit popped into my head. I got off track."

"Ah." She watches me with a faint smile. "My head does that, too."

"Okay. Great." I spear a hand through my hair, trying to reel in my wayward thoughts. "Uh, I wouldn't… I wouldn't require physical intimacy as part of the contract."

Her brows arch again. "No?"

"No." Just as I stated in my business plan. And it took a long damn time to find a phrase as benign as *physical intimacy*. Not that it matters when the next thing out of my mouth is, "There's no reason why we'd need to talk to each other much, let alone fuck."

"Hmmm," is her only response and she looks out the window again. While I sit in this little chair with a hot iron pipe wedged behind my zipper. *Hmmm.* Then she turns back to me with a "I don't believe that would be satisfactory."

Big surprise there. "What part?"

"Failing to consummate the marriage." Taking her seat again, she faces me across the wide desk. "Or at least, failing to *appear* to consummate it. If the purpose of a marriage agreement is to prevent the Wyndhams from acquiring the estate in the unlikely event of your demise, we should not give them reason to argue that our marriage was an illegitimate one. Failure to consummate a marriage is a common reason for annulment."

Is she just yanking my chain now? We both know there isn't going to be any goddamn marriage. If people like her married people like me, I wouldn't even be here.

I never meant for her to take my proposal seriously. Yet it isn't a joke, either. None of this is. Not from the moment thirty years ago when Robert Wyndham told a young maid working in his family mansion that he loved her and wanted to marry her before knocking her up. Not from the moment he wrecked his yacht, drowning himself and the rich fiancée he proposed to after getting what he wanted from my mother. Not from the moment the Wyndhams closed ranks and told my pregnant mother that she'd never work in a respectable house again.

And this shit about consummation? There isn't a chance in hell Audrey Clarke would ever let someone like me touch her. So she's either amusing herself—or this is payback. Wasting my time just like she probably believes I wasted hers.

Now she continues as if she's still considering this. "It wouldn't be difficult to create the appearance of a legitimate marriage, however. A honeymoon, followed by sharing the same home. Preferably my house, as I'd be more comfortable there."

As opposed to living in the shithole that she assumes my apartment is? "Why not lie? If it ever became an issue, just say that I fucked your pussy raw every single night."

Her hand jerks. With a soft *fwap*, the rubber band breaks and shoots across the desk, landing between my feet. Audrey blinks once, twice. Then says, "I'm a terrible liar."

"Yeah, right." A powerful businesswoman who can't lie? "What if someone asks a question you don't want to answer?"

"I don't say anything at all. And sometimes I look at them like this."

Holy fuck. I thought she looked at me with ice in her eyes before? That was a tropical heatwave compared to the withering, glacial stare she levels at me now. If I wasn't so fascinated by the change that comes over her, my dick would have shriveled up and I'd have been tempted to slowly back away.

Instead I laugh. "So without saying a word, you tell them that you can't believe they ever had the balls to ask you such a stupid fucking question."

She grins, and all that withering disdain vanishes.

"It's a useful tool."

"I bet." Because it's bothering me, I bend over and sweep up the broken rubber band, then don't have a clue what to do with it. There isn't a trash in sight, and I'd feel like an asshole tossing it onto that spotless desk. I *am* an asshole, so feeling like one shouldn't matter. But I shove the band into my pocket to toss later.

She drums her fingertips against the presentation folder. "Have you finished your pitch or are there other points you want me to consider?"

"Basically, the property is the only point. Either you want it enough to fight the Wyndhams in court, or you don't." Briefcase in hand, I stand. "I suppose you'll need time to read through my proposal and to consider any changes to the—"

"I don't need time to consider it."

Shit. If she had any intention of entering into an agreement—even one as simple as paying for the legal fees—she'd consult her lawyers first, get an estimate of cost. My jaw clenches, then I force out a polite, "I understand. Thank you for your time, Miss Clarke."

"Mr. Moore." She remains in her chair, her voice amused but her gaze intense. "I'm accepting your proposal."

I stare at her, uncomprehending. "You are?"

"I am."

"What part?"

"All of it," she replies easily. "With necessary amendments regarding our living situation, since the arrangements you suggested weren't satisfactory."

The fuck…? "But the marriage part was satisfactory?"

"It was." Her eyebrows twitch into a slight frown when I slowly sink into my chair, drag my hands through my hair. "Mr. Moore?"

"Caleb," I tell her gruffly. Since we're apparently getting married. "Call me Caleb."

"Caleb," she agrees. "I'm Audrey."

Audrey. Who will soon be my *wife*. What the hell have I done? What the hell has *she* done, accepting me? That wasn't part of the plan. Not really. I only came looking for a slice but she gave me the whole damn pie.

But that's good. That is damn good. Because that means the Wyndhams are fucked.

Still. *Holy shit.* I pass a rough hand over my face to make sure I'm awake. Eyes open. Not dreaming.

I drop my hand back to my side. "What now?"

Her lips quirk. "Did you not plan beyond this point?"

"I didn't really think I'd get to this point. So, no. That's my only plan." I gesture to the folder on her desk.

Nodding, she states, "That's probably for the best."

"It's for the best that I'm unprepared?"

"Yes. So that our plans won't be in conflict as I decide how to take on the Wyndhams. From this point on, Caleb, we'll be doing this my way." Reaching forward, she taps a button on her desk phone. "Jessica, Jeremy— please join Mr. Moore and me in my office."

Doing this my way. Fair enough. I came to Audrey Clarke because she can stand against the Wyndhams. But I don't think there's a chance in hell that Audrey and I won't soon be in conflict. Because this is already grating against my nature. I'm not the type to stand back and let someone else handle everything. Especially when it's my shit being handled.

But for now, I'll grit my teeth and let her do her thing. Because even sitting still, she moves fast.

So do her assistants. The woman—Jessica—could have been a transplant from the law firm I visited a few weeks back. Everything about her says 'serious business,' from her stylish pantsuit to her sensible heels. The kind of assistant I expect to see here. But Jeremy, he's something else. Beneath his suit jacket, he sports a Star Wars tee. And his scuffed pair of red Converse sneakers aren't the shiny dress shoes I figured an executive assistant would be required to wear.

Which means Audrey must not care. At least, not too much. There's probably a line, though. I bet that if I'd come to this meeting in my work clothes, she sure as hell wouldn't be considering marriage. It's a long way from geeky T-shirts under a trendy suit jacket to Carhartt work pants permanently stained with motor oil.

Marriage. I still can't believe she's considering it at all, no matter what I'm wearing. She must want that mansion real fucking bad.

Styluses poised over their tablets, her assistants

come to stand on either side of my chair—which feels awkward as hell with me seated between them. I don't like sitting while other people are standing nearby. But I might as well be a part of the chair for all the attention they give me. Their entire focus is on Audrey.

She starts right in. "Contact the Methodist church on Alder and secure the first available date that Reverend Foster can officiate a wedding ceremony—unless you prefer another venue or have a different religious affiliation?"

The last part is directed to me. "None," I tell her.

She nods and tells her assistants, "The Methodist church, then."

Beside me, Jessica scribbles onto her tablet screen. "And who should I say is getting married?"

"Caleb and I are."

"Congratulations!" they cheerfully say in unison, not missing a beat. Which is fucking incredible, because *I* still haven't caught up to the idea yet. But maybe they're used to Audrey Clarke throwing crazy shit their way.

"Thank you," she replies and rises to her feet, heading over to the window again. Now I'm the only person in the whole damn office who's sitting. Getting up isn't an option yet, though. Not unless I hold my briefcase in front of my crotch. Because my dick still isn't playing nice inside these too-tight pants, and the view she presents of her sweet ass isn't helping any. "As soon as you've nailed down the time for the ceremony, create a guest list. I want the invitations printed and sent out within two days."

This time, with her back turned, I see the "oh shit" glances that her assistants exchange.

"Within two days?" Jeremy echoes with a faint squeak in his voice. "Printed and mailed?"

"Yes."

"And the guest list should include…?" That comes from Jessica.

"After we've finished here, Caleb can give you the names of his friends and family. More particularly, however, I want every single adult Wyndham to receive their own invitations, each one delivered by a special courier who is instructed to give it directly to the recipient." She glances back at me. "We'll put the family on notice right away."

With a hand delivered invitation to go fuck themselves. "Sounds good."

Jessica scribbles again. "And your guests will be…?"

"Every Clarke employee. And my local social contacts—but only the ones whose company I enjoy."

"All five of them?" Jeremy asks, sharing a quick grin with Jessica.

I assume he's teasing her but Audrey answers as if he is serious. "Yes. All five."

"And…your parents?" Jessica asks that with a slight hesitation.

There's no hesitation in Audrey's flat answer. "No."

"All right," Jeremy says with a warning glance toward Jessica. They both wipe their expressions clear when Audrey turns back, taking her seat again.

A frown creases her brow as she gazes at me. "Two days isn't fast enough. I want the Wyndhams to be on edge even before they receive the invitations. Are there any events tonight that Caleb and I can attend and either the Wyndhams or their friends will also be present?"

"The mayor's tree lighting ceremony is tonight at seven," Jessica answers immediately. "It's followed by a cocktail party in the atrium of the Clement Hotel. No doubt several people from that social circle would be there."

"Did I receive an invite?"

"You declined it."

"Then un-decline it. And add a plus one—if you are free tonight, Caleb?"

"Yeah." Jesus. A cocktail party? "Do I need a tux for that?"

I'm going to end up blowing a week's paycheck just on clothes. But it'll be worth it, I remind myself. When the Wyndhams start panicking, it'll be worth every penny and every second I spend in a monkey suit.

"Just put on what you would normally wear for a date," Audrey says to me, and it's real fucking adorable that she thinks I'm the kind of guy who has the time or money to take women out on dates. "I'll get my lawyers started on the marriage contract. Jessica and Jeremy can keep you apprised of what will need to be done before the wedding—the license, tuxedo fittings, and so on. And if there's anything you need, simply contact them. Or… me. Jessica can give you my number and you can, uh, text. Text my phone."

She lifts the device awkwardly, as if to demonstrate what a phone is—or as if she's not used to giving a business associate permission to contact her directly. Judging by the way her assistants blink and look at each other, it might be the very first time.

It's odd. And kind of cute. But I'm more than ready to get the hell out of here and figure out what just happened. "Sounds good," I say and grab my briefcase. "What's the plan for tonight?"

She glances at her phone, checking the time. "Will six-thirty be long enough for you to get ready? My driver can pick you up then. Just let Jessica know where."

Hell no. I'm not going to be picked up anywhere by some fancy driver in some fancy car. "Since we're running short on time, how about I just meet you at the tree lighting ceremony?"

"Very well." She stands at the same time I do, and extends her hand over the desk, smiling. "I believe it will be a pleasure doing business with you, Caleb."

Yeah. A pleasure. I don't what the fuck it'll be, but 'a pleasure' isn't on the list of descriptions that jump into my head.

But touching her hand? Shit. That feels real damn

good. It's a shame there won't be more of that. Her fingers are soft and cool and surprisingly strong.

And because this isn't just a business arrangement we're agreeing to, a handshake doesn't seem like enough. So when it's over, I bring her hand to my lips, press a kiss to her knuckles. Gruffly, I tell her, "Thank you."

For a long, long moment, she only stares at my face. Like she did when I first sprang the proposal on her. But this time her silence doesn't last three minutes. She abruptly comes back to herself—then yanks her hand away, shaking out her fingers before sliding it into her pants pocket.

Crisply she says, "I'll see you at seven, Mr. Moore."

All right. Message received loud and clear. *Don't touch me.* That message should have felt just fine. Seeing her shake off my kiss shouldn't dig at my gut and have my teeth gritting in frustration. This marriage doesn't have a thing to do with touching her. It's about making sure the Wyndhams get what's been coming to them for a long damn time.

Anything else is a whole other pie. A pie that I won't ever get a bite of. So only a stupid fuck would waste time wondering how it tastes.

My proposal isn't about wanting Audrey Clarke. It's about spite.

That's all that I'm here for.

AUDREY

I'M PUTTING ON MY LIPSTICK WHEN, IN THE MIR-ror's reflection, I see Jessica sweep into the apartment I keep in my office building. She stops dead, her eyes widening.

"Oh my god," she exclaims in wonder. "You're finally wearing that smokin' hot red dress!"

Because the only reason Caleb and I are attending this cocktail party is to draw attention and put the Wyndhams on notice. But my clothes probably aren't the reason why she came in. "Did you secure a date for the ceremony?"

"Almost." She gestures to her headset. "I've got the church on hold. They can squeeze you in at two p.m.

on the twenty-fourth, but they have a Christmas Eve service at four, so we have to be finished by three-thirty. And they are asking us to leave our decorations there—which means we need to go with a Christmas theme."

"That's fine." Or is it? Jessica and Jeremy have the twenty-fourth off, as do all of my employees, because even the most efficient ones become easily distracted that close to the holiday. So I shut down the offices from Christmas Eve to New Years' Day. "Would you be willing to work that day?"

"Whether I'm officially on the clock or not, you couldn't keep me away. And Jeremy wouldn't miss it, either."

"Good." Before she turns away, I pick up Caleb's presentation folder from the vanity. "Send a copy of this to Bradford right away so that he can draw up the marriage contract. I've written my amendments in the margins and included a brief description of how I want him to proceed regarding Eleanor's will. I'll follow up with an email later tonight."

"Will do." She takes the folder and glances down at the cover page—and the title of the proposal. A grin splits her face as she reads it, then she flips through the rest of the business plan. "Oh god. He even put in information about the Wyndhams and their lawyers under the 'Competition' section. This is so cute."

No, it's not. And Caleb Moore isn't, either. I turn back to the mirror as Jessica heads out, still smiling and reading through Caleb's proposal—a proposal which isn't like him at all. Instead, it's what he wanted me to think he was. But just like the broad shoulders that strained the seams of his suit, the person Caleb Moore really is kept pushing through the image he attempted to present. As if he couldn't keep that person contained, no matter how hard he tried. Some of the language he used was straight out of that business proposal—but the way he really speaks slipped through, too. So did his resentment and anger toward the Wyndhams.

Certainly, he took an unusual approach by asking me to marry him. But that tepid business proposal does not faithfully represent a man who admits he's pursuing his inheritance out of spite. No one has *ever* given a reason like that to me before. Yet Caleb Moore did.

He could have lied and given me some other, altruistic reason—a lot of people try to—yet he didn't do that, either. Caleb probably *can* lie; he just doesn't bother to. He'd rather say what he thinks.

And I like that about him. A lot.

I head into the closet to search for a pair of boots suitable for both a freezing town square and a cocktail party. This isn't the first time I've had to go directly from the office to a social function, so I keep a selection of clothes and shoes in this apartment, which is essentially a glorified dressing room. I don't sleep here, even if I work past midnight—and that happens far more often than I attend social functions.

The knee-high leather boots I find won't do much good to insulate my feet from the snow, but unless the mayor decides to give a long speech—and he usually doesn't—I shouldn't be outside long. I zip them on and step in front of the mirror, critically assessing my appearance.

Smokin' hot, Jessica said. I want Caleb to think so, too. But even if he does…if he's anything like other men that I've dated, he might start off saying I'm hot. But he'll end the night telling me that I'm too cold.

An unfamiliar emotion pangs deep in my chest. A touch of fear accompanies it. Is it nervousness? I'm not sure what to call it. But some part of me must recognize what the emotion is, or fear wouldn't follow in response to it.

If it is nerves, though, that's strange. I don't get nervous. I'm usually never worried or afraid, either. That's part of the reason many people—not just men I've dated—call me cold.

I'm not cold. But I don't express myself in the same way many people do. I can barely tolerate people touching me or touching them in return. Affection isn't physical for me; it's mental and emotional. So I show affection by showing interest—and it's impossible for me to feign interest if I don't care about what someone is talking about or doing. But even when I do care, I know my manner comes off as lacking in warmth. If I could act, maybe I could fake it. But I'm not any better at pretending than I am at lying. So I can't be anything other than who I am.

Caleb seems to be the same. Not that his brain works like mine. But that he can't help being himself.

Who that person is…I guess I'll find out. But so far, I know that he's a man who'll kiss the back of a woman's hand.

And the effect of that kiss had been a stunning onslaught of curiosity and desire. During our meeting, everything about the way Caleb looked and moved and spoke made me think of touching him. Yet actually doing so never crossed my mind—not beyond my usual handshake. I can tolerate those because handshakes are governed by rules that almost everyone understands and follows. A handshake is used as a greeting or to seal a deal—and it should be brief. So they're only uncomfortable when someone lingers too long.

Caleb lingered. And I can still feel his warm breath against my knuckles and the firm press of his lips. Yet it didn't make me want to pull away and put space between us again. Instead all I could imagine was those lips making their way up the length of my arm. Instead sheer lust nearly blazed through my skin.

Because I'm not cold. My emotions are always raging. But from an early age, I learned to contain those fiery outbursts of emotion—because when I didn't, I was the one who got burned.

And that's what most people see, I suppose. The

container. Which, combined with all of my other tendencies, puts most people off.

But it apparently didn't put Caleb off. Because he could have easily come in with a different plan and I probably would've agreed to it. Yet he wanted marriage. *For spite.* A proposal as unusual as it is fascinating—and as ballsy. Much like the man himself seems to be.

I like that about him, too. Very much.

Enough to marry him, at least.

If liking Caleb Moore was my only reaction to him, though, I might have proposed an alternative to his plan. But liking mixed with sexual attraction? That's more than enough for me—and more reason to marry than I ever expected to have.

Especially since I never expect to marry for love. I wish for love, of course, yet I know the bulk of my appeal lies in my bank account. No one has loved me before and I don't expect anyone to start now. So I always assumed that when I married, it would be a partnership rather than a love match—and the most I hoped for was liking the person I partnered with. A relationship of mutual respect and friendship, perhaps, while understanding that someone would only settle for such a tepid marriage because I'm rich.

Yet nothing about Caleb Moore is tepid. And although he needs my money to defeat the Wyndhams, he doesn't seem to want a fortune for himself. Which means the entire arrangement is far more exciting and fascinating than anything I ever imagined for myself.

So is my body's response to him. Because I don't show affection physically, but sexual attraction is much different. And I cannot stop thinking of what he said. *Just say that I fucked your pussy raw every night.*

I know he didn't mean it literally. That would be painful and not very sexy. He meant that I should say he fucked my pussy long and hard and repeatedly—and it made me yearn for something I never have before. A man who takes a woman long and hard and repeatedly must want her desperately. The thought of ever being wanted like that hadn't ever occurred to me, yet the possibility must have occurred to Caleb for him to say such a thing.

Perhaps he will never want me that badly. He might find my manner as cold as every other man does, and turn away from me. Yet he kissed my hand…so maybe he'll want to kiss me again, in many other places.

I would like that very much.

And after the wedding, we'll be living together. If he's attracted to my appearance, perhaps he'll want to consummate the marriage, too. Perhaps he'll want to fuck my pussy raw.

I think I would like that very, *very* much. So if I can tempt him with my looks as well as my money…I will.

After a final check of my lipstick, I collect my coat from my office and head downstairs, where Jeremy and Jessica are both at the reception desk. Working late, and they probably won't go home anytime soon. Not after what I just dropped on them.

Jeremy holds up a small black box. "Pierre came through with an engagement ring for you to wear tonight—and it's as ostentatious as you requested. No one at that party will miss seeing a rock this big. He'll return tomorrow with a selection so you can pick out a design you like."

"Thank you." I don't like wearing rings because I can always *feel* them. As if the band around my finger constantly calls attention to itself. But I'll ignore the discomfort as best I can.

As I slip the diamond on, Jessica asks, "Do you want one of us to come and help you deal with the crowd?"

"No. I'll ask Caleb to stay at my side. So I should be okay." And I couldn't ask for better assistants. But since my gratitude might not be as obvious to them as it feels to me, I say it aloud. "I realize that giving you less than two weeks to plan a large wedding creates a substantial amount of extra work for you both. Please know that I deeply appreciate your efforts."

Jessica grins. "We'll earn our Christmas bonuses this year simply by getting these invitations out on time."

"You earn your bonuses every year, or I wouldn't give them." I glance at her tablet. "Did Caleb send you the names of his guests or should I remind him?"

She shakes her head. "He said he doesn't have any family. So I asked if he wanted to invite his friends and he said not to bother."

"Ah." I pull on my coat, considering that. "He was surprised that I accepted his proposal and hadn't thought beyond that. So perhaps he also isn't prepared to think about inviting anyone yet. Ask again in a few days. We can send those invitations later this week. It's only the Wyndhams' invitations that I want to rush."

"About that..." Jeremy starts off hesitantly before plowing ahead. "When the city council looks at the rezoning request for your camp project, Christopher Wyndham is likely going to be the deciding vote. At least, that's what you said before."

"Yes. I said that." Because it's true. A few of the city council members are making noises about my project potentially increasing noise and crime in the area, along with a bundle of other ridiculous complaints that I've already countered with studies and data from similar projects. I suspect they fear losing donations from wealthy constituents who are concerned about property values on that side of the lake. A worry that I've also countered with data, but it's an unfortunate truth that many people believe what they want to believe, regardless of statistics and logic.

"If you go in with Moore against the Wyndhams," Jeremy continues, "that might piss off the councilman."

"I'm sure it will."

He looks at me in confusion. "This project is your baby. Yet you're going to risk him voting against you?"

"Yes." *And do everything I can to make sure he doesn't.*

Jeremy and Jessica share a stunned glance, then she laughs and says, "You must *really* want that property."

I'm not good at lying. So I say nothing and let them believe what they like. But it's not the Wyndham estate that I want.

I want Caleb Moore.

CALEB

Wʜᴀᴛ ᴛʜᴇ ʜᴇʟʟ ʜᴀᴠᴇ I ᴅᴏɴᴇ? Between the time I leave the Clarke building to the time I arrive at the town square, that question pops into my brain a thousand fucking times. The answer's easy enough—I'm marrying Audrey Clarke to make certain the Wyndhams get what they deserve—but I can't wrap my head around it. But by the time seven o'clock rolls around, it finally starts sinking in.

I'm marrying Audrey Clarke.

Which might be the biggest goddamn mistake I'll ever make. But if the Wyndhams lose their shit, even a nightmare of a marriage will be worth it.

Maybe it won't be so bad, though. She wants me to move into her place, wherever that is. Probably some giant house on the lake. I'm not the kind of shithead who's going to complain about living in a mansion. She probably has an army of cooks and housekeepers, so it'll be like staying in a fancy hotel. And she'll likely stick me into a room as far from hers as she can. Chances are that our paths won't even cross on a daily basis.

But whether the marriage is a mistake or not, how much time are we talking about—a year? Maybe two? It's not like I'm doing anything else important in that time.

I won't be doing anyone else in that time, either. Maybe that won't be so easy, especially since Audrey will be so damn close. But I've got a hand. So I'll invest in some lotion.

Lotion that smells like she does. Not that she'll ever let me get close enough to smell her. *Don't touch me.* That message was clear after I kissed her hand.

And I've got to keep reminding myself of that, because the second my gaze lands on her pale blonde head, I'm acutely aware of the hot weight of my cock. As if it's a dog ready to sit up and beg for her attention. Christ. It's one mutt that better behave. And hopefully it'll learn real damn quick not to react to her presence, because she's sure as hell not going to offer us any treats.

She's tall enough that she can see over most of the crowd—and I'm tall enough that it isn't hard to spot me as I make my way toward her. She stays where she is, not a part of the crush of people but standing at the edge of the square, a slender figure wrapped in a cream trench coat, her hands tucked in the pockets. It's not snowing anymore, but the wind off the lake is bitterly cold, brightening her pale cheeks and nose.

She's wearing lipstick now, a velvety red that makes it impossible not to notice how lush and soft her mouth is. Especially when a smile lights up her face as I draw close.

And there goes my fucking dick. Not hard yet, but feeling real damn thick and heavy.

A high school band is playing some shitty-ass Christmas music as loud as they can, so I don't try to speak until I'm only a few feet away. Then I greet her with a "So I guess you didn't change your mind, then."

"Change my mind?" She frowns slightly. "Of course I didn't."

As if she didn't even *consider* changing her mind in the past few hours. But I did. A hundred million fucking times. And each time I reminded myself why I brought that ridiculous proposal to her in the first place.

And because backing out on the deal now might ruin the whole damn thing. Rescinding an offer of marriage might sting her pride and fuck everything up. Probably not, because she obviously wants that estate. So she'd likely agree to a different deal and offer to just pay the lawyer fees in exchange for a reduced sale price.

But I still want that whole pie and the certainty that the Wyndhams won't squeeze their way out of this. No matter what happens.

She continues frowning at me, and the wind picks up a strand of her blonde hair from her ponytail and blows it against her cheek. She brushes it away. "Have *you* changed your mind, Caleb?"

"No." And I see she came prepared to announce our engagement to everyone. "Nice rock."

She glances at the giant diamond before shoving her hand back into her pocket. "It annoys me. And I couldn't put my gloves on over it. But if we are to be…"

Whatever we're to be, she doesn't finish. Instead her pale blue gaze settles on something behind me. I glance back, see a teenage couple exploring each other's tonsils with their tongues, and look away again because no one wants to see that shit out in public.

But Audrey is still watching them, and she says, "I should have done that. Right?"

"Done what?"

"Kissed you as a greeting." Now her gaze returns to me—and settles on my mouth. "That is what engaged couples do. Kiss each other hello."

Shit. All at once, tonsil hockey in a public place isn't such a turnoff. Because the crowd seems to disappear as she takes a hesitant step forward, her attention focused on my mouth.

Moving in to kiss me. But not because she wants

to. Because she should. Like wearing that ring, even though it's annoying her. And no matter how badly I'm aching to taste her, I'm not interested in a kiss from a woman who doesn't even want to touch me. Who's just doing it for show.

"No," I tell her abruptly and she immediately freezes. "You don't need to."

"Oh?" Her gaze searches my face for a brief moment, then she turns to face the tall pine tree set up in the middle of the square. "Okay."

I expected relief, but that sounds like disappointment in her voice. Is it? I study her profile but she's hard to read. I decide the disappointment was just my imagination when she starts talking again, because she's obviously not thinking about my mouth the way I'm still thinking of hers. Of tasting all that sweet heat, then watching those lush red lips suck their way down my cock.

Christ. I'm hard as hell now, but it's not my dick that needs to heel. It's my brain. I need to stop thinking about fucking her.

I force myself to focus on what she's saying. About our wedding. And a date. Followed up by a "Will you have any scheduling conflicts?"

"On Christmas Eve?" I shake my head. "I've got the day off. Christmas, too."

"And what of the following week? A honeymoon will help sell the appearance of consummation and a legitimate marriage. We could stay that week at my lodge—unless you would rather travel? We can stay anywhere in the world you wish to go. Perhaps you prefer the tropics over the snow."

"A lodge is fine." A snowy lodge where we'll be bundled up in heavy clothes and I won't have to watch her prance around a beach in a bikini. But I let myself imagine that bikini for a second—then reality slips in and I shake my head. "Hold up. I work that week. So I'll have to ask for the time off first."

"Or you could quit your job," she suggests. "You'll be a wealthy man soon."

"I would be if I was keeping the Wyndham money. But I'm not. So I better keep my job, instead, because I sure as hell like to eat."

"As do I." Amusement lightens her voice and a slight smile curves her mouth. "You'll always have plenty to eat if Wyndham Trash becomes profitable."

She seems to enjoy saying 'Wyndham Trash' almost as much as I do. "You don't like the family, either?"

"Not particularly, no."

"Why? What'd they do to you?"

She shrugs. "Nothing to me. But if you need a complete accounting of reasons to dislike them, my lawyers will soon compile a list to help bolster your case."

An entire list? "You don't fuck around, do you?"

"No. I don't." Eyebrows furrowing, Audrey casts me a glance that seems a little confused—or a little hurt.

"And I won't after our marriage, either. Will you?"

Did she think I meant fucking around as in literally *fucking around*…? "I— No," I answer, but cheating wasn't even what I was talking about. Shit. But the mayor gets up on the platform and starts speaking into the mic, and I can't figure out how to tell her she misunderstood me. Not that it matters. Because we've just established that we won't be fucking other people and we won't be fucking each other while we're married.

Only the Wyndhams are getting fucked. And that's just fine by me.

Except I'm a damn liar. It's *not* fine by me. I can pretend that it is for all of ten minutes, as we watch the tree light up and then head to the fancy hotel that over-looks the town square, where the cocktail party is being held in a huge ballroom with a glass roof. Then Audrey hands off her coat to an attendant and I see what she's wearing beneath it.

And Christ help me. Her long-sleeved red dress is sexy enough from the front, softly clinging to her breasts and her hips before hugging everything down to her knees, where her boots finish the job of making her legs look a mile-fucking-long. Then she turns, and I realize the dress doesn't have a back. The material drapes from her shoulders and gathers at the base of her spine, and in between there's just skin and more skin.

No bra strap. Which doesn't mean no bra, not with all the shit women have available to boost and cover their tits, but hers are small enough that maybe she didn't bother. And I can't stop myself from glancing down when she faces me again. The red material of her dress is soft and thick and mostly conceals everything, unless you're really looking. And fuck knows, I am *looking*. Hard enough to notice the subtle protrusion of her nipples, to see that they'd be like fat berries against my tongue.

"That looks soft and comfortable," she says, and it takes me five full seconds to realize she's talking about the flannel shirt I've got on, because nothing else about me is soft or comfortable. And I'm real fucking glad that I changed out of that damn suit, because my heavy twill pants do a better job of concealing what she does to me.

She told me to dress for a date, so I settled for what was clean and might stand up to the cold outside. And I suppose I look like some giant lumberjack escorting a sexy fairy princess into this damn party, but I can't bring myself to give a shit if we don't match. She takes my left arm as if declaring that I belong to her, sliding her fingers into the crook of my elbow and pressing up against my side until I can feel the curve of her hip against mine and the softness of her breast against my arm.

Putting on another show, like the diamond she's wearing—and the kiss she intended to give. But I can't say no to the way she's clinging to me now.

"I need you to stay with me until we leave the party,"

she says as we enter the ballroom.

"Afraid I'll start trouble if I'm on my own?"

Or maybe thinking that I'll get tossed out of here, since I clearly don't belong. Everyone else is wearing business suits or what I assume is the golf club version of casual, with sweaters over white collared shirts and charcoal slacks. And there's no high school band here. Instead an ensemble of string musicians are making Christmas carols sound like Mozart.

"I'm not afraid that you'll misbehave." She glances over at me, her brows arched and her gaze sparkling with curiosity. "Should I be?"

"Nah. I'll be good." I'll try to, at least.

That incredible smile curves her red lips again, and I am so fucking screwed. A year or more of being any-where near this woman—and not touching her the way I want to? It'll be torture. I should call off this wedding now.

But I won't. I know damn well I won't. So maybe I'll have blue balls for a year. Wah wah. A man who can't control himself around a woman isn't much of a man. So I'll deal with it. Her effect on me will probably fade, anyway. My dick's been hard before. But that's just lust or whatever. Arousal. That shit always goes away. Eventually.

My hatred toward the Wyndhams isn't going away. Not in a year, not in thirty years.

Audrey steers me toward the bar, where she orders

sparkling water in a champagne flute. Pale eyes glittering with humor, she raises her drink. "To spite."

"To spite," I echo with a short laugh and clink the neck of my beer bottle against her glass.

She takes a sip, her icy gaze scanning the room. Searching for any Wyndhams or their acquaintances, most likely. Judging by the crowd that's already gathered, most of the people here didn't bother to attend the tree lighting ceremony, or they watched it from the balcony overlooking the town square. I don't recognize anyone but that's hardly a surprise.

And we're already snagging attention. I can't miss the glances being thrown our way. Because of my size, I'm used to those quick looks being followed by hesitation before someone approaches me. Sometimes there's even a little fear. But the incredible thing is…in this ballroom, it's not *me* who's making them hesitate. I'm not scaring anyone.

Audrey is.

Their eyes follow her as if she's a dangerous animal—though a beautiful one. Like a snow leopard that they want to get close to, maybe close enough to touch. But they don't, as if worried she might rip them to shreds.

I glance down at her fingernails. They're short and painted a glossy black. Not scary at all. And I'd kill to feel them clawing up my back.

Now I'm curious to see who around here *isn't* afraid of her. "Are any of your friends attending this thing?"

"My friends?"

"Yeah. Your assistant said you have five."

"Oh. Yes. Well, here is one now." That gorgeous smile spreads across her lips again, and she lets go of my arm, stepping forward to greet…a priest. Small and wiry, with a lean face and black suit and a distinctive white collar, he wears the kind of gentle, amused expression that I usually see on grandfathers who are showing off pictures of their grandchildren.

Well, shit. That's not what I expected. And despite her smile and the way she approached him, Audrey doesn't hug him or kiss his cheek. She only holds out her hand for a brief handshake before reaching back and entangling her fingers with mine.

"Caleb Moore, this is Reverend Foster," she introduces him. Not a priest, then, but a pastor—and now I remember that she mentioned the Methodist church about two blocks away from here. "He'll be performing the marriage ceremony."

His gaze flicks down to our joined hands and his smile broadens. "Our Almighty Father truly does perform miracles," he says and extends his arm. "I'm pleased to meet you, Caleb."

Audrey's fingers are still tangled up with mine, so I put my beer bottle aside and wipe the condensation from my palm before shaking his hand. "Reverend."

"You're a lucky man." His gaze returns to Audrey. "And you caused quite the uproar in the office this afternoon, young lady. You couldn't have made these arrangements before today so that you'd have more time to prepare? Christmas Eve isn't far away."

"It's too far away, in my opinion," she replies. "But Caleb only proposed to me today. So unless we visit a justice of the peace, Christmas Eve is the earliest date available."

"You got engaged *today?*" His brows shoot upward. "Then why the rush?"

"I don't think you'd approve of my answer, pastor," she says in a serious tone.

He chuckles. "Perhaps I wouldn't. But it certainly wouldn't be the first time I've heard that answer from an overeager young couple. Still, I approve of how you are swiftly taking the appropriate responsibility."

Shit. I start to laugh, because the preacher is thinking that we're pregnant, and she's just thinking that he won't appreciate our reason for marrying. And I suppose spite and money aren't the best answers to give a reverend.

Though she briefly appears puzzled by my reaction, after a second Audrey grins. "Ah," she says and then laughs, too. "You mistake me, pastor. Caleb and I haven't had sex."

His mouth opens but nothing comes out for a moment. Then he nods and declares, "Then I heartily approve of your restraint, Audrey." Amusement seems to shake through him as he glances at me. "Yours as well, Caleb. Resisting temptation is not always easy...

but I think I better understand your need to rush the wedding."

He really doesn't. But before Audrey can set him straight on that score, too, a man joins us. And him, I recognize.

"Mayor Espinoza," Audrey greets him, but doesn't let go of my hand this time.

"Merry Christmas, Audrey. And to you, Reverend Foster. How good of you all to come." Like any politician, he nods to me and pretends to care who I am when the reverend introduces us, then glances back to Audrey. "Can I steal your attention away from these gentlemen for a few minutes?"

"No," she tells him bluntly, yet disentangles her fingers from mine. "But I will give it to you for a moment."

Her attention. Because he asked to steal it. Now she folds her arms over her chest and walks a few feet away to talk with him in relative privacy—and I realize she takes almost everything literally. Which explains some of the responses she's made since I've met her.

"She's a special woman," the reverend says beside me.

I nod, my gaze drifting down over her bare back and settling on her sweet ass. "Damn special."

There's a light snort of laughter, then he says in a more serious voice, "I've heard that the mayor plans to set off fireworks at eight o'clock."

Is he thinking I want to do something for Audrey then? Some romantic gesture, maybe—like it's New

Year's Eve? I've got no clue, but I nod again. "So noted."

Audrey and the mayor turn back toward us, Espinoza casually placing his hand against the small of her back to guide her. Against her bare skin. She stiffens as if he jabbed her with a hot poker and I can't stop my reaction. A growl rips from my chest as I step forward, fists clenched.

Instantly Espinoza pulls his hand back, grimacing and holding it up as if to show me he's not touching her anymore. Tangling my fingers with hers, I pull her in close again.

"Forgive me, Audrey," he tells her. "It's just habit."

I snarl. "I suggest you break that habit."

"Of course. You're right," he agrees easily and offers Audrey a toothy smile. "My office will contact yours regarding that donation. And please accept my congratulations on your engagement."

Her fingers tighten on mine. "Thank you."

"Mr. Moore. Reverend." He nods at us both and takes off, already aiming that toothy smile at his next target.

"I'd best go butter up my other donors, as well," the pastor says with a grin. "Congratulations again, Audrey. I'm very pleased for you. And Caleb, I hope we will soon have the opportunity to speak again."

I nod, then wonder if that'll be more often than I assume. Like maybe every Sunday. When he's out of earshot, I ask Audrey, "Do you attend his church?"

"No. But he has been a good friend since I was

fourteen, and once said that if I ever got married, he would like to officiate the—"

"Audrey!" On a waft of musky perfume, a red-haired woman dripping with diamonds appears out of nowhere and rises up on tiptoe to kiss the air beside Audrey's cheeks.

Audrey stands stiffly, not returning the gesture, and greets the woman with a cool, "Hello, Jennifer."

Either oblivious or ignoring that icy response, Jennifer titters and exclaims, "You *never* attend these parties! So tell us, how did Paul persuade you to come tonight?"

Paul, the mayor. And 'us' is apparently the man who's catching up to her, a bourbon in one hand and a glass of champagne in the other.

"Look, darling. It's Audrey. And..." Jennifer swipes the champagne from her husband and casts me a speculative look from head to toe before dismissing me. Her gaze catches on Audrey's ring and then shoots back to me, her voice dropping to a purr. "Well, well, Miss Audrey Clarke. Is there something you'd like to share with the class?"

"I don't share," Audrey says bluntly.

She eyes me curiously again. "Not even a name? You seem so familiar. Have we met before?"

"No." Not unless she brought her car in for service. Which I doubt.

Her husband steps forward, extending his hand to me. "Dan Pearson, head of Pearson Electronics."

"Caleb Moore," I answer. "Head mechanic at Phillips Auto."

"Oh?" His wife seems to freeze for the barest moment, faint distaste twisting her lips. Then she looks me over again like a piece of meat. "How…interesting. Isn't it, darling?"

Pearson grunts and checks out Audrey's tits.

"The Pearsons are good friends of the Wyndhams," Audrey tells me before informing Jennifer, "Caleb is Eleanor's sole heir."

"O…ohhhh?! Is that so?" Her eyes flare wide, then a grin of sheer rapacious delight splits her face, and Pearson tears his gaze from Audrey to give me another look over. "I *knew* you looked familiar. So you are Christopher's…?"

"Bastard?" I offer bluntly. "No. I'm Robert's."

"The dead brother?" She seems taken aback, but only for an instant. "That's *fascinating*. And you are engaged?"

Audrey answers. "We are."

"Does Meredith know?"

"I don't see how she would. You are among the first people we've told."

"Oh." Eyes glittering with excitement, Jennifer clutches her hands to her chest, the champagne sloshing dangerously near the rim. "Will I be treading on your toes if I share the news? Everyone will be so"—her gaze slides over me again—"*astonished*. And thrilled for you, of course!"

"Tell anyone you like."

I suspect she would have even if Audrey hadn't given permission. As it is, the woman damn near breaks a speed record pulling a phone from her tiny bag.

Audrey leaves her to it, turning away and glancing up at me. "Robert Wyndham didn't marry your mother?"

"No." When I said bastard, I meant it literally.

"Ah." Her gaze searches my face. "Is that what's behind the spite?"

"Some of it." Though not most of it. The truth is, my mother's life would have been a living hell if she'd married him and lived in that house with the other Wyndhams. They'd have destroyed her.

Just like they tried to do anyway.

So it's not that he didn't marry her. It's that the love and marriage he did offer was a lie, because he didn't think she was good enough to become his wife. Or good enough to even offer her some support, despite her being pregnant with his kid. And the rest of the family thought the same.

But they didn't leave it at simply *thinking* she was trash. And they didn't leave her alone, either.

Audrey tilts her head, studying me. "If he had married her, would you be like the rest of them now— just another Christopher, Meredith, or Sylvia?"

"My mother would never have let me become what they are."

Something in her eyes clouds. "She was a good mother?"

"Yeah." My voice roughens. "She was amazing."

"You were fortunate, then." Her fingers gently squeeze mine and she begins leading me away—but we don't get more than a few steps before we're stopped by a "Miss Clarke!"

After that, the floodgates open. As if everyone watched the Pearsons approach her and walk away unscathed, so they line up to do the same. Though most of them aren't as bad as the Pearsons, just about every single one shows a marked change in attitude toward me when they discover a mechanic might be worth a couple hundred million dollars. At first, it's amusing. After a while, though, it just pisses me off.

I can't tell if it bothers Audrey. Mostly she doesn't seem to give a fuck—about anything. After a while, people are lucky to get more than a "hmmm" from her in response. Yet her fingers cling tighter and tighter to mine.

Finally I've had enough of this shit. If our purpose here was to give the Wyndhams a heads-up, we accomplished that just by talking to the Pearsons.

I'm pretty sure the next person to come up reads how irritated I am, because he gives a hesitant smile before slowly backing away. I glance down at Audrey. "We ready to get out of here?"

"Almost." Her gaze is fixed across the room. "There's Neil Prescott."

The Wyndhams' lawyer. And speaking to him is

someone I finally recognize. "He's talking to the fucker that I tried to hire."

"Keith Shayne?"

"Yeah. He said I didn't have chance in hell of winning against the Wyndhams, wouldn't even take me on. Because I couldn't afford his firm's fees."

"Be glad of it," she tells me. "He's lazy and incompetent, yet arrogant enough to believe that he's worth five hundred dollars an hour."

"So he's a shitty lawyer?"

"I'd say so. In fact, telling you that he would have lost is probably the only time he was ever right about anything."

I frown. "You think I'll lose?"

"No. *He* would have. My lawyers won't. Because they *are* worth what I pay them." Pulling me forward again, she adds, "They would also tell me not to speak with opposing counsel at all. So instead we'll take up space on the dance floor right in front of them, and you can watch Shayne weep as he realizes that you have an incredibly wealthy fiancée, and that the thousands of hours his firm could have billed you just slipped through his incompetent little fingers."

More spite. Which makes me laugh and washes away most of my irritation—but the second I've got Audrey Clarke in my arms, I don't give a damn about the lawyer. I don't even look in that direction to see his reaction. Because all that matters is hers.

She doesn't stiffen when my hand flattens over the warm, bare skin at the small of her back. Instead she sighs and her upper body seems to melt against mine, her head resting on my shoulder, her warm breath skimming my throat. Her fingers lightly stroke down my arm, petting me. Petting my *sleeve*, I realize. As if enjoying how soft the flannel is. But, hell. I don't care why she's touching me. As long as she is.

And fuck me, she smells good. I don't know what fragrance that is. A little bit like the green tea she was drinking earlier, but sweeter. And so subtle that I want to chase the scent up to her skin, and bury my face in her neck or anywhere else she sprayed that perfume.

We aren't doing much more than swaying, but she doesn't seem to care that I'm not pulling out the ballroom moves that some of the people around us are. The extent of my dancing talent begins and ends at rubbing up against a woman's ass while some heavy bass thrums in the background. And slowly rubbing up against Audrey's ass to a string version of "White Christmas" might sound damn good to me, but I doubt it would to her.

I glance down, tilting my head so I can see her face. Her eyes are closed. She's not watching Shayne, either— or the other lawyer, Prescott. And when we slowly rotate back around in that direction, I see that they've moved to another part of the room, anyway.

So we're done here. But I'm not in any rush to leave.

"Holy shittola!" A familiar voice and laugh sound from behind me. "Here I was thinking that I'm pretty fucking special, but now I see they're just letting anybody in."

Grinning, I swing around with my hand still at Audrey's back and holding her against my side. "Did they actually let you in or did you crawl in through a bathroom window again?"

"Those days of drunken revelry are over, my friend." Patrick brushes his hands down his front as if sweeping away the sawdust that usually covers him from head to toe. He appears real sharp tonight, sporting a suit and a crisp red tie. "I've got a classy girlfriend to keep happy. Not that you'd know what keeping a woman happy is like—" His gaze lands on Audrey and the grin he's wearing drops into stunned disbelief. "Well, fuck me. You crazy bastard. You actually asked her."

"I did." I'm feeling like a goddamn king as I introduce him. "Audrey, this is Patrick Connell—a friend of mine from way back when."

And she looks straight through him. Completely ignores the hand he sticks out, and looks through him.

His grin fading, he pulls back his hand and drags it through his red hair. "Yeah, so." But he's a good-natured fucker, so he adds, "So you're getting married? For real? Congratulations and all that."

"Thanks." Though a pit opens up in my gut when Audrey doesn't react to his sincere congrats. Not even with the *hmmm* she gave to all the rich assholes we've talked to. "It's just for that thing with the inheritance."

"Uh uh." He gives Audrey's figure a once-over before glancing back at me, brows rising. "Right."

She's not even looking through him now, but staring off into the distance at nothing, as if she's bored as hell. Molten lead starts filling up my chest.

I fight to keep the anger out of my voice. "Where's Karen?"

Patrick gestures vaguely behind him. "Talking to some people from work. I'd bring her over to introduce her… But yeah, I think not."

Because he doesn't want Audrey to pull this pretentious shit with the girl he's crazy about. Doesn't want some rich snob insulting her. Just like she's insulting him.

My throat aches with fucking *shame* as I agree, "Yeah. So maybe later?"

He laughs. "Sure. In a couple of years, maybe. Whenever Elsa releases you from her castle and lets you play with the filthy rabble again, yeah?"

Fuck. Jaw clenched, I nod.

"I hope it's all worth it, man. See you around."

My throat's so tight I can't say a damn thing. I pull her into my arms again, but I'm not enjoying it now. I'm not enjoying *any* of this now. My first impression of Audrey Clarke wasn't the best, thinking she wouldn't ever associate with someone like me, but I changed my mind about that after we met up in the town square. Hell, I started liking her. And although she was reserved with everyone, she didn't act like she was better than them. Or better than me. But the past hour should have taught me why that was, too. Just like it did to every other fucking person here, that inheritance made all the difference to her. Made me acceptable. But obviously my friends aren't.

Yet I'm still hard as fuck, holding her. This cold woman who looked straight through my best friend as if he didn't exist. I'm so fucking disgusted and it's not all directed at her. A whole lot of it is aimed at myself.

I hope it's all worth it, man.

"Caleb?" She's blinking up at me, her brow furrowing as she searches my face. "Are you…upset?"

"Pretty fucking pissed, yeah."

"Why?"

"Because I don't really give a shit if you're a snobby little ice queen with me. Be as pretentious or as frigid as you want, act like I'm not good enough to even lick your feet. I'll put up with any goddamn thing if it means the Wyndhams get what's coming to them. Unless you act just like them and treat my friends like trash again. Then we're going to have a serious fucking problem."

"Like trash?" Her face goes utterly still. "I did that?"

"Yeah, you fucking did."

Pulling away, she looks out over the crowd. "Where are they—and what were their names?"

"Christ. He was that invisible to you? It was just one guy. There." I point him out. "Patrick. And he didn't deserve the condescending shit you pulled. Yeah, maybe he only works in a furniture shop, but he's one of the best men I know." And just saying that truth unleashes the rage and disgust building up in me. I'm choking on them as I tell her, "Fuck this shit. I'm going to get some air."

Before I completely erupt. Tearing away from her, I head for the nearby balcony. A dozen pairs of French doors are open to the outside, where the cold air slaps my face and some sense into me. The fireworks that suddenly explode overhead are like the ones going off in my brain, a goddamn epiphany of color and light.

This marriage isn't going to work. And it's *not* fucking worth it.

If it was just the money, just the lawyers, yeah. But marry someone who'll treat my friends exactly the same way the Wyndhams treated my mother? I wouldn't be any better than them. And I'm no fucking saint as it is.

I can and would tolerate a whole lot of shit if Audrey's snobbery was just aimed at me. But the way she treated Patrick—and would probably treat anyone else I know and care about? No. I won't accept that. Not even to destroy the Wyndhams.

Fuck this marriage. If she still wants to pay for the lawyers, I'll let her. If not, I don't give a shit. I'll find some other way or just let this all go. And try to get over the shame of wanting a woman who would have looked at my mother the same way the Wyndhams did.

It's time to call off this bullshit engagement.

People are streaming out onto the balcony to watch the fireworks, but I push through the crowd and return to the ballroom. Audrey's not where I left her. I scan the tops of heads, searching for a pale blond ponytail. She should be easy to spot.

I don't see her anywhere. Goddammit. I just want to get this over with. Tell her the wedding isn't happening—and then go and get so fucking drunk, I forget the way she felt against me. The way she smelled.

"Hey, man." Patrick stops beside me, Karen on his arm—both of them heading toward the balcony. "You looking for your girl? She just took off that way. Looked kind of freaked out by the noise."

My chest tightens. "Freaked out?"

"Yeah. Was all"—he hunches his shoulders and sticks his fingers into his ears before straightening up again—"so maybe you better check up on her. And she explained about earlier. About having a tough time with crowds, then being overstimulated and spacing out. So, you know. It's all good."

"We invited her to our ugly sweater party next Saturday," Karen adds. "And she said that would be fun. So make sure to bring her."

"Yeah," I tell her, barely listening. Searching for Audrey again. "Which way?"

He points and I surge through the crowd in that

direction. Remembering the reverend telling me about the fireworks.

Not telling me about them. *Warning* me about them.

And remembering Audrey, saying that she needed me to stay at her side until we left the party. But I abandoned her right in the middle of a crowd—which she apparently has a tough time dealing with. Now I don't see her anywhere.

Because she was freaked out. Was she afraid?

Or *hurt*?

With worry clawing at my stomach, I stop at the coat check. She's not there. But how hard can it be to find a woman who looks like she does?

To the attendant, I rasp out—"Blonde ponytail. Red dress. Fucking beautiful. Which way?"

"That way," he says immediately, pointing.

So I'll ask every person in this hotel until I find her. And when I do…

I don't know. Not anymore.

Not that she's likely to give me any choice in the matter. Not after what I said to her.

But I'll deal with all that after I find her. After I make sure she's all right.

As soon as I know she's okay, I'll follow my original plan. Get drunk, and try to forget. But not her scent or her touch.

Instead I'll try to forget how I just fucked everything up.

AUDREY

T HE HOTEL ISN'T CURRENTLY HOSTING A CON-
ference, so it isn't difficult to find an empty
meeting room to hide in. I sit in the quiet and
the dark, on the floor and with my back against the wall.

I know now what the unfamiliar emotion is, the
pang in my chest that's accompanied by fear. It's vulnerability. Because I opened myself up to being hurt by
Caleb. And hurt me, he did.

A snobby little ice queen.

He's so different from anyone else I've dated—and
different from most people that I know. So I hoped he
would see me differently than most people do.

But the only difference is that I'm marrying him.

If he still wants to marry me after I was rude to his friend. I suppose it'll depend on whether his need for revenge against the Wyndhams is stronger than his anger at me. And he'd been *furious*. Believing that I'd deliberately insulted his friend. Believing that I'm the same as the Wyndhams.

That pang strikes again, deeper. My throat tightens until the ache there matches the one beneath my breast.

From across the room comes the sound of the door opening. A light flicks on, a burst of dull red through my closed eyelids.

Without opening my eyes, I tell whoever it is, "This room is in use. Please shut off the lights and close the door behind you."

Darkness falls again. The door snaps shut.

But I'm not alone. Footsteps come toward me. Only hotel employees have access to the electronic keys that can open these rooms. But I know without looking who this must be.

My throat feels raw. "They let you in here?"

"They let you in, too," Caleb points out softly. "So apparently all anyone has to do is ask."

"I don't have to ask. I own this hotel."

He falls silent for a moment. The gravel in his voice seems rougher as he says, "They let me in because I told them you're my fiancée and I was worried about you. I came to make sure you're all right."

"I will be." But I'm not yet. And I can't pretend that I

am. "In a little while."

"Do you want me to stay with you?"

No. It should be so easy to say. Just a little lie. But I'm no good at lying, so I remain silent. That usually works as well as a lie, because people assume the answer I don't give.

Caleb ignores that unspoken answer. I hear him moving closer, the shuffle of his boots and the slide of his back against the wall as he sits on the floor next to me.

Then his hissed—"Shit, goddammit. What the hell did I just sit on…?" His voice flattens. "Is this your engagement ring?"

"Yes."

"You took it off?"

"It was bothering me."

He makes a sound of relief. "Okay. Good. And what else is…is this a handkerchief? It's damp." A bleak edge scrapes through the observation. "Were you crying?"

"It's a pair of panties," I tell him. "They were bothering me, too. So I took them off."

"But…they're damp." Incredulity rings through the statement.

"I know. That's why they were bothering me. I could *feel* them. And it was…distracting."

"But they're *really* fucking damp."

"Of course they are!" I snap, my frustration boiling through. "I'm sexually attracted to you, and you were touching my bare skin and holding me close. So I was physically aroused. But then I hyperfocused on the wetness and I couldn't feel anything else, or think of anything else. So I spaced out and was rude to your friend."

"You didn't talk to Patrick because you were focused on how wet your pussy was?"

"That's what I *just* said."

"And I'm making sure I heard it right. Because you just blew my fucking mind—and I don't want there to be any more misunderstandings between us, especially when we're talking about how me touching you gets your cunt so hot and wet."

Not just his touch. His voice, too. Especially when he talks like that. I squirm against the floor, suddenly too aware of the needy ache between my legs. "Don't," I tell him, my breath shuddering. "Don't talk about it. I'm trying not to think about it now."

"All right." His tone gentles. "You told Patrick and Karen that you don't do well in crowds?"

"I don't."

"Because of the noise? You get overstimulated, you told them."

"That's different. I have difficulty interacting with a lot of people even in a quiet room." Sensory overstimulation just makes it harder. "It's too much to process."

"So you have, what—social anxiety?"

"No." I don't get anxious. "I get overloaded, trying

to figure out what people mean. Because they rarely just *say* what they mean. And sometimes they say the opposite of what they mean, and I can't easily parse their body language and tone and make it match their words. Like Jennifer Pearson. She says 'interesting' but that's *never* what she's really saying. So many people do that. And sometimes I know how to respond. If someone asks 'How is your day going?' I know it's an empty question and they don't want any answer except 'Good.' But most of the time, it's not like that. And it's exhausting trying to follow along."

"That's why you take things so literally."

"Also why people think I'm too blunt." *Or frigid and condescending.* "I say what I mean. You do, too, mostly. So it's easier talking with you."

"Mostly?" He pauses. "I'll be more direct with you. And just ask me if you're not sure of my meaning."

Warmth blooms in my chest, big and bright and beautiful. "I will. I appreciate it so much," I say to make my gratitude explicit. "Thank you."

"Ah, fuck. Baby, you don't need to thank me for that."

"I know I don't." Then I laugh. "See? Whenever people say, 'You don't need to do that,' it's not what they mean. Usually they mean, 'I don't want you to do that.'"

"I meant 'You shouldn't feel obligated to thank anyone for treating you with a basic level of decency.' With no effort on my part, I can make your interactions with me easier. And if you *ever* need something from me, I'll give it to you. It's that fucking simple," he says gruffly. "So you better tell me what works for you and what doesn't."

"All right. But don't go and look up any of this on WebMD. Because there's no neat diagnosis or category for me. So you might think I have Asperger's but I just share a few of the same tendencies—but only a few. Like I don't have any trouble making eye contact. And I have some obsessive compulsive behaviors. But so many people try to figure out what I am based on a few things they've observed me doing, and then act shocked when I do something they didn't think I would. It's irritating."

"So I shouldn't play online psychiatrist."

"Please don't. I don't need you to figure me out. My doctors and I have done a good job of it already."

"I won't, then. But tell me what you think I should know."

The bright warmth in my chest swells. *What you think I should know.* Not demanding everything. But asking what I want to give. "I have trouble understanding non-verbal cues—and I prefer it when social interactions follow rules and are easy to make sense of."

"Like conducting a business deal?"

"Yes. That's easy. But I don't always understand the rules of personal interaction. Sometimes I think there *aren't* any rules, and that's so frustrating to me. So it's easier when I have a context, because there's usually a guideline for that interaction. Employer, employee. Donor, donee. Investor, investee—"

"Or a marriage engagement?" he suggests in a low voice.

"Yes," I say softly. "Though I'm still figuring out those rules."

Like how to choose endearments, because he's apparently already settled on one for me. *Baby.* As if he wants to hold me and take care of me.

Or whether to kiss him hello. To which he said, *You don't need to* but meant *I don't want you to.*

That deep ache opens up in my chest again. I try to ignore it, because I'm supposed to be telling him—"I don't react well to pain. And I don't like things that aren't in the right place, or out of order, or cluttered, or physically uncomfortable. And sometimes I get distracted by those things. But it's not really a distraction. It's more that I become hyperfocused on that thing, and that hyperfocus means that I'm not paying attention to something I *should* be paying attention to."

"Like Patrick."

"Yes. Though maybe that was also overstimulation because I was *feeling* so much. Usually it's loud noises and flashing lights that do it. Then I have to give my brain a break."

"Like now," he says gruffly. "In the dark."

I nod.

"Is that what the rubber band on your wrist was for, too?"

"That's for when I feel myself hyperfocusing on

something—that little bit of pain pulls my focus in a different direction. Long enough for me to realize what I'm doing and stop. So I have coping mechanisms that mostly work. And I usually recognize when I'm becoming distracted or overstimulated."

"But not always."

"No. That's why I typically bring Jeremy or Jessica to events like this."

"But tonight you had me. Fuck." He exhales a breath that sounds forced through clenched teeth. "I should have stayed with you like you asked me to. And I shouldn't have called you what I did."

"Why? You meant it." *Snobby little ice queen.* That vulnerable opening in my chest starts to ache again. Because even before he promised to speak directly to me, Caleb said what he thinks. *Frigid and pretentious.* "Didn't you?"

"I meant it then." His voice hoarsens. "But now I know that I was badly fucking mistaken."

Knowing that he changed his mind should ease the ache, but it only deepens. As if I'm becoming more and more vulnerable simply by sitting here in the dark with him. And more afraid of that vulnerability.

Prodded by that fear, I scramble to my feet. "I'm ready to leave now."

Almost instantly Caleb is at my side, an enormous shadow looming next to me in the dark. "Then I'll help you find your car."

"My driver will pull up to the front of the hotel. I can find that alone."

"I'm sure you can." He reaches the conference room door and opens it for me. I don't look up as the light from the corridor falls over us, don't let myself become distracted by his fascinating face. "But there are rules about this. An engaged man makes sure his woman safely gets where she's going."

His woman? "That sounds like an antiquated rule."

"That doesn't mean it's not worth doing."

Perhaps. "All right. You may escort me to my car."

"I *may?*" A deep laugh rumbles from him. "I would have anyway. But hold up for a minute."

His fingers catch mine, and he swings me around to face him—then backs me up a single step. My back hits the corridor wall and he's all around me, his head bent toward mine. I lift my gaze but only as far as his mouth, my breathing shallow and my pulse racing.

His voice is low and intimate. "What do you want me to do with this?"

The diamond ring. He holds it in his palm, the gold band looking ridiculously small in his big hand.

I sigh. "I should wear it."

"Because that's what engaged women do? But I say there should be some rules that we won't give a fuck about. If a ring bothers you, don't wear one."

"Yes, but...I only borrowed this one for the night. I shouldn't risk losing it. And I'm more likely to if I'm not wearing it."

As it is, if he hadn't brought the diamond with us, I'd have forgotten it on the floor.

"All right, then." He lifts my left hand, and my heart thumps as he slowly slides the ring onto my finger. As if this gesture has more meaning than simply putting on a ring so it won't get lost. As if he's righting something that almost went wrong.

He settles the band into place, then turns my hand over and draws a slow circle in the center of my palm with his thumb. "Okay for now?"

"Yes," I whisper as his thumb circles again. I can't even feel the ring. Only that caress.

"And what about your panties?" He reaches into his pocket with his other hand and, a moment later, black silk dangles from his fingers. "I'll happily put those back on you, too."

Immediately I imagine his rough hands sliding their way up my legs, tugging my skirt up and dragging that tiny scrap of silk into place. My inner muscles clench in response. An erotic shiver works its way over my skin, tightening my nipples, as if his thumbs were stroking those taut buds instead of my palm.

Sheer longing fills my chest, but I shake my head. "Not if they're still damp," I tell him. But even if they aren't, soon they would be again. Especially if he's the one who puts them on me. "I'll feel them and won't be able to think about anything else."

He gives a short, pained laugh. "Then we're a good match, baby. I can't think about anything but these wet panties, either." Which he slides into his pocket again—and before I can protest his thievery, he entwines his fingers with mine and we begin heading down the corridor toward the coat check.

Holding hands. This is clearly something we'll do as an engaged couple. I like it very much, just as I enjoyed clinging to his arm and standing close to him in the ballroom. At first it was only to make certain everyone saw that he belonged to me—and to offer my protection. So many people within this social circle can be vicious, but my presence alone should stop the worst of it. And although I can't detect the more subtle insults, people don't know that. If any jabs slipped through, however, Caleb never seemed to be intimidated by them…and gradually, it was *I* who felt protected, standing there beside him. As he if was a solid wall between me and the crowd. As if I were safe with him, even as I was slowly overwhelmed by the constant interaction with everyone else.

Safe *with* him, yes—but only safe from others. Because even as I feel protected by him, Caleb Moore makes me so vulnerable. Just in a different way.

We are almost to the coat check when he asks, "When will I see you next? I want it to be soon."

He does? Happiness and anticipation skip through me. "I don't know. I haven't looked at my calendar since this afternoon—and that was before we established a date for the wedding. So everything will have changed." And will need to be updated again, after I send Jessica a message about Patrick's ugly sweater party.

"Then look at it while I get our coats."

I can't look at my calendar until he returns with my trench, because I didn't carry my phone into the ballroom. I scroll through my new schedule as we make our way to the hotel lobby.

"I don't have anything else scheduled with you before the wedding."

A scowl darkens his face. "Do you have any free time?"

"Before or after the wedding?"

"Both."

"Not much. But I can tell Jessica to change that."

"Then tell her I want to see you every damn day. Even if you can only manage a few minutes."

I would like that, too. And I can certainly manage more than a few minutes, but I'll let Jessica figure that out. I tell her what I want to do but don't attempt to create my own schedule, because I begin obsessing over the details—such as how long it'll take my driver to get me from one appointment to another—and spend more time planning my schedule than working. Far better to just place all of that into my assistant's capable hands.

Outside, it's snowing again. My driver's waiting for me, and as Caleb walks with me to the car, one of the hotel attendants opens the rear door with a flourish.

A tug on my hand brings me to a halt. "Hold up, baby."

Standing in front of the open car door, I turn to face Caleb. He glances at the attendant, who blurts a "Happy Holidays!" before vanishing.

His dark gaze returns to mine before falling to my lips, and the gravel in his voice seems to abrade my nerve endings, bringing my entire body to raw awareness. "A man should kiss his fiancée goodnight."

A horrible ache re-opens within my chest. "No," I tell him. "You've already established that you don't want me to kiss you hello. A good-bye follows the same rules as a greeting."

The skin over his cheeks draws taut. "You think I don't want you to kiss me? Because I really fucking do."

I frown in confusion. "Then why tell me no before?"

"I didn't want any woman kissing me because she felt obligated to and not because she wanted to."

My brittle smile feels as fragile as my heart suddenly does. "And you thought I didn't want to...because I'm an ice queen?"

"Because I'm a stupid piece of shit," he rasps. "*Did* you want to?"

"Yes."

His eyes close briefly, as if in regret. "And now?"

Yes. But how vulnerable will the truth make me? I don't know—but I'm terrified that I won't simply be opening myself up to hurt. Caleb Moore might be able to completely tear me apart. Because I already feel as if I've been shredded.

Yet I can't lie. So instead I remain silent and let my eyes answer with the cold stare that's so effective in these circumstances. Too late, I remember that I told him exactly what I use it for.

But he doesn't seem to remember. Because his jaw clenches and he nods before replying as if I'd said the word *no* out loud. "You don't want to. All right. No kiss."

He steps back, his big hand clenched on the top of the open door frame as I slide into the car's seat. My throat aches and my eyes burn as I tell him, "Goodnight, Caleb."

Softly he replies, "Goodnight, Audrey."

The door swings shut. I close my eyes, fighting the hot sting of tears.

I liked it better when he called me 'baby.'

CALEB

I DON'T SLEEP FOR SHIT. IN THE MORNING I STUMBLE into the shower and stroke one out to the memory of Audrey's lush red lips. But as my cum washes down the drain, another image sticks in my head. The same image that haunted me all fucking night. Of Audrey looking up at me with that withering, icy stare. The stare she uses instead of saying a lie.

Because she still wanted to kiss me. But she didn't want me to know it. And there was no hiding the wariness that accompanied her every response after we emerged from the dark room.

Afraid. Because I hurt her last night. And not just once.

A handful of text messages greet me when I leave the shower, and a tight band of tension wraps around my chest when I see the name of Audrey's assistant, Jessica. Maybe calling everything off. Notifying me that the Wyndham mansion isn't worth putting up with my shit.

Instead sheer relief hits me when I see it's a group message titled 'Audrey's Little Helpers' that includes Jessica and the other assistant, Jeremy. And I must be crazy about this woman, because group messages are stupidly fucking annoying and yet here I am, glad to see it. I carry the device into my kitchen and begin reading while I pour my coffee.

Jessica: Good morning, Mr. Moore. I'm attaching a calendar to this message. When you click on the link, it should sync with your phone's.

Jessica: I've cleared most of my employer's evenings per her request. At your convenience, please send me your work schedule and let me know of any social events you'd like her to attend with you.

Yeah, my schedule's not exactly hopping with 'social events'—and I'm not likely to drag her to any of my friends' parties. Not if she doesn't do well with crowds and loud noise. But I'm damn pleased that Audrey opened up her evenings.

I pull out a griddle and continue to the next message, then start grinning when I hit the assistant's name for her.

Jessica: Please understand that this calendar is extremely flexible. Audrey Motherfuckin' Clarke (AMC) can do whatever she wants, whenever she wants, wherever she wants, however she wants. But she likes the structure of a schedule. So if you've planned something, let me know. Updating the calendar is no problem.

Jeremy: Also—though she might have a different preference with you—generally AMC prefers texts and emails to phone calls.

That last one came in while I was looking at the screen, so I type out a response.

Caleb: Who doesn't?

Jeremy: Truth. Also, if your reply is rhetorical, or if the tone of your message might be easily mistaken or is unclear, AMC appreciates emojis that can clarify your meaning. If you are joking or teasing her, I recommend the winking emoji.

Caleb: Got it.

Jessica: For the upcoming wedding, would you like us to schedule tuxedo fittings, arrange transportation to church and honeymoon, make sure you and AMC obtain a marriage license and have all necessary documentation, hire movers to take your belongings to her house, etc.? Before you say no, or that it's not necessary, or that you can do it, consider that we make AMC's life easier by making YOUR life easier—and that we are very good at it.

Caleb: You can do it.

Jessica: Great. We'll accomodate your work schedule as much as possible. Also if your employer is reluctant to give you the week off between Xmas and New Years', let us know. AMC's name can be very persuasive.

Caleb: Absolutely fucking not.

Jeremy: Hard limit noted and accepted.

Jessica: AMC is scheduled to attend the Bennet Foundation's Christmas carnival tonight from 6 to 9ish. Do you wish to accompany her?

Caleb: Yes.

Jeremy: This evening's fundraising festivities include a raffle drawing, a pie-eating contest, several wintertime sports activities, a Polar Plunge, and—if you've been a good boy—you can sit on Santa's lap.

Caleb: Pass. What will Audrey like?

Jeremy: Ice skating!

Jessica: Hot chocolate with marshmallows.

Jeremy: Manly yet sensitive displays of strength!

Jessica: Anything soft and fuzzy.

Jeremy: Correctly punctuated signage!

Caleb: Thanks.

Jeremy: Our pleasure! We look forward to helping you become Mister AMC, husband to the beautiful and successful woman who gives us a tremendous bonus at the end of every fiscal year.

Jessica: I'll send updates to your schedule as I arrange them. Do not hesitate to contact us if there is something you need or if you have any questions regarding

ANYTHING.

Caleb: Will do.

Though not often. I'm not using Audrey's assistants as a go-between for me and her. But they're obviously invested in making her happy—and they know her likes and dislikes better than I do.

But that'll change. If I get my way, I'll know her inside and out.

I get dressed for work, then pick up my phone again. Audrey's number is the newest entry in my contact list but our message history is blank. Not anymore.

Caleb: Tell your driver to take the night off. I'll pick you up from work around 5:30 and take you to the carnival, and then drive you home. Bring your ice skates.

It feels like a goddamn year passes before the reply comes. I'm on my way out the door when my phone buzzes and the message notification pops onto the screen.

Audrey: Okay.

Fuck. Is that a happy okay? An irritated okay? A disinterested okay? I wish she'd used an emoji. Because I can read that simple 'okay' a million ways.

And I don't know what the hell to write next. *Sorry I hurt you? I'm a fucking asshole? I want to kiss you hello and goodnight and I don't want you to be afraid that I'll hurt you again?* But that's not the kind of shit you say over a message. That needs to be said face-to-face.

So… We'll just leave it at 'Okay.'

For now.

* * *

AT FIVE-FORTY, I PULL UP TO THE CLARKE BUILDING. When I saw it yesterday under a gray sky and in the drab winter sunlight, it struck me as an unwelcoming sculpture of glass and steel. With night falling and warm light filling the windows, the building looks more like a flame rising against the dark and the cold.

Christ. Even her building is telling me how wrong I was about her.

It's a damn good thing she needs that Wyndham property, because it'll give me a chance to make it right. And since I left her last night, the only thing on my mind has been how I should go about doing that. The main thing is—taking it slow. Let her see that I'm not going to hurt her again. Build up her trust. Because she might be sexually attracted to me, but her icy stare last night told me that she doesn't think I'll take care with her emotions. Not after I treated her like she doesn't have any.

So I'll go slow. And luckily, I have time to go slow. She agreed to marry me to get her hands on that property. So we're stuck together for a while.

Earlier, Jessica sent a text telling me to park directly in front of the main doors, so I do. Feels damn strange, but the way the security guard in the lobby greets me by name and some of the looks I'm getting tell me that the word is out. That I'm not just Caleb Moore anymore, but the soon-to-be Mr. AMC.

"Miss Clarke says not to bother coming up. She'll be right down," the security guard says—Reginald Johnson, according to his name tag. "And congratulations on your engagement, sir."

"Thanks. And it's Caleb."

"No can do, Mr. Moore. Just like she'll always be Miss Clarke here, whether she invites us to call her Audrey or not. The employees of Clarke, International like anyone coming in from outside to know how much respect they ought to be showing her. Now that respect extends to you—along with other privileges." He holds out an envelope. "In here is a key card that'll give you access to the building after hours and allows you to take the elevator to the executive levels. It'll work in combination with your thumbprint, so if you'll let me scan that now, we'll get that all set up. There's also a parking sticker. You have a designated spot in the garage, but the truth is, your spot is called 'anywhere you like.' Though we'd appreciate a heads-up if you change vehicles."

"I'll do that." I stick my thumb on the scanner. "I guess these are the perks, huh?"

He grins, then with a lift of his chin gestures behind me. "*That's* your perk."

Audrey. Looking fucking beautiful as she crosses the lobby toward us. She's wearing a thigh-length puffy coat over a long white sweater and black leggings, with heavy snow boots that look twice as big as her feet. Her blonde hair is braided this time, with a fuzzy red hat pulled down over her ears. She's carrying a canvas bag that I assume holds her ice skates, and I take that small burden from her as she draws near.

"Thank you, Caleb," she tells me in a soft voice, her pale eyes searching my face. Still wary, and seeing her fear tears at my gut. After a second she pulls her gaze away and glances at the security guard. "Did you get everything you need, Reggie?"

He nods. "We're all squared away."

"Thank you. Have a good evening."

He wishes us the same as we head for the exit. I open the passenger door of my truck and take her hand to steady her as she steps up into my cab—because it's not a big step, but I'll use any excuse to touch her. Even buckling her in. I feel her gaze on my face as I lean in close to perform that simple task, aware of her soft pink lips and her incredible smell and the way she's holding her breath.

And that quick, I'm hard as hell. Jesus. Taking this slow is going to kill me. But I suppose it's what I deserve.

I toss her bag behind the seat and slide in behind the wheel. The directions to the carnival are already loaded into my GPS. We're quiet as I fire up the engine and head out, and I don't know what the hell to start with aside from a, "How was your day?"

"Good," she replies.

"Was it?" Because that remote response doesn't sound like it was good. Then I remember what she said about questions like that. "That's not an empty question. I'm really asking, baby. Because if you had a shitty day, you can unload on me. And we'll make sure the rest of your day is better."

Her eyes brighten. "It wasn't a shitty day. I spoke to my lawyers regarding your case. They're confident that they'll prove the will's validity, since Eleanor wrote it almost ten years ago—and she reaffirmed the contents of the document with her lawyer every year afterward. So it will be difficult to argue that she wasn't in her right mind, which is what the Wyndhams are trying to do. And her intentions were clear. She made several statements to witnesses that echo the reasons she gave for disinheriting the other Wyndhams. So her habit of speaking bluntly will work in our favor."

"I guess that's good news for us both." Otherwise Eleanor Wyndham can go fuck herself all the way down to Hell.

"Yes." She glances at me curiously. "Did you ever meet her?"

"Once. At my mother's funeral."

Her brows furrow. "Only once? How long ago was that?"

"Twelve years." My throat tightens as I say it, because it feels a hell of a lot longer than that—and also like it was only last week. "And meeting Eleanor once was enough."

"You didn't like her, either?"

That understatement drags a harsh laugh from me. "After the funeral was over, she came up to me and said, 'Your mother might have been a thieving slut, but obviously she wasn't the liar that I believed she was. You're the spitting image of Robert.' Then she asked me to lunch."

"But you declined, obviously."

"*Declined* is a very nice way of putting what I said to her."

Her pink lips curve into that gorgeous smile. "You must have been surprised by the will, then."

"Yeah, I was. And my first impulse was to tell the executor to burn the damn thing, because I didn't want anything from her."

"Burning the document wouldn't invalidate it. And there would be copies."

I grin. "That's what her executor said, too—and that I'd have to officially disclaim the inheritance. But then those Wyndham fuckers contested the will and I started rethinking. Because I don't want them to have it, either."

She nods, then casts me a speculative look. "How many times did Keith Shayne contact you today?"

The lawyer I tried to hire? Laughing, I shake my head. "I blocked him after the third message."

"Jessica and Jeremy told him that I'll eventually return his calls," she tells me with a mischievous little grin. "They probably have a bet regarding how long it'll take him to realize that a call from me is never coming."

"When would your guess be?"

"That he'll realize it on the day that we run into each other at some event." She shrugs. "I'm not good at stringing people along."

No surprise there. It might amuse her that Jeremy and Jessica do, but she would tell Shayne flat out that she'd never hire him. Thinking of her assistants, I ask, "What's your middle name?"

"Madison. Why?"

I can't stop my grin. "Just curious."

She eyes my grin for a long moment, as if wondering what I'm not saying. Then she asks, "Why do you drive a pickup truck?"

The first thing that pops into my head is wondering whether she thinks a pickup's not classy enough to ride around in. The same kind of shit that popped into my head last night.

I've got a big fucking chip on my shoulder. Knowing that never bothered me before. But I've got to knock it off. At least with Audrey. Or I'll risk hurting her again.

"Because I spend a lot of time in junkyards," I tell her. "And it's better for hauling auto parts around in than a car or an SUV is."

"Ah," she says as if my answer solves a mystery. "So you also use it for work, then?"

"Not usually. The shop where I work has its own vehicles."

Her brow furrows. "Then why haul auto parts around?"

"Because restoring vintage cars is a hobby of mine." Or a side job, maybe. Just not one that's very lucrative. "I pick up an old junker for cheap, rebuild it, then sell it off for a profit. Then pick up another junker and start again."

"That's what I do, sometimes. But with junker corporations. And usually more than one at a time."

I laugh. Yeah, I'm sure that's exactly the same. "You enjoy that?"

"Very much. Do you enjoy restoring cars? You must, if that's how you spend your free time."

"I do. How do you spend your free time?"

"Working, usually. Because my job is also my hobby."

"So you really like what you do."

"Making money? Yes, I like it very much. Because then I can spend it on whatever else makes me happy."

"Making and spending money are good hobbies to have," I say with a grin, then follow the GPS's directions to pull into a long driveway. At the top of the hill sits the big mansion that overlooks the city—the Bennet House. I've seen it a million times but have never been here before. "So how does this Christmas carnival thing fit in? Are you making money or spending money?"

"Giving it away—because I enjoy that, too, and even after I reinvest some of my earnings into the company, I keep making far more than I could ever personally need. So I donate a few billion every year to a variety of foundations and charities around the world. And ice skating is also fun."

I can't argue with that. The snow-covered lawn in front of the house looks like a parking lot. I find a spot alongside a school bus, then shove her bag into a backpack containing my hockey skates.

She's already out of the truck and zipping up her coat when I make my way around to that side. I frown at her hand as she begins pulling on her gloves.

"You're still wearing the ring? I thought we agreed that you'd say 'fuck you' to that tradition."

"It's a different one." Now that she says so, I notice that the diamond is much smaller, too. "I told the jeweler that the feel was annoying me, so he suggested a comfort band. This one feels okay."

And with those gloves on, she's clearly not wearing it just for show, like she did last night. Shit. I should have been the one to get a ring for her. Not that I could afford the one she's wearing. But I can probably swing the other rings we'll need—the wedding bands.

Because I'm marrying this woman. *Holy fuck*, I'm marrying this woman.

"Caleb?" She's frowning up at me. "Are you all right?"

"Yeah," I tell her and hear how hoarse that sounds. Because I just got the wind knocked out of me. "Just, uh…realized something."

Again. But this time, I'm not wondering if I've made a huge mistake. Instead I'm wondering how I got so damn lucky. It's the one thing I'll ever be grateful to Eleanor Wyndham for: leaving me the property that

Audrey Clarke wants to buy.

Slinging the backpack over my shoulder, I take her gloved hand in mine. The Bennet mansion is lit up, but everyone's heading around the house instead of into it, so we join the crowd of people moving in that direction. Speakers are blaring Christmas music, and already I can hear little kids screaming and laughing. "Is all this noise and shit going to be all right?"

She squeezes my fingers. "I'll let you know if I'm not."

All right. And the way her face lights up when we step through an arbor and into a winter wonderland of a garden tells me that nothing's bothering her yet. A lady dressed in an elf costume hands out a little map, where different sections of the estate grounds are given labels like "Santa's Village" and "Reindeer Rink" and "Sugarplum Pond."

"Where will the raffle drawing be held?" Audrey asks the elf.

"At the Gingerbread Gazebo in Mistletoe Midway, at eight-thirty."

She thanks the elf and tells me, "We need to be there at eight-fifteen. Since I donated the prizes, I'm scheduled to draw the tickets."

So not just here to spend money and have fun, but also to work. Yet if it's all the same thing to her, it'll be all the same to me. "So that gives us about two hours at Reindeer Rink," I say and scope out the map.

"I saw how to get there." She tugs me toward a

snow-covered path, anticipation brightening her face. I pocket the map and let her lead the way. The place is a blur of Christmas lights until we reach the skating area—which includes two temporary rinks, one for figure skating and the other a hockey rink surrounded by a safety net, complete with skates and gear provided for the kids lining up, and a bevy of attendants. I'm thinking the Bennets must have spent a pretty penny on this carnival until I see the "Sponsored by Clarke, Incorporated" written in small letters on the banners over the entrances to the rinks.

Giving away money here, indeed. So maybe the second rink is how Audrey makes sure she'll get to do what she enjoys most. I hand over her bag, and she sits on a bench to pull off her boots.

"You prefer hockey or the other?"

"The other," she says, then glances at the black skates I take from my bag. "But if you prefer to play, go ahead. I'll be fine on my own. And if I finish skating before you do, I don't mind waiting. I enjoy watching the game."

And I love playing it but I'm not at all tempted. "I'd rather spend the time with you."

A touch of pink brightens her cheeks. Ninety minutes later, that pink is a deeper flush from the cold and exertion. And I knew I'd enjoy being with her, but messing around on the ice with Audrey turns out to be even more fun than I expected, because she might not play hockey but she's still damn competitive and apparently loves a race. Plus I skate a hell of a lot better than I can dance—and since lifting her up in my arms and spinning until she's breathless with laughter allows me to perform a manly display of strength, I figure it's a win overall.

To keep my streak going, I jog over to the concession stand as soon as I've got my boots back on and while she's still unlacing her skates. With two hot chocolates warming my hands, I walk alongside the hockey rink on the way back to the bench, then stop short as an arc of shaved ice flies in front of my face.

"Holy shi—eeeoooot." A Santa goalie in the hockey rink abruptly seems to remember how many kids are around. "Caleb Moore? *S'mores* Moore?"

I haven't heard that nickname since high school. The big guy has to remove his beard and Santa hat before it clicks, and even then it's his size that clues me in before his face does. Only one friend from back then had any inches on me. "Cole Matthews? Fuck me. I thought you were long gone."

"Just to the other side of town." He nods to the two cups I'm carrying. "You got someone waiting for you? Let me get all this gear off and I'll meet you by the benches."

Shit. "For a minute, maybe. We can catch up another night."

"So it's like that?" He grins and skates backward, hand over his heart. "I won't fuck it up for you, man."

I know he wouldn't. But I'm not here to spend time with anyone but Audrey. I can meet up with Cole some other day.

She smiles when I return with the hot chocolate, and her sigh of pleasure as she takes a sip goes straight to my dick. Her eyes are bright and her nose is pink, and I've never wanted to kiss anyone so bad in my life. But even though she hasn't given me that wary look in a while, the plan is still to go slow—and now there's goddamn Cole. I turn to greet him.

"Caleb, damn." Still in that Santa suit, he gives me a solid handshake, slapping my shoulder. "Fuck, it's been a while. How you been?"

"All right." I step aside a little so he can see Audrey behind me, wishing I didn't have to share her. "This is—"

"Audrey?" he asks, his eyebrows shooting high.

"Hello, Cole."

He looks from me to her and back again before he starts laughing. "Where the hell did you pick this asshole up?"

"Caleb picked me up." As if thinking she needs to protect me from that insult, she slips her hand into mine—still ungloved after unlacing her skates, and her left hand holding her cup. His gaze lands on her ring and his laughter stops.

His eyes narrow. "That's an engagement ring."

"Your observational skills haven't failed you, detective," Audrey replies with laughing curve of her lips.

"How long have you and Caleb known each other?"

How long have *we* known each other? How long has *he* known Audrey? *How* does he know her? "We grew up on the same street," I tell her.

"Ah," she says. "Friends or enemies?"

"Friends," Cole says, apparently getting over his surprise, and now enjoying the hell out of this situation.

"I'm glad. It means I won't have to destroy your life." She smiles sweetly at him. "We were just on our way to find Mia. Are you heading in that direction, too?"

"Yeah," he says with a grin, then falls into step with Audrey between us.

"Mia?" I ask.

"My wife."

"No shit? How long?"

"A little less than a year."

"Congratulations."

"That seems to be going around." He glances at Audrey. "Does Mia know about your engagement yet?"

"I sent her a message today. And you should receive an invitation tomorrow," she tells him.

Which means this Mia is one of the five people in Audrey's social circle that she enjoys being around, I realize. Which also means Cole will be part of that circle.

Sounds damn good to me. "Did Audrey call you 'detective'?

"Yeah. I'm at the station downtown. And you?"

"Still working at Phillips Auto, still restoring shit in

Patrick's garage."

"Patrick?" Cole grins. "What's he doing?"

"Woodwork at Crenshaw's. We get together with that crew at Murphy's most Fridays. You should come."

He nods. "I'll do that. How's your mom doing?"

"She's gone." The raw edge to my voice tells him exactly what that means.

Abruptly stopping, he stares at me. "Ah, fuck no. What happened?"

I shrug and feel Audrey moving in closer beside me, as if trying to protect me again—or comfort me. "She hit a patch of black ice driving home from work one night. They say it was quick."

"Shit." Jaw clenched, he shakes his head and we all start walking again. "I'm so fucking sorry, man."

"I am, too," Audrey says softly.

"You'd have liked her," Cole tells Audrey. "Hell, everyone liked her. There was a reason why his house was the most popular in our neighborhood."

"Because she was always gone," I say. Working her ass off, holding down two or three jobs just to pay the bills.

"Nah, that wasn't why. Not for me, anyway. She'd come home at, what—midnight?—obviously tired as hell and wanting nothing more than to get some sleep, yet she always made sure I'd be all right if I went home that late. And told me to come back and wake her up if I wasn't."

Because Cole's father had been an abusive drunk.

We never hung out at his house because it was never safe. But my home was. We didn't have any of the shit that kids love—no snacks, no video games—because my mom couldn't afford them, but I always figured it was the lack of supervision that made my place a haven for my friends. Now, though…I can see my mom being a big part of that. Because Cole wasn't the only friend who sometimes stayed a few days.

"I think I would have liked her very much," Audrey says.

How could I have ever thought this woman was cold? Throat tight, I lift her hand and press a kiss to her ungloved fingers, then enfold them in mine to warm them. We reach Mistletoe Midway and Cole leads us to a gazebo covered in fake gingerbread and icing.

Inside, Cole leaves us behind and heads straight for a tall, raven-haired woman. Clearly more congratulations should go around, because his big hand cradles her swollen belly as he leans in to kiss her. As he does, I'm greeted with the sight of one the toughest nuts I've ever known cracking open.

"That's fucking adorable," I tell Audrey with a grin. "He used to call me S'mores because he said I had a gooey marshmallow center. Now look at him. So sweet and soft with her."

Audrey's laugh is soft and sweet, too. "Yes, he is."

"And you're a friend of hers?" Because Mia's got that same air of class and money around her that Audrey has.

"Did you go to high school together?"

"No, my parents sent me away to a boarding school," she replies, sipping her hot chocolate. "I've been acquainted with her for several years, though, mostly through the Bennet Foundation. But her father was the foundation's director and I didn't like him. His business practices were too sleezy. And she works in the county morgue, so our paths don't cross professionally."

Mia is a Bennet? So Cole just doesn't happen to be here at this carnival with his wife. She's one of the people in charge of the whole thing—and maybe the one who lives in that mansion. Jesus.

Audrey continues, "Then last year, Mia had her father arrested on charges of fraud and for embezzling the foundation's funds. I liked that very much. So I sent her a list of all of the reasons why we should become friends."

I almost choke on my cocoa. "You sent her a friend-ship proposal?"

"Yes." She arches a brow. "Via email. And she accepted it. Then we went to lunch and became friends."

"Now you're getting a husband the same way."

"No. You didn't send an email." Her sly look is a teasing one, her eyes brimming with laughter. "But a business proposal does seem an efficient way of forming relationships."

"Considering that I gained a sexy, brilliant fiancée, I have no complaints," I tell her, and watch delight spread through her expression before she bites her lip and glances away. Still not sure of me. But I'll keep working on that.

Mia's widened gaze is all over me as she and Cole head our direction, then she exclaims to Audrey, "You wouldn't believe how many people left messages for me today, trying to find out if the rumors were true. Apparently Jennifer is telling everyone that you snagged the Wyndham heir."

"The Wyndham *what?*" Cole bursts into laughter—laughter that dies as abruptly as it started, his gaze arrested on my face. "Hold up. You are?"

"I am," I tell him. "One of those assholes was my dad."

His jaw drops. "Holy shit, man."

"Oh…my," Mia breathes, then begins giggling. "This will be fun. Now I wish we'd gone to the tree lighting party. Please tell me that you and Caleb are coming to our New Year's Eve gala, too, because the Wyndhams will be there and I would *love* to see their faces."

Audrey shakes her head. "We'll still be on our honeymoon. But if you come to our wedding, you can see their faces then. If they come, too."

"Oh, I'm not missing *that* for anything. Even if they don't come." Mia clenches her fists in front of her chest and seems to vibrate with excitement for a moment. "Oh, I *would* hug you but I won't! I'm just so happy for you, Audrey." To me she says, "Cole says you're all marshmal-low-y inside."

And he hasn't seen me in more than a decade. "If I still am, I'm one of those marshmallows that are burned up instead of toasted golden brown."

"The burned ones are the best," Audrey says matter-of-factly. "You pull off the charred skin and what's left is all gooey and warm. The others don't get gooey enough."

"There you go," Mia says with a nod, then grins and looks to Audrey again. "You must be kicking yourself now for buying that Sandpipe property for your camp project."

"No. The overall acreage is smaller, but there are more woodlands at Sandpipe than on the Wyndham estate. And the lake access is better."

"How's the rezoning going?"

"No problems yet. It should be finalized after the next city council meeting."

"Good. Jason's looking forward to helping you move the project into the next stage. Especially after *this*." She gestures around us and then looks to me, explaining, "Jason is my brother—and with my father gone, he's living here in the manor house and acting as the Bennet Foundation's director, and he decided the grounds should be put to better use than simply being decorative. So this is the first year for the carnival. But we couldn't have done as much if Clarke hadn't sponsored it all. Which reminds me, Audrey—we have raffle tickets to draw."

Mia grasps Audrey's coat sleeve and pulls her away, while everything she just said keeps sinking in. And sinking in. Until it settles in my stomach like a leaden weight.

Audrey *doesn't* need the Wyndham property for her project? So why does she still want it? Just as a good real estate investment—get it for cheap, turn a profit? Enough of a profit that she's willing to marry me?

The profit she'd make on the house can't be *that* appealing. Not to someone who buys and sells corporations for fun. So maybe she just wants the house for herself.

My gaze lifts to the Bennet's mansion. I haven't seen the Wyndham house yet, but my guess is that it's similar. The kind of place that screams old money. Someone might want to get their hands on a house like that, sure. Especially if they were new money. Owning a house like that is a symbol of prestige or whatever.

But that doesn't seem like something Audrey cares about.

Cole joins me, leaning back against the low wall of the gazebo and idly watching the goings-on near the raffle table. "So you're the Wyndham heir?" Chuckling, he shakes his head. "Shit. That makes me the only working class asshole in this place."

"I'm not quitting any time soon. And I don't think working class changes, anyway." No matter how much money you get. "From what I've seen so far, these people live in a whole other world."

"Yeah, they do." He sobers up, his gaze on his wife.

"But you'll learn that it doesn't matter a damn bit. Not when *she's* your whole fucking world."

How can Audrey be my whole world? I've only known her a day. Yet there's not a thing inside me that's laughing at the idea, or saying it's not going to happen. Instead everything in me is agreeing. Like it already *has* happened.

"How long are we talking about?" I ask him. "This 'learning that nothing else matters' part?"

"For me? The very first second I saw Mia."

A laugh busts out of me. "Bullshit."

Wanting her, I believe. But knowing she's going to be everything?

"To be fair, I'd just been shot by some asshole with a semi-automatic rifle. It was a high adrenaline moment." His grin fades into something more serious a second later. "But I couldn't stop thinking about her. Then I said some stupid shit and she slammed her door in my face. I knew for sure, then. Because I'd have done any goddamn thing to make it right. Anything except not see her again."

Fuck me. I don't know if I said it out loud or Cole just reads my face.

He gives me a knowing look. "Sound familiar?"

Too damn familiar. But I'm not getting into it with him now. "You were shot?"

And obviously came through all right. But still. That's a hell of a thing.

He scowls at me. "The incident was all over the news last year."

Yeah, and there's breaking news about one shooting or another every damn week, it seems like. "I prefer to get my daily updates from the little songbirds that chirp outside my bedroom window every morning."

"They should be chirping about how I'm a fucking hero."

"I'll be sure to raise a glass to you at Murphy's then," I tell him with a grin—then push away from the gazebo wall, because Audrey's finishing up. "This Friday or next… Shit, not next." I'll be at Audrey's lodge…on my honeymoon. That sense of unreality slips over me again, because I can't understand how this happened. I thought I had a handle on it, but if she doesn't need that property, then I don't have a handle on anything. "Maybe we'll catch up after the new year."

"Sounds like a plan. Good running into you, Caleb."

"You, too." Though I'd give just about anything to have run into him a week ago. To have seen Cole and his wife—a man from my world and a woman from Audrey's—looking so damn happy. Maybe that could have nudged the chip from my shoulder a little and I wouldn't have said what I did to Audrey.

But maybe it wouldn't have made a difference. Because it wasn't just that Audrey was rich. I read her wrong from the beginning. I'm still reading her wrong, because everything I assumed about her motivation for marrying me is way off.

I don't know what to think now. But one thing I'll never be accused of is being indirect. And Audrey likes that about me.

So I'll be real fucking direct now and find out what the hell is going on. As soon as we leave the gazebo, I pull her off the main path and into an alcove of tall shrubs wrapped in tinsel and Christmas lights, then swing her around to face me.

That delight has returned to her face, her eyes sparkling. Until I ask her, "You don't want the Wyndham property?"

Her expression dims a little, her brow furrowing. "I do. At the price you're selling it, I'll make a substantial profit."

"Yeah, but you don't *need* it anymore. For your camp project." Which I've heard mentioned but still don't know what it is. "Do you?"

"No, I don't *need* it."

Fuck. Because she could still get that profit if she wanted to. She has to know that. No need to marry me. Just pay for the lawyers and I'll agree to sell the property at whatever price she wanted.

My chest tightens. I thought I had something she wanted. Something she *needed*. And that was my hold on her. But I don't know what she wants.

But I need to know. "Why are you marrying me, then?"

"Because you *asked* me to marry you, Caleb."

As if I've forgotten that part. "So you'd have said yes to anyone?"

She frowns at me. "No. Of course not."

Of course not. As if there's some certainty here. But I'm not feeling certain about anything. "Then why say yes to me?"

"Because if your goal is to spite the Wyndhams, your proposal is sensible—and a marriage for business purposes is, too. Spite has never been my goal before, but I thought it sounded fun, especially since the Wyndhams deserve it. Though I wouldn't have accepted if I hadn't also liked you and been attracted to you."

The grounds seems to shift. But it's just her admission, staggering me. Because from what she's saying… the only thing she wanted that she couldn't easily get another way was *me.*

And all I want to do is haul her up against me. Kiss the hell out of her. Show her that I want her, too.

Yet I can't touch her. And that's my own damn fault. "But I fucked it up last night," I tell her hoarsely. "Hurt your feelings. Didn't I?"

She doesn't answer. Just gives me the icy stare that tries to say I didn't hurt her at all. But I know it's a lie.

"Didn't I?" I say again, softly this time. "I'm sorry for that."

Her throat works before she averts her face. "I appreciate your apology."

Which sounds like polite shit most people say…but most people aren't Audrey Clarke. And accepting an apology doesn't mean all is forgiven—or that she likes me anymore. But she hasn't called this marriage off.

Yet.

Maybe I've still got a hold on her. Because she's attracted to me. So screw going slow. I'll use any advantage I have to make sure she still wants to marry me. But I already fucked that up pretty good, too. No kissing hello and goodnight. And a kiss is the best way to get started on the rest. Because I might not be going slow anymore, but skipping over the kissing might be *too* fast.

So I've got to give her another reason to kiss me. And we're in the perfect place for that. Mistletoe Midway. Because she likes it when interactions have context and this is a context that everyone knows.

I glance up. A little bush is right over my head, tied with a red ribbon to a string of lights crossing the entrance to the alcove. Remembering the delight on her face, I realize that Audrey already spotted the mistletoe. Because she thought I was bringing her over here to kiss her. And her delight suggests that she wanted me to.

But I'm not taking a single thing for granted now. In a low voice, I tell her, "It's traditional to kiss someone under the mistletoe."

Her gaze snaps up to meet mine, and she stares at me for a long moment, utterly still, before replying softly, "Yes, it is."

"But that's not why I'm kissing you, Audrey." Gently I cup her jaw in my hands and a tremor races through her. "It's because I want to. Real fucking bad. But that's not all I want."

Her focus drops to my mouth. "No?"

"No." I drag my thumb across her bottom lip, and the way her breath shudders across the moistened tip blows my dick into a length of hot steel. "I want to consummate this marriage."

She trembles against me. "You do?"

"I do. It doesn't make any goddamn sense otherwise. I want you, baby. You want me. And we'll be living in the same house." Slowly I lower my head, watching her face tilt up, her eyes closing. They fly open again when I say gruffly, "Every day, I'll get my mouth on your pussy and eat you up. Then I'll fuck you deep and hard, and I won't stop until I feel your cunt squeezing my cock as you come. So if you want that, you better say yes right now—"

"Yes." She pants the word against my lips. "Yes."

Arousal roughens my voice as I demand, "Now tell me you want it by letting me taste that beautiful mouth of yours."

Even as she rises up on her toes, she fists her hands in my jacket and drags me closer. Her lips open beneath mine, but although I'm not taking this slow anymore, this isn't something I intend to rush, either. Not our first kiss.

Gently I brush my mouth over hers, teasing before nipping at her full lower lip. Her little gasp and chocolate-scented sigh slip over my tongue as I lick past her teeth. And fuck. I should have known. Should have known she'd be hot and sweet and this kiss would mark the end of Caleb Moore and the beginning of Audrey and me. Because Cole was right. My old world is suddenly gone, along with everything else around us. Now there's just her body pressing closer to mine, her soft little moan filling my mouth and echoing deep inside my chest, where my heart pounds with a rhythm that sounds like her name.

Hunger rips through me, a ravenous urge to lift her up and wrap her legs around my waist and grind my rigid cock into the softness between her thighs. Through that red haze of lust, I force myself to recall that the world isn't really gone. That this is a family-friendly event. That I can't fuck her right here.

I ease back and groan at the sheer perfection in front of me. Those icy eyes glazed with desire. Her cheeks flushed with arousal. Her pink lips parted and glistening.

Needing another taste, I allow myself a sip from her mouth and the tip of her tongue before rasping against her lips, "Are your panties wet again, baby?"

Her entire body shudders against mine. "Yes."

That breathless answer might as well have been a hot tongue down the swollen length of my cock. I bite back a tortured groan and steal another kiss from her panting mouth. "Then how about I take you home, so I can get those wet panties off you?"

This time her answer isn't spoken. With her fist still clenched on my jacket, she turns and starts dragging me toward the exit. Eager to take me home. And fuck knows, I'm just as eager to get there…though this night won't end like she thinks it will.

Because if Audrey Clarke wants me? Then I'll give her what she wants.

But not until she marries me.

AUDREY

MY PANTIES AREN'T THE ISSUE HERE. CALEB is. Kissing me like he did. Saying things like he did. *Every day, I'll get my mouth on your pussy and eat you up.* How could anyone be expected to function after that? Or think about anything else at all? When his voice is a gravelly promise and he doesn't just kiss me but sucks on the tip of my tongue? That is *not* a mistletoe kiss. That's a make-Audrey's-heart-race kiss. That's a make-Audrey's-pussy-ache kiss.

And that's the other issue. Because my panties are wet but they aren't bothering me. I can't even feel them. I can't feel anything but slick hot need, and even though he's not kissing me now, the need isn't fading. Because I feel it and feel it and feel it, with my memory revisiting the heat of his mouth and the stroke of his tongue and everything he said, and *everything's* aching now, and on fire, and I can't breathe.

We reach his truck. He unlocks the door and inside the cab is quiet and dark, and that will be good, but we're at least thirty minutes from my home. Thirty minutes of not touching him or kissing him and just burning and squirming and trying to hold it in.

It's too long. But if I'm going to burn, then I'm going to burn as hot as I can. So when Caleb helps me up into the seat, I shove my fingers into his hair and kiss him again. It's wet and greedy and his reaction is exhilarating. A harsh groan rumbles against my mouth and his rough hands grip my hips and drag me closer, sideways on the edge of the seat with him standing in the open door, so I can wrap my legs around his waist. So I can grind against him, against his thick erection, and I feel my panties now, between us, there shouldn't be anything between us. I whimper with frustration, and the sound of his groan is suddenly deeper, rougher.

He stops kissing me, with my braid wrapped around one of his hands—I don't know when he did that but now he's using it to hold my head in place, preventing me from kissing him again, his forehead resting against mine, his chest heaving.

"Ah, fuck. Fuck. Audrey." His voice is ragged. "You get so hot so fucking fast."

And I'm dying from it. On a sobbing breath, I tell him, "Don't stop. I can't stop like this."

"Shh, baby. We'll just take the edge off. All right?"

I can't agree because I don't know what he means. But what he does is all right, more than all right. He lifts me against him and turns, sitting on the passenger seat. There's a few seconds of awkward movement as he pulls his legs inside while still holding me. Then he closes the door, and suddenly everything is very all right, because I'm straddling his hips and our mouths are so close. Our hot breaths frost in the cold air, and it's so dark but his eyes seem to glitter with their own heat.

And I want my panties gone but I also don't want to stop what he's doing now, his hands sliding beneath the back of my coat and sweater and grabbing my ass, holding me in place for the upward thrust of his hips. And there's *so much* friction. From his cock and his jeans and my leggings and my panties and all of it dragging against my clit. My strangled moan against his lips is answered by a feral snarl, followed by Caleb's taut, "Is that the right spot, baby?" and my "yes, yes" that I would have kept saying forever if I hadn't desperately lunged for his mouth. Because I understand the edge he means to dull now, letting me masturbate against him to orgasm, and this is so much better than my fingers have ever been.

But not better than *his* fingers. And I never want to stop kissing him, but when Caleb brings one hand forward around my hip and pushes down the front of my leggings and his thumb dips into my panties to tease my clit, I don't have a choice. I can't kiss him anymore. I can't do anything but feel him touch me, can't breathe or think. I can't do anything but fist my fingers in his hair and hold on as he rocks beneath me and curses about how I'm soaking wet and his thumb circles and rubs that slippery knot of flesh.

Can't do anything but shake, and chant out a "You're making me come, Caleb. Oh god, you're making me come. You're making me—" before I *do* come in a convulsing, white hot flash, my head tilted back and my scream trapped behind my clenched teeth.

Then he pulls me back down against him, our foreheads together, our frozen breaths harsh and ragged. I think of kissing him again, but the edge is gone—and I don't want to risk it returning until we're home.

Maybe Caleb's thinking the same, because when he does kiss me, he holds my face in his palms but only presses his lips to my forehead and then to both of my cheeks. "All right now?"

I nod into his hands. "Thank you."

He grins. "I ought to be thanking you. Watching you come so hard and so fast was the goddamn sexiest thing I've ever seen."

Warm pleasure blooms inside me and I grin back at him. "And it made me tired." Utterly sated, with lethargy stealing into my limbs. "I'm going to nap until we get home. Do you have my address?"

A chuckle rumbles through him. "Yeah, I do. Do we need to stop for dinner? Maybe pick something up?"

"I should have something ready at home. If you want, you can eat there."

"I definitely want to eat," he says gruffly. "And I'll even settle for food."

"AUDREY. I'M SORRY, BABY, BUT I NEED YOU TO WAKE up."

I do, sitting up and wiping the drool from my cheek. Immediately I see the problem. A gate blocks the narrow lane ahead. My hands dig into my pockets searching for my phone.

Caleb's frowning at his, the screen open to a mapping application. "The GPS brought us here, but we're apparently on a nature reserve. Should I have turned down the last road or—"

"No. This is where I live." I tap the gate code into my device.

His brows rise. "In a park?"

"It's a private reserve. Most of it's open to the public. Just not this part."

He huffs out a laughing breath, shaking his head. "All right, then."

Unfamiliar nervousness flutters in my stomach. Because I forgot—this is where he'll be living, too. And his reaction seems somewhat...ironical. As if he's laughing at a joke I don't understand.

"You don't like the forest?" I ask him hesitantly.

"I do. I just didn't expect that you'd live in one, especially so close to the city." He pulls forward through the gate and into the snowy wood, following the gravel lane. "How long have you been here?"

"I had the house built about eight years ago." And because that nervous flutter still hasn't gone away, I add, "It has a big garage that I don't really need. You could take it over and use the space for your restoration projects."

He glances over at me with a quick smile. "Yeah, maybe."

That smile eases some of the tension in my stomach, but not all of it. I watch his face as the truck begins climbing the incline toward the house. The structure is visible now, though at first he doesn't seem to see—

"What the…?" Slowing the truck, he brings it to a halt and stares through the dark, as if trying to make out the shape of the house. "You live in a waterfall?"

Not exactly, but…kind of. "The water actually falls behind the house. And then flows through the different levels, so it just appears as if it's part of the waterfall."

"But your house is built into that cliff?" The disbelief has returned.

"Right up against it." And designed to look as if it's an extension of the cliff. "I wanted the house to seem like it's a part of the natural landscape."

"It does that," he says in that ironically amused voice again. "Where do I park?"

"The garage entrance is around the side, but the front entrance is under that overhang. We can just park there, instead. And I'll show you inside."

Where Caleb seems to fall uncharacteristically quiet. The house isn't built into the cliff, but more like a semicircle sitting with the flat side against the cliff, and made up of several levels. The main living space is on the second level, so I take him there before running upstairs to change. I strip off my leggings and my damp panties, drag on a pair of fuzzy socks, then head back down.

When I spot Caleb, I'm reminded of the first time I saw him—standing silently with his back to me, his hands in his pockets, gazing through the enormous windows that look out into the snowy forest. Except he doesn't unbalance this space. He seems to fit right in, as if he belongs—and I suspect that now this room will only feel wrong when he's *not* in it.

As if he spots my reflection in the window, he turns. My stomach drops as I see his expression. Not a frown, exactly. But also not pleased.

My chest tight, I tell him, "If you don't like it, we can buy a different house."

"Not *like* it?" he echoes before dragging his hand through his hair, shaking his head. "Audrey, this place is fucking beautiful. I mean, these windows. You only have a view of some trees, but it's just…like nothing I've ever seen. Like we're not even in a house, but outside in the forest, and there just happens to be some"—he waves around us—"really comfortable furniture and stuff around."

The tension in my chest eases. "So you like it?"

"Yeah. Yeah, baby, I do." His voice deepens and his brows draw together as he looks at me—as if suddenly realizing how nervous I am. "Did you think I wouldn't?"

"I didn't know. You sounded…*something*. When you found out where I lived. And what the house looked like."

Nodding abashedly, he rubs the back of his neck, looking around again. "I'm still adjusting to the reality of what a whole lot of money can do. And…I didn't expect *this*. In any way."

"It's an unusual house," I agree.

"Not the house. Though, yeah, it's unusual. But I pictured something like the Bennet place. Up on a hill—or maybe one of those giant mansions on the lake. And this is a big place, relatively speaking, but still a lot smaller than I expected. How many bedrooms does this have?"

"Four. But only because the architect pointed out that I might want a family someday. I originally asked for one."

"So you must want a family someday?" Gaze suddenly intense, he doesn't wait for an answer before continuing, "I also thought it might be like your office. Empty and sterile. But this isn't at all."

"Oh. That's just because the office is where I work—so I minimize distractions as much as possible. I don't ever work here at home, though. And I don't guard against becoming hyperfocused here. If it happens, it happens. But the spaces *are* similar."

"Because of the giant windows?"

"Yes. Because nature is the one thing that's never *wrong*. Or too cluttered. Or unbalanced. Or out of order. It just is what it is. And that's very soothing to me."

"So when I move in, I shouldn't go shifting stuff around and unbalancing everything?"

When I move in. Relief pours through me. "You can change anything you want to. But if it bothers me, I might move it back."

He grins and comes closer. "You don't need to worry that I'll change much of anything. I don't own much stuff, and what I've seen of this house seems perfect as it is. Especially if you've got a kitchen. Are you hungry?"

"Very." My stomach has been growling since we got here.

"Then I'll get you fed before getting you into bed," he says and a shiver of anticipation races over my skin.

I lead him to the kitchen, which has its own wall of windows, though part of the view is blocked by my Christmas tree. I head for the refrigerator. "My house-keeper always leaves a dinner for me. Looks like we have…peanut chicken skewers and a chopped salad." I read the label she left on the container, then consider the size of the portion, then Caleb's massive size. "Do you want this? I'll eat one of these yogurt and granola things."

"Just a yogurt? Let me see how much is in here." Frowning, he takes the container from me. "Ah, yeah. Okay, how about we split the chicken, but I'll cook up something else to go with it." Opening the refrigerator door wider, he scans the contents. "We can work with this. Do you have any rice noodles?"

"I have no idea."

"Can I look through your cupboards?"

"They're your cupboards now, too," I point out, and that seems to stop him for a long second, his gaze arrested on my face. Then he gives me a brief, fierce kiss before beginning a search for the noodles.

Remembering that he ordered a beer at the party yesterday, I find one in the beverage cooler and pour him a glass. It doesn't take long before he's got a small collection of ingredients on the counter.

"Do you need me to cut anything?" I ask, moving in to examine the bottles and spices. "I can cut. And peel."

"I've got it covered. But you can keep me company. And you should eat some of this salad to hold you over until it's ready." With thrilling ease, he hefts me up onto the counter. My sweater's long enough to cover my bottom, but the granite's cold under my bare thighs— yet it quickly begins to warm from the heat of my skin. "Those fuzzy socks are adorable."

"And comfy." Which is more important.

"Your bare legs are gonna kill me, baby." He skims his hands down my thighs before bracing his hands on the counter on either side of my legs. "In the very best way. Is this the kind of thing you usually wear around the house? Just a long top and some fuzzy socks?"

"Yes. Though I usually wear underwear, too."

His eyes close and he groans as if tortured, his head hanging low. Then my stomach growls and he abruptly backs away, shaking his head. "Feed you first. After that…"

Anticipation heats my blood. Because he doesn't finish that thought now, but he already told me. *I'll get you fed before getting you into bed.* I don't see why we can't just do the rest in the kitchen, but I can wait for the bed, too.

And enjoy myself here. I especially like looking at his hands. His fingers are long, the tips blunt and his movements deft as he begins preparing the noodles. He rolls up the cuffs of his flannel shirt before filling a pot beneath the tap, his forearms like sinewy steel.

"Do you cook often?" I ask him, taking a bite from the chopped salad.

"Most nights. So tell your housekeeper she doesn't need to keep making dinners for you."

Because he would cook for me? Warmth fills my chest. "Or I can ask her to make two, if you don't want to take the time."

"I enjoy it. But you don't?"

I shrug. "Hot stoves and I don't make a safe combination. I learned that fairly early. So I don't cook. But I *can* cut and chop and peel."

"Can you stir?"

"Like a three-star Michelin chef."

He grins, opens a few bottles and pours a measure of their contents into a small bowl. A dollop of reddish-brown paste goes in before he hands me the bowl and a whisk. "Get to work."

It only takes a minute before it all smooths together, the scent of the sauce slightly sour and slightly fishy. "When did you learn to do this?"

"Cook? When I was twelve. Though when I first started, it was usually mac-and-cheese or spaghetti. Sure as hell wasn't pad thai."

"Only twelve?" I assumed it was when he began living alone—learning out of necessity.

"Yeah. I remember it pretty clearly." He pauses to take a swallow of his beer, then cracks a few eggs into a bowl. "My mom worked most nights until pretty late. It just made sense for me to cook something for myself and have enough left over for her, so she'd have something ready when she got home. Once I got the hang of it, I started reading recipes so I could surprise her now and then with something new. As long as the ingredients weren't too expensive."

Oh. On a soft sigh, I tell him, "You *are* all

marshmallow-y inside."

He barks out a short laugh. "Yeah, no." His jaw tightens briefly before he shakes his head. "The reason I started? Is because I was a lazy little dick. Because one night she came home late, just fucking exhausted. And the first thing I said to her was that I'm hungry and where's my dinner. So she went into the kitchen and started heating up a can of soup. Then she hid in the bathroom and began bawling, because she was so damn tired, but her work still wasn't done. And all that work she did *for* me. But it was no effort for me to learn and have it ready on those late nights for her, to make her life a little easier. So I stopped being such a dick and gave something back."

"Ooey-gooey S'mores," I tell Caleb quietly, my heart swollen with all the sweet emotion I feel toward him. "You didn't start cooking because you were a lazy little dick. You started because you loved her."

"Yeah, I did," he says gruffly.

Of course he did. And being loved by Caleb sounds completely, utterly wonderful.

Not being loved by him is completely, utterly wonderful, too. Simply being with him makes me so happy. When I accepted his proposal, I believed that I'd be marrying a forthright man I liked and was attracted to. But Caleb is so much more. He's a man who apologized when he hurt me. Who makes me catch fire with his kisses. Who so easily accepts my tendencies and doesn't demand typical responses.

I didn't expect that I might start falling in love with him. But I think that I am.

I don't expect Caleb to fall in love with me, though. That's no more likely than being loved by my own mother. But I'll take what he gives. I'll take this desire, this closeness, this happiness—and give him everything I can in return.

I know it won't be enough to keep him forever. His marriage proposal stipulated that the marriage would be temporary. I was reminded of that today when I saw the first draft of the marriage contract based on his business plan. He only wants to be married until he receives his inheritance.

It was so difficult not to take that stipulation out of the contract. To demand that our marriage should last forever. But I know all too well that demanding more than someone wants to give can destroy a relationship. So I need to accept that I'll only have a little while with him.

I can be content with a little while. It's far better than no time at all.

"So what's your story?" he suddenly asks.

I look at him in confusion. "My story?"

"You asked when I started cooking. I told you the story. So what's the story of you building a house in the forest? Because I understand that it's soothing—but how do you end up knowing something like that? Did you grow up in the woods or go camping a lot as a kid?"

"Neither of those. It was at my boarding school. They had extensive grounds, including some woodlands. So I used to go out hiking alone and…" I don't think there's anything else to this story. "I liked it."

"So why didn't you become a forest ranger or something similar, instead of working in an office?"

"I wouldn't have been a good forest ranger. But I *am* good at business, and the money I make allows me to establish nature reserves and hire forest rangers."

"So you're like someone who enjoys art but can't paint. You're a patron, instead."

That analogy is literally accurate, too. I support many artists. But instead of confusing the issue, I simply nod and scoop up another bite of salad. "Unlike you."

"Me?"

"Fixing vehicles and restoring them," I say, then try to use his analogy. "You work in the art museum but you are also a sculptor."

"Yeah, I guess so." A smile quirks his mouth before he flicks a glance at me. "Is that forest story also the story of this camp project of yours?"

Essentially. I nod while chewing.

"So what kind of camp is it?"

"It'll be a summer camp for neurodivergent teens. During the rest of the year, it'll offer outdoor school programs and science education for local underfunded school districts."

"So you're trying to give a bunch of kids the same experience that you got at your boarding school?"

I shake my head. "Just a different experience from what they usually have. Whatever they get out of it will depend on them."

"Speaking as one of the kids who came from an underfunded school district, I'd have loved an opportunity like that." Admiration fills his voice. "That's a fucking fantastic project."

"It makes me happy." And hearing him say that makes me even happier.

"It should. And if you still want the Wyndham property for that project, I'll just give it to you. You don't have to buy it."

Touched by that generosity, I smile up at him. "The property I have is enough."

"All right." He reaches for a colander hanging on the pot rack and I take another bite of salad. "So what's the story with your parents?"

It suddenly becomes hard to swallow. "My parents?"

"You told Jessica not to invite them to the wedding."

"Because I don't want them there," I say woodenly.

His gaze fixed on my face, Caleb comes closer, bracing his hands on either side of my legs. "Why?"

I don't talk about why. "I shut them out of my life."

My voice is icy. And I know how it comes off. The billionaire who cut off her family and refuses to reconcile. I've heard the whispers. My parents are vocal about my rejection of them, telling anyone who listens that I'm a cold ungrateful bitch who cares more about money than I care about family and human connections. Maybe Caleb is thinking the same.

I only wish that I could truly shut them out. That the mention of them wouldn't affect me at all. That I could sit here without a lump in my throat and a dark ragged hole in my chest.

His eyes search mine before nodding. "All right."

It's with relief and regret that I watch him move away from me again. He busies himself at the stove, scrambling the eggs. His profile is a beautiful arrangement of hard angles and surprising softness in the shape of his mouth, which feels firmer than it looks. But there's no softness in his jaw, shadowed by a heavy growth of stubble. And with his collar looser than it was yesterday, I can see a little more of the tattoo peeking up along the muscled column of his neck. Still not enough to determine what it is, but I try to mentally extend the shape, searching for a design that seems right.

"Audrey." Caleb's directly in front of me, his big hands gripping my thighs just above my knees. "Audrey, baby."

I blink up at him.

"There you are. You weren't kidding about spacing out." A slow grin widens his mouth. "Dinner is ready."

"Okay," I say and reach for his collar.

He goes still as I unfasten the first button, then the next. His rough hands begin a slow slide up my legs, and my name is a low groan. "Audrey…"

"I want to see your tattoo." I smooth the left side of his shirt back, revealing part of the design, but need to unfasten more to expose it all. The tension in his body increases with each button I undo, until his shirt is hanging open and I can push the flannel completely over his left shoulder and halfway down his arm.

"Do you have a tattoo under your sweater that I can look at?" Despite his clear amusement, hunger deepens his voice.

"No tattoos. I don't handle pain well."

"The needle's not as bad as you think it'll be."

"It doesn't matter if it's really bad or not. I still don't handle pain well." As if in reaction to my touch, his heavy pectoral flexes beneath my fingers when I trace a stylized wing. "It's a bird?"

"A phoenix."

"Why?"

"I like the idea of second chances. Or rising from the ashes." His short laugh reverberates beneath my fingertips. "Or fucking up a first date, but still ending up at a woman's house the next night after making her come in your truck."

I like all of those ideas, too. My hands range down over his stomach, gliding over the ridged muscles that harden to corrugated steel beneath my touch. My fingers hook beneath his belt.

He catches my wrists. Voice raw, he tells me, "There

aren't any tattoos down there."

I'm not looking for tattoos. Instead it's the thick bulge behind his zipper that interests me. I glance up into his face. His eyes are a fevered gleam of arousal.

Need sparks across my skin. "I'll race you to the bed."

That's all the warning I give before shoving him aside and taking off. His bark of laughter comes from behind me, then the sound of his pursuit. I sprint up the first flight of stairs, giggling and already breathless, then nearly wipe out as I turn the corner in my socks and start up the next flight. That slip allows him to gain on me, his hands snagging my hips, just enough to make me stumble before I catch myself on the steps, still trying to climb but forced to use both my hands and feet on the risers. Abruptly he curses and his grip tightens, bringing me to a sudden halt.

His deep groan sounds from behind me. "Fucking hell, baby. You think you can tease me with a glimpse of this pink pussy and get away easy?"

I hear the muffled thunk of his knees hitting a step below, then he pushes my sweater up over my ass. My heart thunders as a ragged exhalation passes over my exposed flesh.

Time stops as I feel Caleb's mouth against me—and his hot tongue. Oh god. Licking through the seam of my pussy. Pushing *into* me. My head swims from the sheer stunning pleasure, then I cry out when his firm lips close around my clit and he sucks on that aching bud, just like he did to the tip of my tongue when we kissed, but the kiss didn't feel like *this*.

"Goddamn, you've got a delicious little cunt." His harsh voice penetrates the silky haze of ecstasy he just wrapped around me. "Now you keep running. And we'll see what happens when I catch you again."

My knees wobble unsteadily as I start off. I'm still reeling from the pleasure of his mouth, the flesh between my legs slick and hot—but I like to win, so I push past the lust and run. I hear Caleb following, taking the steps two at a time.

But I've got a head start and the advantage of knowing exactly where I'm going. I burst onto the fourth level and sprint for the bed, leaping the last few feet to secure my victory, letting loose a triumphant laugh when I safely land before he closes in. From my perch atop the mattress, I spin to see how far ahead I was.

And…oh. He's not far behind me, but he's not running. Instead he's prowling closer, his hot gaze fixed on my face, his thumb wiping a glistening smear from his chin. His shirt is still unbuttoned, his hard chest framed by soft flannel, but he's only a step away when he drags the shirt the rest of the way off.

"You beat me here," he says in a gravelly voice, then licks my arousal from his thumb. "But I'll still catch you."

So easily. Because I don't even try to get away, sinking down on the mattress as his hands grip the hem of my sweater and pull it over my head.

Abruptly he stops, staring at my nude form kneeling on the bed. "God help me. You're so fucking gorgeous," he groans as if that's a terrible thing, then spears his hands into his hair and pulls at the short strands in frustration. "Waiting is going to kill me."

"Waiting for what?" I grab his belt and tug him forward. He makes that tortured sound again but sways closer, his hands catching my face and his head lowering.

He rasps against my parted lips, "Waiting until we're married before I fuck you."

A giggle ripples through me. My mouth curves beneath his…but he's not laughing. Was it *not* a joke, then?

"Are you serious?"

"Yes." His thumbs stroke my cheeks, and his voice deepens. "It's traditional to wait until the wedding night before consummating a relationship."

I scoff. "It's an old-fashioned tradition."

"I'm an old-fashioned guy."

"Really?" I pull back, narrowing my eyes at him. "So does that mean you're a virgin, too?"

"No. But I didn't intend to marry any of them, so there was no need to wait for a wedding." Even as I snort derisively at that answer, he goes utterly still. "Hold up. Did you mean 'too' as in 'Are you old-fashioned and *also* a virgin, Caleb?'—or did you mean 'too' as in 'Are you a virgin like me, Caleb?'"

I give him my coldest stare.

"Holy fuck." His disbelieving gaze searches mine. "But you're not old-fashioned—or religious."

"No." And not shy or prudish, either. "But I don't like people touching me. And I don't like touching them."

Tension abruptly whitens his jaw. "You don't?" Gaze stricken, he jerks his hands away from my face. "I'm so sorry, baby—"

"Except for *you*, Caleb." I catch his hands and guide them back, until he's cupping my cheeks again. "I like it when you touch me. I like it very, *very* much."

He exhales a relieved breath, then pulls me closer, resting his forehead against mine. "Then I'm going to touch you so damn good. So you tell me what you like and what you don't."

I will. But I don't get the words out before he kisses me, deep and hot and hungry. And I do like this, so much, as he eases me onto my back, his mouth ravishing mine all the way down. His tongue slicks past my lips in rhythmic strokes, drawing a low moan from my throat as my hands roam up over his strong arms, his broad shoulders. I want to touch him everywhere, the wondrous pleasure of his warm skin under my palms blending with the ecstasy of his kiss.

His weight settles between my thighs, and the burning need becomes a wildfire. I break the kiss, gasping, "Your jeans. Take them off. Let me feel you."

Laughing and groaning at once, he buries his face against my throat. "If I feel your wet pussy against my bare cock, I sure as hell won't last until the wedding. So they aren't coming off until we're married."

I hiss with frustration, then he's kissing me again—but this time my neck, trailing his lips downward and finding a spot so sensitive that a single lick seems to swipe over every nerve within my skin, making me tighten and shiver all over.

"I won't leave you aching, baby," he promises on a soft growl before moving lower, cupping my breasts in his big hands and pressing them together, giving me more cleavage than I've ever had. His thumbs sweep across my hardened nipples before he lowers his head to my right breast. He teases me with a swirl of his tongue, then moves to the left and teases again.

"I like this, Caleb," I tell him on panting breaths. My nipples had been tight but now they throb with restless heat. "I like this so much—"

Lightning snaps through my veins as he draws hard upon one taut peak. A strangled cry breaks from me, my back arching.

"Oh god, and *this*. This, too."

Caleb groans his agreement, as if his pleasure is as sharp and electric as mine. And now it's clear why he pushed my breasts together, so that he could suck hard upon one nipple before hungrily feasting on the other, back and forth, back and forth, while my fingers dig into his shoulders and my hips writhe beneath him. Between my legs, I'm so slippery that there shouldn't be any friction. But there is, rough and just as good as it was in his truck but here it's adding a layer of sheer frustration.

"I'm getting your jeans damp," I point out breathlessly, hoping that'll change his mind and he'll take them off.

"I know it, baby. I hope your pussy juices soak them through," he says gruffly. "It'll be like wearing a badge of honor, because I made you this hot for me."

"So hot." My skin on fire, my pussy all molten heat. I rock up beneath him, seeking the hard ridge of his erection where the friction is best and worst and so good. "And so wet. You make me so wet, too."

A tortured groan rumbles through him. "You make it so hard to hold out."

"Then don't."

"I have to. But I'll take care of all these pussy juices for you—and I'd rather have that badge of honor all over my face," he says gruffly and moves lower, his tongue tracing down my stomach, but I catch his hair and bring him up again.

I guide his lips to my left breast. "It wasn't equal. You started on the right side and ended there, and this one didn't get a final turn."

"Not equal?" He chuckles against the bottom swell of my breast before latching on to my nipple, his heavily-lidded gaze holding mine as his cheeks hollow. And as incredible as it feels, the way he looks at me with his dark eyes gleaming with hunger and amusement and challenge—as if he's daring me to find fault with what his mouth is doing now—deepens every sensation, not just touching my skin but also the sensitive, ephemeral parts buried inside me, those feelings that have nothing to do with nerve endings.

With a gentle tug of his teeth, he releases my nipple and rasps, "Better?"

"Yes," I tell him huskily. "And I like watching you."

"Then you keep those gorgeous eyes fixed on what my mouth's about to do."

I do, coming up onto my elbows. My stiffened nipples are a bright rosy pink when he leaves them behind. On a trail of licks and kisses, his dark head slowly moves down over my stomach, my skin tightening with every inch he gains. His hands go more quickly, coasting down my sides and gripping my thighs.

My breath catches when he pushes my legs up, settling my feet on his shoulders. He looks up at me, gaze dark with hunger.

"All right?"

Dizzy with anticipation, I nod.

His hands slide downward again, palming the underside of my legs, thumbs sweeping inward through the wetness glistening on my inner thighs. His gaze drops from mine and his body goes utterly still as he takes in the sight of my most intimate flesh, open and waiting for his kiss.

"I like this," I tell him, my breath coming in erratic gasps. "I like this."

A groaning laugh escapes him. "I'm not even touching you yet."

He is. His hands are still gripping my thighs and his shoulders are bracing my feet, and that's good, too, but that's not what I like best now. "You're looking at me as if you want this more than anything."

"Because I do," he says in a voice thick with hunger. His thumbs slide upward and part the lips of my pussy. A ravenous growl rumbles from him. "Just look at you. So fucking beautiful, and so goddamn wet, and all I want to do is to make you come on my tongue. Now you hold onto something."

Obediently my hands fist in the bedspread as he lowers his head. Tension quivers through my thighs, then my breath leaves my lungs in explosive rush when his tongue drags up through my center and flicks over my clit. His eyes close in ecstasy, as if that long hot lick was even better for him than it was for me, but it couldn't be, nothing could be better.

Until it is, when he does it again. And again. Slowly, as if savoring the taste of me, as if my pleasure is only his secondary goal—because if my pleasure was first, then he'd just focus on my clit, but he's licking me all over. I tell him what I like, and it becomes a chant that I can't stop because I like it all, from the way his tongue slicks through my folds to the way his teeth graze my clit before he licks it again, to the way he groans and orders me to fuck his face when I can't stop myself from rocking against him, to the way he pins my thrashing hips when he focuses on my clit again, sucking and teasing.

And he told me to hold on but I can't support my weight anymore, my elbows giving out and my hands letting go of the bedspread. So I hold on to his hair instead, fisting my fingers in the thick strands and sobbing with frustration and pleasure as he abandons my clit, lifts my hips and thrusts his tongue past my sensitive entrance again and again, fucking into me with each deep lick.

Then his gaze meets mine, and with a long slide of his tongue he slicks his way back up, his mouth and chin glistening with my juices as his lips close over my throbbing clit. And I can't see what he does, only feel it—the teasing licks, and the sweet suction that makes my legs begin to shake. Then his tongue glides over my engorged clit from side-to-side, with pleasure and arousal ratcheting painfully tighter with every sideways swipe.

"That." I can't get any more words out, can't tell him that I like it so much, that it's so good. Instead I sob "that" again and Caleb does it, rougher and harder and faster, his eyes like hot coals locked onto mine as the ecstasy twists higher and higher, his fingers digging into my thighs to hold me in place as my spine arches up with it, his harsh groans vibrating through my aroused flesh and urging me to come.

The orgasms uncoils suddenly, violently, an earth-shattering quake beneath my skin. I scream as it unleashes inside me, my pussy muscles clenching and my body shaking through its release. As my climax subsides, Caleb's mouth gentles, his eyes burning with satisfaction and pleasure. Then I can't hold his gaze anymore, falling back against the bed again. Aftershocks tremble through me as he slowly licks the full length of my pussy, as if gathering up all the wetness of my orgasm.

And I like it, like it so much, but can't bear it now. "It's too much," I gasp and he begins working his way up my belly instead. My feet slip from his shoulders and I don't have the strength to do anything but let them fall, lying beneath him with my legs splayed and my lungs still trying to catch up with what my body just did.

"I think we're both about to take up a new hobby," he says gruffly against my breast. "Because that was a whole lot of fun."

I laugh breathlessly, nodding. And I like what he does now, too—kissing me again with the flavor of my arousal on his lips, then rolling us onto our sides and pillowing my cheek on his biceps. With his head tilted down and me looking up, we're nearly face to face, and somehow I feel closer to him now than when we were kissing. His fingers trace the curve of my jaw, then glide down over my neck. His gaze follows his hand, but I watch him, my chest swelling at the expression that settles over his features, a mixture of desire and wonder and contentment, as if simply being close enough to touch is as pleasurable for him as it is for me.

Until his fingers slip down my upper arm and a frown draws his eyebrows together. "What happened here?"

"Surgery," I whisper. "I fell out of a tree and broke my arm."

"Must have been a bad break."

It wasn't. Not really. Not at first. And the memory halts the swelling warmth in my chest, makes me tense as his fingers pass my elbow and find the scar on my forearm. Then the next.

His head comes up and he lifts my arm to get a better look. His face slowly darkens. "And these scars here?"

Pain constricts my heart and I shake my head.

A dangerous light enters his eyes as he examines the scars again. They're old, a little paler and shinier than the surrounding skin, and not very noticeable except for the difference in texture. But no one else ever touches me. "They look kind of like the burn marks you get after brushing up against a hot exhaust pipe."

I yank my arm away and sit up. He lets me go but I can still feel his gaze on me.

His voice is sharpened steel. "Were those from an accident or did someone do that to you?"

I can't lie. And I can't give him my usual stare because I can't even meet his eyes.

His tone softens. "Who did this to you, baby?"

Averting my face, I reach for my sweater and pull it on, covering the marks. But I feel as if I should tell him *something.*

My throat feels hot and tight as I say, "I don't talk about it."

A muscle works in his jaw. Then he nods. "I won't mention it again."

Relief at his easy acceptance loosens the obstruction in my throat. Hesitantly I suggest, "Should we go down and eat?"

"I already did," he replies with an exaggerated leer— and when I laugh, he kisses me and kisses me and kisses me before swinging me up into his arms. His voice is like crushed gravel when he adds, "Now I'll take care of you."

CALEB

I BEGIN COUNTING DOWN THE DAYS TO THE WEDDING like a kid waiting for Christmas. Except no kid ever wanted anything as much as I want Audrey Clarke.

After that first night at her house, I use her pussy like my own personal Advent calendar, opening up those thighs every day and finding a sweet treat to eat. And that's all I do. By some miracle, I keep my goddamn pants on. I like to think it's willpower, but I don't have much where Audrey is concerned. More likely it's cowardice, because I don't trust myself enough to sleep in her bed— so every night after making her come on my tongue, I return home and remove myself from temptation.

Or it's fear that keeps my pants on. Terror that I'll

lose her. That she'll decide wanting me isn't reason enough to marry me. So I hold out on the desperate hope that if she begins wavering, sexual need will see her through the wedding.

But she hasn't wavered yet. And now there's only three days left. Three more days until she's completely mine—not just because I'll finally bury my cock deep inside her, but because she'll be wearing my ring.

Not long to wait. And she probably won't change her mind now. But I'll feel a lot more secure when I've got her locked down. Today I take one step closer to that—by signing the marriage contract.

I arrive at the law firm's building before Audrey does and wait in the lobby for her. She strides through the entrance a few minutes later, her blonde hair sprinkled with snowflakes, her red lips curving into a smile the moment she spots me.

"Ready for this?" she greets me, her icy eyes sparkling.

"More than ready."

I hold out my hand and she takes it without hesitation. Just like she always does. Ever since she mentioned that she doesn't like being touched, I've paid a lot more attention to when she *does* touch anyone—and when she doesn't. Like when we went out to dinner with Cole and Mia a few days ago. Audrey obviously adores the other woman. Yet all the hugs of greeting and casual, affectionate touches I often see between female friends were absent. Also absent are all the casual touches with me. She'll take my hand as we're walking or standing together, but unless we're alone and focused on each other, she won't reach out and touch me. As if there's nothing at all casual about the way she touches anyone—it's all deliberate. Maybe even an effort. And whenever she's the recipient of an absent touch, even if it's just someone lightly brushing her arm to get her attention, she stiffens up.

Yet she never stiffens up when I touch her. And I figure it relates back to what she told me once about having a context for personal interactions. I'm her fiancée, and she wants me. So me touching her is all part of that. But it's still not easy for her to reciprocate those touches unless we're in a clearly intimate situation—such as standing close to each other in the kitchen. Or snuggled up together on her big sofa and watching a football game. Or while I'm making her come in her bed.

Or in an elevator. Because we still don't kiss hello. I kiss her for better reasons.

As soon as the doors close, I tilt her chin up and tell her, "I'm kissing you now because I can't fucking wait to call you my wife."

That happy smile curves her mouth again just before I claim her lips, pulling her body tight against mine. She moans softly and her fingers tangle in my hair as she hungrily returns the kiss. Only the chime of the floor indicator reminds me to let her go—and if I've got red lipstick smeared all over my mouth now, so be it. Everyone at the law firm of Sullivan & Ellis already knows I'm hers.

She takes my hand again as we exit the elevator. "I told them you're on your lunch break and we need to move through this as quickly as possible. Are you all set for next week?"

For our honeymoon. A full week spent between her thighs, if I have anything to say about it.

"All set." My boss gave me the time off for the wedding and honeymoon, but only after I persuaded the other mechanics to cover my shifts those days. Luckily I possess something valuable to barter with. As lead mechanic, I've got a coveted schedule that gives me weekends off…but I won't be seeing those weekends for a while. I ended up trading schedules with the other employees for three months out, starting with the weekend before Christmas—which starts tomorrow. "I'll be working this Saturday and Sunday, though."

"I will be, too," she says lightly and I laugh before lifting her hand to my mouth and pressing a kiss to her knuckles. Audrey works every weekend, according to her assistants. Maybe that'll change up after we're married, but if it doesn't…well, I keep pretty busy on weekends, too, usually working on my current restoration project. I don't expect Audrey to sit on her ass while I'm messing around in the garage.

Maybe we'll just shorten those working hours on the weekends, though. Staying a little later in bed in the mornings. Coming home early in the afternoon.

"What did you think about the Wyndhams' dinner invitation?" she asks as we enter the law firm's spacious reception area, which resembles one of those rooms you see in movies about rich people in England. "Do you want to accept?"

An invitation that came this morning…for an event scheduled tonight. A celebratory dinner to congratulate us on our engagement, supposedly. "It was damn short notice, wasn't it?"

"It was."

"And you have your company Christmas party tonight, don't you?" I know she does, because this was going to be the first night in a week that we wouldn't spend the evening together. I'm tempted to accept the Wyndhams' invitation just to have a little time with Audrey.

"Yes, but the Christmas party always goes on until midnight or later. I could leave it for a few hours. But you intended to meet up with your friends at Murphy's tonight?"

Which, knowing Patrick, will turn into a stag party for me. "The dinner's early enough that I could still do that afterward. I'm just wondering what the hell they're playing at."

"I might be able to shed some light on that, Mr. Moore." It isn't Audrey who answers. Instead it's the man who's waiting for us—who also looks like he might have come out of a movie about rich people in England, though his accent places him closer to home. He gives my hand a firm shake. "Bradford Sullivan."

Audrey's lawyer. "Caleb Moore," I respond. "Shed what light?"

He gestures for us to walk with him and says, "We've argued that only the estate's executor should have access to Eleanor Wyndham's assets while the will is in dispute. The probate judge agreed. So the Wyndhams received a notice to vacate the mansion within two weeks."

"They've been kicked out?" This was already a good day, but now it's even better.

"Essentially." Bradford opens the door to a conference room. "So I suspect the dinner invitation is an olive branch that they are extending out of sheer panic."

"Because they assumed they'd win this case, yet one of the first motions filed resulted in their eviction," Audrey says and glances at me. "Do you want to accept that olive branch?"

"Fuck no. But I'll go to the dinner."

Her pale eyes glitter with amusement. "For spite?"

"Pretty much." And because I've never even met these assholes. I should probably get a look at who I'm dealing with. "We might as well let them know where they stand. Maybe give them a U-Haul brochure."

"I like your style, Mr. Moore," Bradford says, then introduces me to a man who is his blond clone. "Our senior partner, Nathan Ellis. Typically, we'd ask that you bring your own attorney to advise you, but we understand that time is short and you've had difficulty finding competent representation. So Audrey requested that Nathan and his team act as your unofficial representatives in this matter. They've already asked for several revisions to this premarital agreement on your behalf, and after a week of back-and-forth, this is what we've arrived at for today—so please consult with Nathan if you have any questions or concerns. The agreement itself is based on your original proposal to Audrey."

I don't really give a shit what it is, as long as she marries me. I take a seat at the conference table with Audrey and her lawyer sitting across from me, then begin reading through the contract. And, yeah. It's damn similar to my proposal, but a hell of a lot more comprehensive. I skim over the long sections about her paying the legal fees and the sale of the mansion. The only new section is the part she added after a conversation we had about protection and birth control, the same conversation that had me heading in to the health clinic last weekend. And the lawyers are damn thorough here, too. She'll continue with the pill that she's already taking, and we'll use condoms if needed, with changes to be made at our discretion and by mutual agreement. Copies of our clean test results are even included in the—

Snap.

My head jerks up. Across the table, Audrey's icy gaze is focused on the contract in front of me. But I don't see what about it is distracting her. "Audrey?"

Her eyes meet mine and a little smile plays around her lips. She glances at the lawyer sitting beside her, then pulls out her phone. I look at mine when the text comes in.

Audrey: Every time you turn the page, you lick your thumb the same way you tease my clit.

Oh fuck. Instantly I'm too damn aware of the fit of my jeans. I shove the phone back into my pocket—and I don't even know if I've finished reading this page. But I don't give a shit. I lick my thumb and turn to the next.

A sharp *snap!* follows while I grin like a motherfucker. I glance up again when I hear her move. Her smile is a full curve now, but she's rising from her chair, turning toward the windows overlooking the city, her arms crossed beneath her breasts. Suddenly I'm tossed headlong into the memory of the first time we met. Sitting across from each other—not at a table, but at her desk. Where she did the same damn thing. Snapped that rubber band while looking at me. Then got up and looked out the window.

At the time I thought she was cold, distant. But now I know better. She's standing over there with her pussy as hot as my dick is hard.

And it was hot when she accepted my proposal, too.

Her hands rub up and down her sleeves, and my grin fades. That's another thing I've paid attention to this past week. Maybe she always wears long sleeves because it's winter. Or maybe it's habit from a time when her scars were a lot more visible than they are now. But whatever the reason for the sleeves, I've also noticed there are only two things she doesn't talk about: those old burns on her arm, and her parents. It doesn't take a genius to figure out that they're connected.

Someday, I really fucking hope to meet them. Not so I can do or say anything to them, because I've got a feeling Audrey wouldn't like it. But for the same reason I'll be seeing the Wyndhams tonight—I'd like to put faces to the people I hate.

I look down at the contract again, my stomach tightening as I realize this page starts the section regarding the dissolution of our marriage.

This is all straight out of my proposal, too. At least the first part is, where it says that as soon as probate is granted and Eleanor's estate passes into my possession, the marriage agreement will be considered complete and divorce proceedings can begin without either party being in breach of contract.

There's some other shit about infidelity voiding the agreement but I'm never going to cheat on her. I keep going back to that bit about divorce proceedings beginning after I receive the inheritance.

With acid eating away at my gut, I glance at Nathan Ellis. "How long do you figure it'll be before this thing with the Wyndhams is settled?"

"We estimate between six to twenty-four months."

Two years with her. Maybe.

Because this was based off my proposal. I told Audrey at the beginning this marriage would only be temporary. But that was before I got to know her. Before I kissed her and tasted her.

Is this what she wants, too?

I look to Audrey, who's still standing at the window. "Did you read this thing?"

"Yes." She faces me again, her expression unreadable. "Several times. I had to approve each revision."

Each revision. But if this was based off my proposal, this part was in here since the first draft.

And she approved it each time.

A thick knot fills up my chest as I start skimming the rest. Barely seeing it. Something about shared custody if we have kids. Something about keeping the assets we came into the marriage with, and the same for assets we earn or inherit during the marriage. Something about a settlement if I don't win against the Wyndhams—

"Hold up. What the hell is this?"

Ellis glances at the paragraph. "In the event that we don't secure your inheritance, then upon the dissolution of your marriage to Miss Clarke, you will receive a settlement of five hundred million dollars."

"Absolutely fucking not."

Audrey frowns at me. "You are entrusting me—and through me, this law firm—to secure your inheritance. Eleanor's will is clearly valid. The only way we can lose is if my lawyers make a terrible mistake during proceedings, and failure means that I have made a gross error in judgment asking Sullivan & Ellis to handle this matter."

Beside her, Bradford appears pained but nods. "She's not wrong."

Audrey's gaze doesn't leave mine. "So if we fail, you would deserve compensation for my error."

"No." And because that one curt word clearly doesn't convince her, I add, "You were my one chance of going up against the Wyndhams. This was all a gamble for me. If I lose, I don't expect to walk out with money in my pocket."

"The courts are not a casino, Mr. Moore. You don't win a lawsuit by chance but with a strong legal argument," Nathan Ellis says. "The Wyndhams might create a delay by contesting the will, but it's all a bluff—and in this type of game, we can see their cards. We know they have nothing. They were relying on you not having either the money or the stamina to fight them. But their claims are pathetically weak in the eyes of the law and they *are* going to lose."

So maybe the inheritance is a sure thing. If so, this clause won't even matter. But I can't let this shit stand.

"I don't give a fuck. Take it out." My gaze burns across the table to meet Audrey's. "I'm not marrying you for your goddamn money."

"Yes, you are," she replies succinctly. "You asked me to marry you so that you could gain access to my money and my lawyers. Is that not so?"

"No, it's *not* so. The marriage proposal was just to get your attention. I never figured you'd go for the whole thing."

Lips parted, she stares at me for a long second, her expression utterly still. Her throat works before she asks, "Your proposal was a *gimmick?*"

That makes it sound sleezy as shit. "No, I just…asked for more than I figured you'd give. I wanted a business partner. I wasn't looking to fleece money out of a rich wife, or to get anything more than what I was supposed to inherit. Any money you spend helping me, I intend to pay it all back. I sure as hell don't want half of a fucking billion dollars out of you."

Nathan Ellis slides in again. "Mr. Moore, marriage to a woman like Audrey will come with certain drawbacks and sacrifices. You'll have to endure public attention, and your personal relationships might suffer if any of your friends or family become resentful or envious of your new situation. I advise you to consider—"

"No. This bit where I get money from her? It's a deal-breaker. If it's in here, you better tear up this fucking thing because I won't sign it."

Ellis glances over at Audrey, who's up at the window again, her back to all of us. "Audrey, you originally suggested the terms of this settlement. Do you have any objection to removing it?"

There's a long silence. Dread clutches tight around

my chest when I see how stiff she is—her spine rigid, her body unmoving.

Finally she says, "Please give Caleb and me a few minutes alone."

Fuck. Heart thumping, I push back from the table and head over to the window while the others quietly leave. She stares straight ahead through the glass, giving me nothing to go on. Just her profile and the stiff set of her shoulders.

The inside of my throat feels like I swallowed gravel when I ask her, "So you put that bit in there, making sure I get money after we divorce?"

"Yes."

"And is that what you expect—that we'll split up after this legal shit is all over with?"

"Yes," she says quietly. "That's what I expect."

All that gravel is ripping up my chest now. "When this marriage is over"—I can barely fucking get that out—"I don't want your money."

"I know. You just made that very clear." She glances at me with a sad sort of amusement touching her mouth. Amusement that vanishes only a moment later, and she worries her bottom lip between her teeth before looking out the window again. "Do you want to tear up our marriage contract completely? I will still help you with the rest…and be the business partner you hoped to find."

Because when I brought that proposal to her, I didn't really know what I was looking for. But it was Audrey all along. For however long I can have her. Six months. Two years. It'll never be long enough.

I should have known a man can't have a whole pie and eat it, too. So I'll take what I can get.

"No," I tell her hoarsely. "I don't want to tear it up."

Her eyes close briefly. She pulls in a deep breath before glancing at me with another little smile. "I suppose there is still the matter of your unlikely demise. We need to make sure that inheritance stays out of the Wyndhams' hands."

"Yes." I'll agree with any reason she wants to believe.

A bit of sparkle returns to her gaze. "And spite."

I try to dredge up a smile but can't manage much. Because spite isn't anywhere near the top of my list of reasons to marry her. Hell, I've barely even thought of the Wyndhams during this past week. Only of her.

Only of making certain she still wants to marry me.

"And this, too," I tell her gruffly—and she doesn't stiffen when I catch her chin, doesn't pull away when I softly kiss her. Instead her eyes close and she melts against me.

Her cheeks are flushed when I lift my head. Her eyes search my expression, then she glances away, her gaze settling on the contract I abandoned on the table.

"Caleb, we can change the agreement—but you should know that, in my mind, this is when our marriage begins. When I sign this contract. Not the ceremony or the license. To me, that's just…" She seems to cast about for words before settling on, "That's just the handshake after the deal is made, because there's no going back for me after this. So if you have any doubts—"

"I don't. And I'll sign any damn thing you want me to." Especially if a contract is what locks her down. "But I still want the ceremony. Because that's what's important to me."

The vows that talk about forever. Not just a short time.

She nods. "Of course we'll have both."

"All right, then." I stalk over to the table and grab a pen, start flipping to the end of the contract. "Let's do this."

"Not yet!" Her exclamation and soft laugh follow me. "We need witnesses. And we'll ask them to print a copy that doesn't include the paragraph about the settlement."

"Oh. Good."

Her face serious again, she collects the contract from the table. "But are you certain, Caleb? If we lose against the Wyndhams, you'll end up with nothing when our marriage is over."

"I'm sure," I tell her.

Because it'll be the same either way. Win or lose, when our marriage is over…

I'll have nothing at all.

AUDREY

AUDREY: I'M LEAVING THE CHRISTMAS PARTY now. I'll be there in about fifteen minutes.

Caleb: I'll be ready.

In the backseat, I click off my phone and lean my head back, closing my eyes. The driver's closed partition, privacy screens on the windows, and soundproofing shut out the light and noise from outside, but I can't shut out the pain that's been growing inside me all afternoon.

I'm no good at lying to other people, but I apparently have no problem lying to myself. I told myself that I would be content with the short time I have with Caleb. Yet I could barely breathe as I watched him read through the second part of the marriage contract today.

Hoping with everything in me that, after spending this week together, he'd modify his original plan to dissolve the marriage after the legal battle ended.

But he didn't. He let that part of the contract stand while everything inside me felt as if it was breaking apart.

That wasn't even the worst of it, though. I thought it would be. But I had a week to prepare for that—of reading that section over and over, of knowing it might never change. I wasn't prepared for the rest.

I want to marry you, he said the first time we met.

But it was a lie.

I never believed the proposal was anything more than a business arrangement. That had been clear from the beginning. He wanted to marry me to spite the Wyndhams. I was never under the illusion his offer meant more than that.

Yet I still believed him when he said, *I want to marry you.* That statement had electrified me. It had surprised me and pleased me and I decided to accept his proposal before I even heard the rest of his pitch.

But he never meant a word—and I didn't even realize it.

I can't always tell when people are lying to me, and I can't always interpret their tone and expression, but I can spot a gimmick like red paint on white canvas. Yet I didn't spot his. I took him at his word. And since then, he's been so forthright that it never occurred to me that his *I want to marry you* was just a way of getting my attention.

But he didn't want to marry me.

Maybe he does now. He says he does. But maybe he just…recognized that marriage was a better deal. Because it is. So maybe he doesn't really *want* to marry but is smart enough to see the advantages, so he agreed to take that step. I know he doesn't want my money, but in this fight against the Wyndhams, marriage to me makes attaining his goal much more certain.

As for the sex that he claims is another reason…we certainly don't need marriage for that. And I don't think he's faking his desire when he kisses me or touches me, and I don't think his thoughtful way of offering protection and comfort is a pretense. But those have nothing to do with marriage. He would be the same if we were only dating. Because passion and caring are in his nature, and his friend was right to call him a marshmallow. Caleb *is* a big, sexy marshmallow. A little charred and rough at first glance but so sweet inside. So he would be the same whether he was marrying me or not.

And I don't know what to believe now. Self-doubt has crept in. Because I mistook what he wanted from the beginning—mistook the words that formed the foundation of this relationship. And it hurts. The painful vulnerability that faded over the past week is once again a giant, aching hole in my chest.

I open my eyes as the vehicle stops in front of a house festooned with Christmas decorations. Movement on the upper level of a detached garage draws my attention. Warmth twists in my belly as I recognize Caleb's big form coming down the stairs, wearing the same black twill trousers and red flannel shirt under a heavy canvas coat that he wore to the tree lighting ceremony. He greets my driver by name before getting in and choosing the rear-facing seat across from mine.

"A bigger car today," he comments, leaning forward to briefly press his lips to mine. "Are we pulling out the stops for the Wyndhams?"

"For my employees. All of my drivers are on call to take home anyone who isn't sober enough to drive." The door closes, leaving us in a cocoon of dark and quiet. "I hope you don't mind if we keep the privacy screens up."

"I don't," he says softly. "Was the Christmas party too much? If it was, we can skip this dinner."

This whole day has been too much. But the dark isn't just to settle my brain. It's how I hide when I'm hurting, too.

I don't want to say any of that, so I simply tell him, "Dinner will be fine. And there's a Christmas present for you on the seat over there."

"You shouldn't—"

"It's not from me." I know he doesn't want anything from me. That was made clear today, too. "It's from Jeremy and Jessica. They didn't think you had time to shop for an ugly sweater for tomorrow, so they picked up one for you."

"Ah, shit. That's good of them. But they shouldn't have done that."

"They like you. And they enjoy giving things to people they like." Just as I do.

"Yeah, but I was thinking we shouldn't even go to that party."

Patrick's ugly sweater party? "Why?"

"Because the wedding's only two days after that. I'm sure both of us have tons of other shit to do."

"Not according to my calendar." And if I needed time to accomplish something, I'd schedule time for it. "Is there something else you need to do? Or you just don't want to go?"

Frustration roughens his response. "I'm just thinking it would be better if we didn't."

"Oh." My throat suddenly closes up. Tight, so tight. Because it suddenly occurs to me why he doesn't want to go. Or rather, doesn't want *me* to go. My voice is a jagged whisper as I ask, "Are you afraid I'll be a rude snob to your friends again?"

"What? No. Fuck no. That doesn't worry me at all."

"Then why?"

"Because of *this*, baby. Because you just got out of a party and you're sitting here in the dark. And it's not all ugly sweaters. There's going to be a fuckton of people, they're all going to be loud and drunk, they'll have music blasting in one room and probably playing a *Die Hard* marathon at full volume in another room, and they'll all be trying to grab you and hug you and shake your hand while congratulating us."

"I like *Die Hard*," I snap before tapping on the overhead light, trying to control the emotions suddenly raging inside me.

Sitting across from me, Caleb blinks a few times, then his brows lower in a dark frown. "Are you pissed off?"

Partly pissed off. Partly touched. Mostly thinking that I *never* want this to happen again.

In a tight voice I tell him, "I appreciate your concern. I do. But you need to understand that I don't accept invitations because I think it's a polite thing to do, or because I feel an obligation to go. I only do what I *want* to do—and this party sounded fun. I also expect the noise and music, and if I thought I wouldn't enjoy myself or be okay, I wouldn't go. As it is, the worst that will happen is that I space out or have to find a dark room for a while. And those aren't such bad things."

"They aren't bad things at all." His eyes close and he gives a heavy sigh, dragging his hand through his hair. "All right. I was just—"

"I know what you were just. You were trying to protect me. And I like very much that you are thinking of me, Caleb. I truly do. But please do not ever think *for* me."

His jaw clenches but he gives a tight nod. "But you'll tell me if you need me, or if it's too much."

That, I can give him. "I'll tell you if I need you."

"And I live right over Patrick's garage—so if you have to escape, I'll keep it open for you."

"Thank you."

He groans. "Don't thank me, baby. It's the least I can do. But while we're at it, is there anything else you want to get off your chest?"

I don't mean to. I don't mean to at all. But my eyes suddenly burn, my throat thickens with tears, and it bursts out. "I didn't know it was a gimmick."

Caleb goes utterly still. "Audrey—"

"And I feel like *such* a foolish dipshit!"

His expression hardens. Instantly he leans forward, catching my hands. His gaze locks on mine. "First of all," he grinds out through gritted teeth, "you are the smartest person I've ever met. Hands down. No fucking question. The most brilliant. So you don't ever think or feel like that. And second of all…" His voice suddenly hoarsens. "I can't say I'm sorry for doing it. I'm so damn sorry it's making you feel like this. But if I only asked you to be a business partner, then I wouldn't be here with you now. I wouldn't know what your pussy tastes like and wouldn't be jacking off every fucking day while picturing you under me on our wedding night. If I hadn't asked for the whole damn pie instead of a single slice, I wouldn't be marrying you in three days. So if I said I was sorry that I went into your office with a marriage proposal that I never believed you'd accept, it'd be a lie."

I swallow past the thick lump in my throat. "So your

only lie was the first one?"

"Yes. Except it's not a lie anymore."

Because he wants to marry me. Maybe not forever. But for now. And despite all this pain and uncertainty…I also know that I love him. I know I'll hurt even more when I eventually have to let him go.

Fortunately that won't be today.

A ragged breath shudders from me. And another. Then I ask, "You jack off every day?"

A short laugh escapes him, as if that was the last thing he expected me to say. "Every day since I met you."

"Why don't you do it with me?" I only get to touch him above the waist or through his jeans.

"Because I'm keeping my pants on with you. But I usually come while I'm eating your pussy, anyway. I've done a hell of a lot of laundry this week."

"I haven't done any," I say and as he grins in response, I demand quietly, "Show me."

His fingers tighten on mine. Heat flares through his gaze. "My laundry?"

"I want to watch you jack off."

His breathing deepens. "We're only about five minutes away from the Wyndham estate."

Not enough time. "Then we'll save that for the trip back. But I want to see you now."

"Me?" His voice roughens. "Or my dick?"

"Both," I whisper huskily. "I want to look at you— and the big cock that I've felt against me but never seen."

His eyes darken. "Say all that again, Audrey. And then tell me you want my long, thick cock balls-deep inside your tight little cunt."

Is that what he wants to hear? But I want something, too, and negotiating is an activity that I do very, very well. "Maybe I'll tell you after you show me."

"Oh fuck," he groans and leans back, sliding down a little in the seat and unbuckling his belt. "You're such a hot tease."

"I'm not the one holding out until the wedding."

A tortured laugh shakes through him. "Trust me when I say that I'd do any damn thing to make Christmas come earlier this year."

Me, too. But I don't think he expects a response, and I can't give one anyway as he unzips and drags his erection free, his fingers wrapped around the base. The heavily veined shaft that juts up through his fist is crowned by a broad, flared head—and all of that is going to be inside me. My inner muscles clench almost painfully hard. I make a needy sound low in my throat, aware of his burning stare locked on my face, but I can't look away from his massive length.

"It's fatter than I thought," I whisper. The shaft is even thicker than the wide tip. As his fist strokes upward, his fingers tighten near the head. "And a little longer."

"The perfect size to fill you all the way up." His voice is taut with strain. "The perfect size to make you feel so damn good."

"Yes," I agree breathlessly, because I don't know what size is right but simply looking at it makes me feel so good. Because every rigid inch is evidence of his desire.

His desire for *me*.

"If we were married, you could climb up on me right here and…" His fist slowly drags down his length as if to demonstrate the way my pussy would take him in. "Or you could turn around in that seat and I'd get up behind you, fuck you so deep and hard."

Oh god. He demonstrates that, too, with his fist jerking up and down his shaft, rough and fast—before slowing, slowing.

"But on our wedding night"—his breathing is heavy, harsh—"I'll be so gentle. Because I want you so goddamn bad but I'll never hurt you. So I'll slowly ease into your hot little cunt when I open you up for the first time."

Thighs clenched tight, I squirm in my seat, my pussy drowning in molten heat. "Caleb," I gasp.

"You want that, baby? Then you tell me. I showed you the goods, so you tell me how bad you want this big cock inside you."

I'm not done negotiating. "Only if I taste it first."

"Christ help me," he groans, his eyes closing. They open again when I slide out of my seat and kneel in front of him. "Audrey. Baby. Your mouth looks so goddamn fuckable. You're killing me."

Not any worse than he's killed me this past week. Softly I say, "Please, Caleb. I want it so much."

"Ah, fuck. Fuck. How the hell am I supposed to resist that? All right, then." His voice suddenly hardens as if he's steeling himself. Gripping his cock just below the crown, he angles the ruddy head toward my lips. "You lick away that little drop right there. That'll give you a taste."

The pearly bead of semen that decorates the fat tip. More evidence of his need for me. Eagerly I lean forward to sip away the drop.

But it's all over too fast. I barely process all the sensations coming at me. The salty flavor. His harsh curse and the small, involuntary jerk of his hips. The taut, slick skin beneath my tongue. His heat and my own arousal, the deep throb in response to it all. And foolishly, I closed my eyes, as if I were kissing his cock. So I didn't witness his reaction.

I look up at him now and see the strain visible across his face. My voice thick with hunger, I request, "One more?"

Jaw clenched, he gives a tight nod. "Just one," he rasps.

But he doesn't specify how long that taste can last. And this time I keep my gaze on him, just like he does when I'm so close to coming and his mouth closes over my clit, when he begins to suckle and lick and I can't see what he's doing but I can feel all of it—and he never looks away from me all the while.

Now I know why. Because I do the same, closing

my lips over the head of his cock, sucking and licking and watching as agonizing pleasure overtakes Caleb's expression. *I'm* doing that do him. Making his teeth grit on a tortured moan and his head fall back. Making his fingers convulsively tighten around his shaft. Making the heavy muscles in his thighs tremble before stiffening.

I swirl my tongue and his breath hisses through his teeth. The tendons in his neck stand in sharp relief before he lowers his head again, gaze locking with mine. His dark eyes gleam with need, an aroused flush reddening the skin above the hollows of his cheeks. For an instant, his left hand hovers above my hair—whether to push my mouth down farther or to pull me off of him, I don't know. Then his hand clenches into a fist and drops to his thigh.

With another groan, he begins stroking his shaft with his right hand. "Fucking hell, I can't stop this. Your mouth feels too goddamn good."

I try to make it better, sucking harder. His curled fingers rhythmically bump against my lips, wrapped around the flared rim, and when I frantically rub my tongue along the underside of his cock head, that rhythm suddenly increases. His breath shudders before he drags in another, his broad chest heaving.

"Baby— Ah fuck." His head bows, lips drawing back in a grimace. The clenched fist on his thigh opens and convulsively closes again even as his right hand pumps faster and faster. "You've gotta stop— Holy shit, I can't…

I'm gonna— Audrey, ah fuck, fuck—"

On a harsh grunt he curls forward before his entire body turns to iron—except his cock, which throbs beneath my tongue as his salty release fills my mouth. He's absolutely beautiful as he comes, his features flushed and taut, his eyes glazed and unseeing. With awe expanding in my chest, I watch the orgasm overtake him.

Immediately I want to make him come again, to witness this one more time. And although my body is on fire, my pussy aching, I feel utterly content in this moment, knowing I've just given him the same ecstasy that he's given to me over and over again. If Caleb felt even half this satisfied after making me come, then it's no wonder he was able to keep his jeans on. I would love to fulfill my own need right now, but it's only physical desire. Emotionally...I feel completely sated. And so pleased.

Swallowing a mouthful of cum is an effort, but as soon as I manage it, I grin up at him. "No laundry this time."

He chokes on a laugh and catches my face in his hands, hauling me forward. His mouth captures mine in a hot, deep kiss that ends far too soon, with Caleb resting his forehead against mine, his breathing still ragged. "Christ, I've never gotten off so fast. But the sight of your lips wrapped around my dick, and the way you were looking up at me... It was too fucking much.

Now you say it."

Against his mouth, I murmur, "I want your long, thick cock deep inside me."

Gruffly he asks, "You want this cock enough to marry me?"

If that was the only thing I wanted…? I still would. "Yes."

That earns me another kiss before he pulls away. "You'll get it, baby. Just three more days. You'll be a virgin for our wedding but I'll be taking your sweet little cherry about two seconds afterward. We're going to shock all the guests."

I laugh, but then a tiny worm of uncertainty wriggles under my skin. Because…I'm a virgin. I don't think of myself that way very often, because it's a label I don't put any real stock into. I don't think it matters much to Caleb either—aside from his planning to be gentle that first time.

Because it's supposed to hurt.

"You okay, Audrey?"

"Yes." I can think about my virginity later. The car is slowing, so I quickly return to my seat and reach under my skirt to peel off my drenched underwear. A few tissues take care of most of the wetness, then I snag a new pair of panties from the small bag of toiletries I brought with me. I slip them on and smooth my skirt down.

Caleb watches the whole process with his expression

showing a combination of lust and bemusement. "You came prepared with dry underwear?"

"Of course. You keep making me wet. So I have a new 'Caleb keeps making me wet' kit. Do you need to wait a few minutes?" I gesture to his cock, which he's shoving back into his pants—still partially erect. "That looks painful."

"Meeting the Wyndhams will shrivel it."

"If I had one, it wouldn't shrivel." Not after what Bradford told us today regarding his investigator's findings. "Instead I'd be rock hard with anticipation and ready to spew loads of spite all over them."

When my driver opens the door, Caleb's still laughing so hard he staggers getting out. Then he staggers a little more—but this time it's because he got his first look at the mansion, I realize.

"Holy shit," he breathes. "I thought it would be like the Bennet House."

Which is Neoclassical in style, whereas the Wyndham mansion is a dramatic Gothic structure of gray stone, with steep gables and gargoyle-studded towers and forty thousand square feet of living space.

Still appearing slightly stunned, Caleb glances at me. "You were going to buy this thing?"

I shrug. "It's not to my personal taste, but I thought students would like it."

"Were you going to build a Quidditch stadium, too?"

"Don't tempt me. I'm a Slytherin, by the way." And

I bet he's full-on Hufflepuff. I take his hand as we head for the front door. "So are you changing your mind about selling it?"

He shakes his head. "If I kept it, I'd burn the fucking thing to the ground."

The large arched door is opened before we reach it, but not by one of the Wyndhams. Instead I recognize Mr. Ferry, Eleanor's butler. Attired in a crisp black suit, the elderly gentleman first greets me and welcomes me back to the mansion before turning to Caleb.

"Mr. Moore, I believe that I speak for the entirety of the staff when I say how very pleased I am to make your acquaintance." He bows slightly, inclining his head. "I am David Ferry, and I am at your service."

"*The staff.* Shit," Caleb mutters under his breath before reaching out and shaking the man's hand. "Good to meet you. We're here to see the Wyndhams."

"Yes, sir. They await you in the drawing room."

"The drawing room. Great."

Ferry's lips quirk. With a sweep of his arm, he ushers us inside and begins showing us down a long hallway. "If I may be so bold, sir—I had the pleasure of knowing your mother for a short time. We were all quite shaken by what befell her."

Caleb's reply holds the same raw edge that always deepens his voice when he speaks of his mother. "She only had good things to say about all of you. Especially the housekeeper, Mrs…?"

"Mitchell," Ferry supplies.

"That's right. Mrs. Mitchell made sure my mother had a place to stay when she was trying to get back on her feet. Is she still around?"

"Mrs. Mitchell retired two years ago, I'm afraid. But I can make certain to pass on her contact information."

"That'd be good. Yeah." Caleb abruptly frowns. "Hold up. Are all of the employees being kicked out when the Wyndhams are?"

"No, sir. I'm pleased to report that this has become a very merry season for us, indeed—and will be even merrier in two weeks. We are employed by the estate, not by Mrs. Sylvia or her children, so we retain our positions until Mrs. Eleanor's will is settled."

When most of them should be able to retire, because Eleanor had been gracious enough to gift each member of the staff a substantial sum and establish a pension. But while the Wyndhams contest the will, their future remains uncertain.

"Mr. Ferry," I ask him, "have the Wyndhams indicated that they'll honor Eleanor's gifts to the staff if the will is invalidated?"

He smiles thinly. "Mrs. Sylvia is of the opinion that, since the staff will still be needed when she and her children inherit the estate, we shouldn't be given incentive to retire so young or require such a large pension when we do eventually leave."

No wonder Ferry was so pleased to see Caleb, then.

And Caleb appears pissed off by that revelation—angered by the injustice done to the staff, not just driven by spite and hatred.

And it's just another reason that I keep falling deeper and deeper in love with him.

"Change of plan," he says in a low voice to me as Mr. Ferry opens the drawing room door and announces us. "I don't burn it down. I let the employees do it—with the Wyndhams still inside."

"The staff will receive their gifts and pensions when we win," I remind him, my gaze skimming the large room as we enter. It's a rather small and quiet engagement party. Only the Wyndhams themselves seem to be here—Sylvia, the new matriarch, and her children Christopher and Meredith—along with an all-too familiar couple seated on a blue sofa.

Ice splinters through my gut. My fingers convulsively tighten on Caleb's.

"Caleb," I whisper through stiff lips. My entire face feels frozen. "I need you to stay right by my side. And don't let *anyone* touch me."

He abruptly stops, ignoring Christopher's greeting as the man approaches us. Frowning, he asks quietly, "What is it?"

I'm on the verge of hyperventilating, yet I can barely manage the breath to answer. "My parents."

AUDREY

C ALEB'S FACE DARKENS AND HE THROWS A DAN-gerous glance in my parents' direction. "Those two are?"

"Yes." I can hear the high-pitched panic in my voice. "We can't stay long. I don't want to stay long."

"Fuck this, then. We'll go now."

"No." I stop him as he pivots toward the door. "Let's say what we came here to say. Just…be with me."

"I will." He presses a warm kiss to my palm before turning to Christopher—who resembles Caleb in his coloring and the overall shape of his features, yet without any of the fascinating rough edges and irregularities. "You invited those assholes?"

Christopher doesn't even blink. With a smooth smile he replies, "Yes, of course. An engagement party should include the families of the happy couple, shouldn't it? We all wish to offer our congratulations."

"Sure you do," Caleb tells him, then looks to Mr. Ferry. "Congratulations will go over better when my fiancée has a glass of champagne. Will you please see that she gets one?"

"Right away, sir."

Warmth fills me, melting some of the ice. Caleb knows I rarely drink alcohol. So he must have noticed the trick I've been using in public to escape touching and too many handshakes—by holding a glass in my free hand while I hold on to him with the other.

I love him so much.

I cling to that love as tightly as I cling to his hand as we walk farther into the drawing room, fighting to keep my gaze away from my parents. It's hard. Because they're so *wrong* here. They're so wrong anywhere. And I'm not looking at them but they're all I can see.

Everyone stands at our approach. Before we reach the group, Mr. Ferry returns carrying a silver tray topped by a single glass, which I gratefully take. But it might not have mattered anyway. Bristling with anger, Caleb doesn't bother to shake hands, either. Introductions go around but I barely hear them. Only his replies. I focus on the sound of his deep voice so I don't drown in the bloody wound that ripped open in my chest when I saw my parents.

The wound was only a scar before. A scar that ached now and then—especially after I met Caleb, as if to remind me of the damage that can be done when your heart is open and vulnerable to someone.

Caleb will be more careful with me, though. Even when our marriage ends, I believe he'll take better care with my heart than my parents did, because he's a rough man but also a good one. The wound might be deep and bloody, but not delivered cruelly or thoughtlessly— and I'm walking into our marriage with my eyes open, knowing it'll end. I'm choosing the eventual wound over never having him at all.

My parents, though…I could have done without them.

We're invited to sit. Caleb escorts me to a love seat adjacent to my parents' sofa, then sits forward slightly on the cushion, as if using his big body to shield me from their sight—or to block them from mine. Whatever his intention, having them out of view helps me begin to relax and listen to what the others are saying.

In an elegant Chanel suit and pearls, Sylvia graces a wingback chair positioned to preside over the conversation. Yet Christopher does most of the talking, seated on the sofa across from us with Meredith at his side. I can imagine what the Wyndhams think of my attitude thus far—and my icy silence—but I don't care. They had to know I've shut my parents out of my life, because it's common gossip in these circles, yet my parents were invited anyway. Which tells me the Wyndhams wanted to knock me off-kilter. Well, they managed that. Point to them. But it's the only point they'll get.

Christopher offers another smile, just as smooth as before but tinged now with melancholy. "Tonight we celebrate a happy occasion, yet we must acknowledge the tragic event which truly brought us together. I'm only sorry we couldn't have done this before my grandmother's passing."

Meredith chimes in, "I believe that it would please her very much to know that we have all come together now."

"Yes, it would," Christopher agrees solemnly. "And it is our hope that—in the healing spirit of the season—we might repair the rifts that have estranged us…and make apologies that are long overdue."

Both Meredith and Christopher turn to Sylvia, who wears a delicately earnest expression. To Caleb, she says in remorseful tones, "To properly apologize, I must first explain how terribly shocked and grieved we were when we lost Robert so suddenly. He came along much later than I did, you see. I was already married and with Meredith on the way when my mother gave birth to him. And so Robert was not like a sibling to me at all, but another son."

"And an older brother to Christopher and me," Meredith adds with a soft, nostalgic smile.

"So when Robert's yacht sank"—Sylvia's voice quavers—"we were simply *devastated*. And in the rage and denial of our grief, I regret that we closed our minds and our hearts to your mother's truth. Because with one look at you, there is no denying your parentage. I know that this apology should have been made to her. I honestly can't say what prevented us from doing it. Cowardice, perhaps. Or a stubborn unwillingness to revisit our loss and pain, and to never consider what we might gain by welcoming you both into our family. Perhaps fear, too— fear that she would never forgive our overreaction."

Throughout this speech, Caleb's fingers slowly tighten on mine. Angry? Affected? I can't tell. But I hope he isn't falling for this manipulative hogwash. Because I *can* usually spot a gimmick, and they are pushing their grief harder than any used car salesman ever pushed a lemon. The only thing their rehearsed apology lacks is a solitary tear rolling down Sylvia's cheek.

Oh oh!—and there it goes. Her lips trembling and her eyes shimmering, Sylvia turns her face away, as if overcome by emotion.

If my parents weren't here, this might be fun.

Christopher picks up the script from there. "So we hope, Caleb, that we might put the past behind us and welcome you into our family as we ought to have done so many years ago."

"In the healing spirit of the season?" Caleb responds, and I still can't read him.

"Exactly."

With a nod, Caleb turns to address my parents. "And you have an apology, too?"

I stiffen beside him. Whatever they feel sorry about, I don't care to hear it.

But apparently the Wyndhams didn't tell my parents that apologies were on tonight's agenda or give them time to prepare. A few moments of silence pass before my mother's stammering, "Well, ah… Of course."

Without even seeing them, I know exactly what's happening now. My mother glances at my father in a wordless plea for help. My father would rather eat rusty nails than apologize for anything, so he leaves it to her to handle such a troublesome matter.

For many years, I was the troublesome matter that he left to my mother. And even after decades of him continually denying her pleas for help, she *still* looks to him first. Perhaps hoping this will be the day he gives her the love and support she so desperately needs. For the longest time, I gave her mine—or I tried to. Because what I had to give certainly wasn't what my mother needed from me.

Now I've got nothing left. Except this raw wound in my chest.

And Caleb, so warm and strong beside me, holding my hand and silently offering his protection. He has no use for my love, either—he's only marrying me for spite and sex. Yet I think we have become friends, too. And simply being next to him softens the wound enough that I can listen without running away to hide from the pain.

Haltingly, my mother begins, "I suppose…that we were also guilty of overreacting. Or *I* was. Your father was…"

She hesitates over what he was, so I suggest flatly, "Weak."

"Audrey!" she gasps, as she always does whenever I speak too bluntly. She gasped often while I was growing up.

I try again. "Selfish?"

"Of course not. You know your father is a very generous man."

Only if generosity is defined by how much money someone gives. "Indifferent, then."

"No," she denies emphatically. "He was *not to blame*. That's all I meant to say. And that I was unprepared for a child like you were, Audrey. I was unprepared for your screaming or your tantrums—or how cold you were."

"Catherine, my dear," my father interrupts tightly. "Perhaps you and Audrey should take this discussion to another room."

"Oh, should we?" I shift forward to look past the shield Caleb made of his body. My father's expression is taut and remote, his posture clearly of a man in extreme discomfort, while my mother's face is flushed with emotion and effort. I got my pale coloring from him and my facial features from her, but in every other way, I can't see myself in them at all. "Is that so you won't have to listen to all these troublesome matters? Or is it because you don't care for the Wyndhams to hear? Are you embarrassed for them to know you had such a difficult and emotional child? I am not embarrassed by it because I don't care what they think."

"Perhaps you don't care that this is making them uncomfortable, either."

"Not really. Though I suspect you're the only one who's uncomfortable, Father, because the Wyndhams are probably delighted by this little drama."

"Of course not," Meredith protests softly, her eyes wide as she follows our every word.

A muscle works in my father's jaw. "I simply do not think this is the time or the place."

"And yet our hosts have explained that this was the purpose of being here—to air old grievances and make new apologies. So go on, Mother. I would like to hear how you were unprepared for such a cold child. Because as I recall, I *constantly* told you that I loved you." Especially after I was old enough to understand how much she needed it. But it still wasn't enough.

"Simply saying it means nothing, Audrey. You must *show* it." Her gaze darts to my father's face as if hoping that her words will sink in with him, too, but he's already locked down, staring straight ahead and waiting for this to be over. Bitterness creeps into her voice when she looks to me again. "You said you loved me, but you could not even bring yourself to hug me, or display any sort of affection that children typically show their mothers."

"I showed you affection," I tell her. "Because I loved you more than anyone and I was desperate for your approval. But you never recognized what I was giving."

"Perhaps that is true—and perhaps, if you will give us the chance, I can learn to recognize it now." Her gaze falls to my hand, still clasped in Caleb's. "Or perhaps in these past years, you've learned to show more affection than before."

"No, I haven't." Easily touching anyone in the way she means will never be something I can learn. "But I *have* learned to give my affection to people who are more deserving."

Her gaze darts to Caleb and rare fury flares through my blood, because I know exactly what rushes through her mind during that brief look—wondering how a rough bastard like Caleb could possibly be more deserving of love than someone like the delicate, beautiful, well-bred creature that she is.

Yet because she's such a well-bred creature, she will only think it and never say it. Instead she continues, "I am encouraged by your acknowledging that you were a difficult and emotional child. Just as I acknowledge that I did…overreact. And you were perhaps right to be angry with us. With *me*. But now that you are beyond your youthful rage, you can look back with the wisdom of maturity and have compassion for a young mother who was simply overwhelmed—and see that I did my best. And considering all that you've achieved in recent years, it's evident that no lasting harm was done. So perhaps you might put aside your anger now, and forgive me for being so young and unprepared, so that we might be a family again."

My anger? I was never angry. I was hurt and afraid.

I *wish* that I'd been angry. Like Caleb is at the Wyndhams. I wish resentment burned so deep that I could take pleasure in spite and revenge. Instead I've simply been afraid that they'll hurt me again.

Not anymore, though. Because I realize they *can't* hurt me more than they already have. They've done their worst—or at least, they've done the worst that I'll allow them to do—and I survived. And I will *never* give them an opportunity to touch Caleb or show him any more of the disdain that my mother just did.

So now I'm just…finished with them.

"I have plenty of compassion for young, overwhelmed mothers who receive no support from their partners. Yet I also have very little sympathy for women who are cruel to their children, no matter the reason—or for weak and selfish men who leave their wives to it," I tell them, before saying as plainly as I can, "I have no interest in renewing our relationship—*ever*. You are my parents but you are not my family. And after this evening, I hope to never see either of you again."

Outrage suffuses my father's face. But he leaves this to my mother, too. Her features pinched with bitterness, she looks to Caleb. "I cannot congratulate you on your engagement to our daughter. Instead I offer my condolences for the cold life you'll soon lead. You've secured yourself a rich, beautiful wife who will never be able to show you love and affection, and who will be impossible to love in return." She casts a sour look at my father, who's getting to his feet, before adding to Caleb, "But no doubt you'll find warmth elsewhere, as men so often do."

"Nah, I won't. And as far as I'm concerned, you can shove your condolences so far up your ass that they'll pop out your mouth again. But they'll probably still be covered in the same amount of shit."

Perhaps my mother meant her final remark as a parting shot, but Caleb's response brings both my parents to a stunned halt. They stare at him, disbelieving.

I squeeze his hand in gratitude for not letting her have the last word. But he's not done.

"Your daughter loves what she does and pursues what makes her happy. The people around Audrey are happy to know her, too—and it doesn't have a fucking thing to do with her money, and everything to do with who she is. That doesn't sound like a cold life to me, and she doesn't sound like a woman who has no love and affection to give." His voice sharpens to a razor's edge. "What it sounds like is that you need Audrey's life to be all about you, to make you feel good about yourself. Luckily, the rest of us who know her aren't as fucking needy as you are."

Gaping at him, my mother begins to shake her head, to say, "I have *never* in my life—"

"That's enough, Catherine." My father grips her arm and steers her toward the door, with my mother still denying and gasping and gaping. "Sylvia, Christopher, Meredith—until next time."

He doesn't acknowledge me as they leave, which is a relief, because my throat is a knot of overwhelming emotion after hearing Caleb's speech. No one *ever* has understood me so perfectly.

I pursue what makes me happy. And *he* makes me happy. If Caleb hadn't proposed to me, I'd be pursuing him even now. He said that he wasn't sorry for using the gimmick, because if he hadn't we wouldn't be here. But maybe we would have been. Because after our initial meeting, I'd have gone after him. Asked him out for dinner—and probably to my bed. Surely he wouldn't have waited for a wedding night then, just as he didn't wait with anyone else he wasn't marrying. And perhaps we would have gotten to know each other in this same way.

Aside from sex, however, skipping straight to a marriage engagement has proved a much more efficient way of getting to know him. And makes me even happier than merely dating him could have.

"All right, then," he says, facing the Wyndhams again. "Two apologies in the bag. So I guess that means it's my turn."

"To…apologize?" Christopher's brow furrows. "If you are sorry now for having us evicted from our home, surely that can be easily amended—"

Caleb barks out a laugh. "Hell no. In her will, Eleanor said she wasn't leaving anything to you all because you're 'lying, cheating, backstabbing, greedy vermin.' I don't know anything about that. But I'm pretty damn sure that Meredith is wearing the necklace you all accused my mother of stealing—the one that got her sent to prison for two fucking years."

Prison? I suck in a breath, my gaze flying to the diamonds around Meredith's neck. She stares back at Caleb, absolutely frozen, before she looks to Christopher as if for help.

Caleb doesn't give her brother time to offer it. "Is wearing that necklace supposed to be a joke? Did you think I wouldn't recognize it from pictures in the police reports? Or that I wouldn't have looked up the court transcripts that could tell me why she missed out on the first years of my life? Or maybe you just forgot how you ruined a woman's future with that necklace. An event so goddamn insignificant to you, but the moment that changed *everything* for her."

"Mr. Moore," Sylvia says placatingly, "please understand how young Meredith was and how she didn't fully understand the consequences of—"

"She was eighteen, which means she knew damn well. So did you. The assistant district attorney who first looked at the case decided not to pursue prosecution because there were too many conflicting witness statements. None of the staff remembered seeing any of the same shit that you all said you saw. Then you asked your district attorney friend to take another look—and those conflicting accounts went away. So did my mother. For two years. Even though you all knew she was pregnant."

Oh my god. I had no idea about any of this. I thought he hated them for being snobs who blacklisted his mother. Which was enough of a reason. But *this*.

"And when she gave birth to me—while in prison for a crime she sure as fuck didn't commit—you all made sure that everyone thought she was a liar for putting Robert's name on the birth certificate. And you"—the furious heat of his gaze lands on Christopher—"claimed to have seen her whoring herself out to every rich asshole she could find at your lakeside club. You give me this bullshit now about welcoming me into the family, but you all sure as fuck made certain that I went into state care as a baby. And even after she got out on parole, it took four more *years* before she got full custody of me again. Working her ass off every goddamn second. Then after she got me back, taking on two or three jobs at a time, because the kind of work a woman can get after a felony theft conviction doesn't pay shit. Those jobs are also why she was on that fucking road so late. Why she was so damn exhausted. Why she had a shitty car and shitty tires. As far as I'm concerned, what you all did to my mother put her on that patch of ice—and you all killed her."

Christopher is shaking his head. "Surely you can't hold us responsible for an accident—"

"You killed her," Caleb repeats flatly. "Don't look for any forgiveness here, because any possibility of that died with my mother. If you'd shown her any mercy at all, I might have reconsidered. Instead I intend to take from you every goddamn thing that I can."

"Ah," I say as it all clicks into place. That small sound draws their attention, so I continue, "Eleanor knew. Didn't she? You told her all of this at your mother's funeral—when you declined her invitation to lunch."

"Yeah, I did," he says gruffly.

I look to the Wyndhams, and direct the remainder to each of them. "Our lawyers wanted to affirm Eleanor's statements that you were lying, backstabbing vermin, but they didn't know what you'd done to Caleb's mother. We knew about Meredith silencing the girl who was recently assaulted at the party her son threw for his lacrosse team by threatening a defamation suit against her family, and about the charities Sylvia uses as her personal piggy bank, and of the bribes that Christopher took from John Bennet in exchange for city council votes. But clearly Eleanor learned how you all framed and discredited the mother of Robert's baby—probably so you wouldn't have to share your inheritance with Robert's son." And I laugh, because that's just too good. "Oh, but Eleanor made you all pay for that, didn't she? Because after discovering the truth, she turned around and gave everything to Caleb—and nothing you all did in the past ten years changed her mind, because you're all horrible people. Ah, that's fun. And I think we're done here. Shall we go, then?"

Caleb rises to his feet, holding my hand. The Wyndhams regard us with a mixture of outrage and fear and worry, and Christopher opens his mouth, yet Caleb doesn't give them another chance to plead their case.

"You start packing up," he tells them. "But keep in mind that Eleanor had the contents of this house and her jewelry collection inventoried less than a year ago. When all this shit passes to me, I'll make certain everything is accounted for. And if one thing is missing, just one goddamn thing, I will have you hunted down like the thieves you accused my mother of being. So Merry fucking Christmas. You have two weeks to get the fuck out of my house."

Oh, that was lovely. By the gleam in Mr. Ferry's eyes as he opens the drawing room door and ushers us into the corridor, he thinks so, too. Yet Christopher's voice brings us to a halt a few steps outside of the drawing room.

"Miss Clarke!" Faintly sweating, he catches up to us

in the wide hallway, his jaw lifted pugnaciously. "Considering the upcoming city council vote regarding the rezoning of the Sandpipe property, you might reconsider the way that you and your fiancé—"

"I'll reconsider nothing," I interrupt, absolutely disgusted. "And you should recuse yourself from the vote. You have a clear conflict of interest."

His smug smile appears. "You need my vote for the rezoning to pass."

"No, I don't. I'll flip Kaser or Andersen when I throw my weight behind the Green Spaces project." Though he knows I'm right, his expression barely flickers. So I apply more pressure. "But since we are speaking of things that ought to be reconsidered, I advise you to think carefully about how you will soon have no access to the Wyndham fortune—which means that your wife's fortune will be your sole means of support. So the pictures that my investigators took of you and a female companion on Wednesday afternoon might disrupt your access to her fortune, as well. Unless you intend to give your wife a Christmas speech about forgiveness and healing, too?"

Now his expression flickers. His face becomes a mask of self-righteous anger. "Are you blackmailing me?"

"No. I don't want to sway your vote—I want you to recuse yourself. And if you don't do it voluntarily, I will explain in detail to the city council how your impartiality is compromised, but only with respect to my fiancé's relationship to you and our current legal battle. Your private business is your own. It might be to your benefit, however, to examine all the areas of your life that could damage you professionally and personally. Because if the court case drags on, with your side questioning Eleanor's mental acuity and judgment, my lawyers might feel compelled to offer evidence that supports Eleanor's assessment of you as 'cheating vermin'…and you can be certain those photos will end up in a publicly accessible docket."

He goes absolutely silent.

"See? Not blackmail. Just friendly advice. Legal battles involving inheritances are notoriously ugly. And this is only after a single week of investigation. Who knows what we might turn up by the end? Though I suppose you and your mother and sister know all the things you each have done and everything we might find. So you all should decide what really matters to you—your past, or your future." I smile at him. "Goodnight, Christopher."

Though Caleb's fingers tighten on mine as we walk toward the front door, he doesn't say anything until we're outside, where fat snowflakes have begun falling. I automatically tip my head back to catch one on my tongue.

He grins at me. "That felt damn good."

Yes, it did. "Christopher *did* say that he brought us together in the hope of healing our old wounds."

His deep laugh rumbles out. "He's probably not real happy with how that healing turned out."

Probably not. But I am. And I feel so much relief after that confrontation with my parents. As if the pain hadn't been an open bleeding wound at all, but a festering boil that needed to be lanced and drained. It's still sore but…it's better. And Caleb has been carrying around pain even deeper than mine, because I've been able to address mine through therapy—and to control their access to me. Yet he's never had the opportunity or the power to confront the Wyndhams before. So laying it all out before them and making them pay for what they did to his mother must have been incredibly satisfying.

And he's clearly not only driven by spite, though maybe there's some of that, too. But I just witnessed something much more powerful—a man seeking justice for his mother and finally being able to deliver it.

Though maybe he could do even more. I glance back at the house just before I slide into the car. When he settles into his own seat, I tell him, "I don't think you should burn it down."

"No?"

"I think you should turn it into a home for women who have been incarcerated and recently released, and who need help getting back on their feet or to regain custody of their children. You could call it the Phoenix House. Where they get their second chance. Or rise from the ashes—oh!"

One moment I'm sitting. In the next I'm straddling his lap, with Caleb's fingers buried in my hair and his mouth opening beneath mine as he draws me down into a hot, deep kiss. Lust immediately flares through my blood, and I can feel Caleb's desire in the thick ridge between my legs. But despite his arousal, he breaks away after only a minute, his breathing rough and close in the darkened car.

"Your parents are so fucking blind, Audrey," he says in a low, urgent voice. "And I know you don't like to talk about them, so I won't bring it up again. But I need you to know that I'm not like your mother. I see you. I see how much you have to give. And how much you *do* give every day. You don't have to go around hugging anyone to prove a damn thing."

Emotion swells inside my chest, so big. So frightening. Because if Caleb sees all that, then he must know that I love him. Must know that, even now, the way that I can sit here so close—not because we're kissing or in a sexual embrace but an emotionally intimate one—is a wordless display of how much I trust him, and how safe I feel…and how I know that he'll take care of my heart, even if I don't hold his.

My voice is thick as I tell him, "Then I want you to know that I'm not like her, either. I won't ever ask for more than you want to give—or for something you *can't* give."

Like his love—or more time with him.

Softly he kisses me. "I know you won't, baby."

That gentle response both eases and deepens the ache in my heart. He's such a good man. How could I not love him? And how can I not yearn for his love in return? But I won't be like my mother in that, either—always throwing my emotions and wishes into his face, so he feels obligated to reciprocate my feelings.

So despite the love bursting inside me, I only tell him haltingly, "But…I do have to ask for something. Because I don't want to ruin our wedding night. And I'm sorry, because I know it's not what you wanted."

"What isn't?"

"We need to have sex after the party tomorrow."

His body reacts, stiffening beneath mine—but for the longest moment, he doesn't respond. I hunch my shoulders, preparing for his rejection…yet when his reply comes, it's only a simple, "Why?"

I draw a shuddering breath, so glad of the dark. "I won't talk about all of this again, but since we'll be living together, you need to know anyway. I don't handle pain well."

"I know." His voice is gentle. "You've said that before."

"But not why I don't, or what happens when I get hurt. Not that I know *why* I don't handle it well. But…" I'm babbling. As if I'm nervous. But I shouldn't be. Because this is Caleb. And he understands who I am. So he'll understand this, too. On a deep breath, I start again. "You just met my mother."

"Yeah, I did." Steel hardens the words.

"She wasn't exaggerating about my tantrums. When I was younger, I couldn't control my emotional reactions. And when I became overwhelmed, I would scream and cry and…sometimes, I was physically violent. Hitting her or kicking her. But you don't have to be afraid of that now," I rush to add. "I learned to control that by the time I was eight."

He softly brushes a strand of hair away from my face. "I'm not afraid."

"I'm glad," I whisper, and draw another ragged breath. "But it wasn't always when I was overwhelmed. Whenever I got hurt, I would go to her for help, and then I would cry and scream—and I wouldn't be able to stop. Even if it was just something like a splinter in my finger or a stubbed toe. She would tell me it was nothing, and I suppose that, rationally, I knew it was. But it didn't matter. Until it stopped hurting, I couldn't think of anything else or feel anything else. And if she tried to help, I would scream more and fight her because I was afraid touching it would just hurt more. Because it always did. Pulling out the splinter, or the way antiseptic burns. And she would get so frustrated and angry and… she would say that if I knew what *real* pain felt like, I wouldn't freak out over a splinter. Then she'd show me. Most of the time it didn't leave marks. Though some did. Like her curling iron. And none of it ever taught me anything, except that I shouldn't go to her for help anymore."

Caleb makes a rough sound in his throat. "I'm so fucking sorry, baby." His palm smooths up and down my back. "What did you do, instead?"

"Hide. Usually in my closet, because I could cover my mouth with a blanket or pillow and scream and cry as much as I needed to until I stopped hurting."

"And it was dark and quiet there."

"Yes."

His body suddenly tenses. "Did she break your arm, too?"

"No. I fell out of a tree."

He releases a heavy breath. "Okay. I'd been thinking that maybe… But I forgot you don't lie."

Though Caleb doesn't finish what he thought, it's easy to guess. He thought I was concealing her abuse. I wasn't hiding it, though. I just don't like to think about it or talk about it.

But that's what we're doing now. This one time. So he can understand what I'm asking from him.

"I didn't lie," I say quietly. "But I didn't tell you all of it. After I broke my arm, I went to my closet but it didn't stop hurting. So I was there for a while and wouldn't leave. And they all thought I was freaking out about another little injury. Until my father got upset that I was causing so much trouble and grabbed my broken arm and jerked on it to drag me out of there." I close my eyes and rest my forehead against Caleb's. "I don't like remembering the rest."

He makes another rough sound and says in a raw voice, "Then don't, baby."

"But it was better after that. Because they sent me off to boarding school. I met Reverend Foster there—he was the school chaplain back then. And he was someone I could go to for help again. Not if I was hurt, because I still just hid. But while I was working through…emotional things. Mostly regarding my parents."

"He didn't preach forgiveness?"

"No. Mostly just acceptance. That they were who they were, and I am who I am—and understanding that, because of who they are, they will always hurt someone like me. And then teaching me to accept who I am. Which was the best lesson I ever learned."

"Because who you are is fucking amazing."

All that sweet warmth fills my chest again. I want to kiss him for that, but I've already gotten off track. And this needs to be settled. "I'm also someone who doesn't handle pain well. I've learned to withstand those mild pains better—or use it, like when I snap my rubber band. But even a splinter can still be overwhelming. And sometimes I still have to run off to hide and cry. And if I have to do something that hurts me—like get an immunization—it's hard. Especially if I might bleed. I panic a little. I don't scream or cry when they're coming at me with a needle but it's really difficult to not run away. You might think it's childish, but I just can't process—"

"I don't," he reassures me, his hand soothing up and down my spine again. "I don't think it's childish."

"Thank you. I appreciate that so much," I say, though words could never convey how much. And my heart thumps wildly, a bit of panic settling in already when I think about the rest. "But having sex is supposedly painful the first time—and it might make me bleed. I didn't think about that until after you mentioned being gentle with me. But even if you're gentle, I might not handle it well. That's why I want to do it after the party tomorrow instead of our wedding night."

For a long moment, the only sound is the soft brush of fabric under his palm as he continues that slow, soothing massage. His voice is all gravel when he finally asks, "If I come at you with my cock, you think you'll panic and run away?"

"Maybe." I pull in a shallow, shaky breath. "But I can probably make myself stay. Like when I learned to ice skate. It hurt every time I fell down, but I wanted to do it so much, so I just…pushed through. As best I could. But I might cry. Then go and hide when it's over."

"When it's over?" He makes a rough, explosive sound in his throat. "Baby, if you're crying, I'm sure as fuck not finishing anything."

"I'm sorry," I whisper thickly. "It's not going to be sexy."

"Don't you be sorry." He falls quiet again before

saying, "You're not really asking me to fuck you. Just to pop your cherry, so it won't hurt the next time. Is that right?"

"Yes. I would do it myself with a dildo or something but I can't…I can't even pierce my ears. And I trust that you'll make it hurt as little as possible."

"Not at all, if I can help it," he says gruffly, then his chest rises and falls on a deep, ragged breath. "So I'll do this. But we aren't going to have sex. We'll still save that for our wedding night. I'll just…open you up. Then I'll take care of you until you're feeling all right again."

I'll take care of you. A torrent of love washes through me, flooding my eyes with the force of the emotion. "Okay. Tomorrow night, then."

"Why not tonight and get it over with? Otherwise you'll spend all day tomorrow worrying about it."

"I'll try not to. And today has already been…overwhelming." First when we signed the contract. Then hurting all day after discovering the proposal was a gimmick. Then seeing my parents. "But we had a victory at the Wyndhams'. So now you should go out and celebrate with your friends. I'll return to my Christmas party and celebrate a fantastic year with my employees. And we'll each end today on a happy note."

Instead of a crying disaster.

"And because cherry popping isn't on your calendar for tonight," he says in the dry tone he uses when he's teasing me.

I grin, delighted by that gentle ribbing. Because I *do* live by my calendar. "Maybe I'll tell Jessica to include it on my schedule. 'After the party, please add in ten minutes for my deflowering.'"

"Ten minutes? Fuck that. I'll send her the message. And it'll be something like, 'Schedule in the whole goddamn night, because I intend to eat Audrey's pussy until she's all soft and wet and dizzy from coming so many times, and then gently open up her tight virgin cunt with my big cock."

My inner muscles clench with sheer need. "You're making it sound sexy," I say breathlessly.

"I'll make tomorrow sexy for you, too," he says in a low growl. "Now you get back over in your seat and lift up your skirt, because talking about eating your pussy is making me hungry."

I moan softly. "And you're making me wet."

"Then you get over there and show me."

I'll show him. But that reminds me—"I was supposed to watch you jack off on the ride back."

"You should have added that to your calendar to make it official before I changed it to a pussy licking. Do you have another pair of panties in that Caleb's-making-me-wet kit?"

"I do." And I already need them. Heart pounding, I slide off his lap and back to my seat, turning on the overhead light as I go. So the first thing he sees is me slowly following his orders, rucking up my skirt to my waist, spreading my legs…then showing him how wet my panties already are, with my fingertips teasing my clit through the damp fabric.

He groans softly and follows me, kneeling between my thighs. "That's so fucking hot, baby. Now we've got about ten minutes before you drop me off at Murphy's, and I intend to end this night on a real happy note by making you come all over my mouth. And that way I'll be tasting your pussy juices all the time you're away from me."

"I'm sure the liquor will wash them away," I laugh, then gasp as he pushes my legs up and hooks my knees over his shoulders. His eyes narrow dangerously as his strong fingers curl beneath the waistband of my panties, and he begins to slowly drag them down my thighs.

"Nothing in this world could wash away your sweetness from my tongue, Audrey." His dark gaze holds mine as he bends his head, his warm breath whispering over my slick flesh. "And by the time I'm done, you'll be feeling my mouth on your pussy all goddamn night."

Anticipation renders me almost breathless, yet I have to tell him—"That's not on my calendar, either."

But when he's done laughing, Caleb's mouth changes all my plans.

CALEB

N O AMOUNT OF LIQUOR COULD WASH AWAY Audrey's taste, but as the crew at Murphy's buys round after round for me, the alcohol makes a valiant effort to turn me into a genius. The first time is when I think back to Audrey saying I should celebrate my victory against the Wyndhams. But even as I'm raising my glass to do just that, my brain kicks in and I realize I can't. Because every win against the Wyndhams is another step closer to the end of our marriage.

Letting the Wyndhams know they hadn't gotten away with what they did to my mother and telling them why I was taking everything from them still feels damn good. But the rest of it… Shit. How can I celebrate? I don't want this lawsuit over quickly. I want it to last to the end of my life.

Because I'm in love with her. That realization slams into me even as Patrick's shoving another glass into my hand. I am madly in love with Audrey Clarke.

That's why I never want to leave her. And never want her to leave me.

I drink a hell of a lot after that, trying to figure out how I'll persuade Audrey not to dissolve the marriage after the terms of the contract are fulfilled. Because I've got her locked down until our wedding night, sure. Then until I receive my inheritance. But after that? Maybe I can get her so addicted to my cock that she'll never give me up. I'll keep her so happy in bed—and out of it—that she won't ever pull the trigger on those divorce proceedings.

But the real genius idea pops into my head around three a.m., just before I pass out facedown on my bed. A fucking brilliant plan. One that guarantees she'll never leave.

I'll just make her fall in love with me.

MAYBE I'M NOT THE SMARTEST ASSHOLE WHO EVER lived, but that plan still seems like a damn good one as I'm dragging myself into work the next morning. Of course, in the cold, sober—and real fucking hungover—light of day, figuring out *how* to execute that plan isn't as easy as thinking it up.

And given the way my chest feels like my heart's being ripped out whenever I imagine the marriage ending, it doesn't even seem like a plan now, but simply a basic need. One as essential as water and food and shelter, and just as critical for survival.

I *need* Audrey Clarke to fall in love with me.

But fuck if I know how to make her do that. Because I don't even know when I fell for her. The word *love* never entered my head until last night. But looking back, the emotion got into me long before that. Maybe first sparking at that cocktail party when she grinned and clinked her glass against mine, then made me laugh with her toast to spite. And flaring a little brighter as I held her close while we danced—though I nearly fucked it all up a few minutes later by thinking the worst shit about her. So my fate was probably sealed in that dark room, while I sat beside her and realized I'd be willing to stay in there forever with her if she needed me to.

Since then, simply being with Audrey has made me real fucking happy. So I've been falling in love from the start.

I can't think of any reason she might have fallen for me yet. But there has to be some way to make it happen. To make attraction and liking become so much more. It's easy to see why Audrey made my heart tip over into love—it was everything about her. Every damn thing.

Aside from my dick, though, what the hell do I have worth giving to a woman like her?

Not much. So maybe I'm a fool to think she'll ever love me. But the last time I was drunk and came up with a plan, it was a marriage proposal—and I never thought she'd go for that. But she did. So maybe I'll get lucky in this, too.

How to do it is a harder question. Obviously I'll need to be a better man. Though what "better" means is a real damn mystery, because she doesn't give a shit about the usual stuff like how much money I have or what I do for a living. Personality-wise, I'm a vulgar asshole at my worst, and miles away from Prince Charming at my best.

My best will never be worthy of her heart. But somehow I'll just be…better. Then maybe she'll need me like I need her. And maybe I'll never have to figure out how to live without her.

I know damn well I'll never be able to.

But figuring out how to make her fall in love can wait at least another day. Because what I need isn't as important as what Audrey needs from me—and I promised I'd make tonight sexy for her. So she sure as hell doesn't need an exhausted, brooding asshole jabbing his cock into her while she's nervous and afraid.

Since she's working today, too, Audrey's driver is bringing her to Patrick's party instead of me picking her up. After my shift's over, I crash out on my bed and try to catch up on a few minutes of shut-eye before she arrives—then, like an asshole, I sleep through my alarm and two incoming messages. One from Audrey saying she's on her way. The other saying she's at the party… almost two and a half hours ago.

Fuck. I haul my ass out of bed and into the shower, then force myself to slow down and shave—because I didn't bother this morning, and my face is going to spend a long time between her legs tonight. I don't want two days' worth of stubble ripping up her inner thighs. I pull on a T-shirt and jeans, then in the last second remember the gift her assistants got for me. The box sits on the breakfast bar where I dropped it last night, wrapped in shiny paper and topped with a festive bow.

And holy shit. My ugly sweater is *really* fucking ugly. A knitted portrait of my face features giant googly eyes and a wide goofy grin. Short strands of brown yarn stick straight out to form the hair. It's all topped off by a collar made of tiny, dancing unicorns in elf costumes, as if I'm wearing a psychedelic pearl necklace.

Jeremy and Jessica don't half-ass a damn thing. I drag it on because I'm sure that Audrey's going to love it.

I can hear the noise from the party as soon as I leave my apartment over the garage. I don't have to go far. Just down the stairs and up the walk to Patrick's front door. Every person that Patrick knows seems to be crammed inside—which means it's also pretty much everyone I know, too.

Audrey's not in the living room. Relief hits me straight in the chest when I spot Jeremy in the dining room talking with Logan Crenshaw, who's one of the crew that regularly gets together at Murphy's. The plan was that Audrey's assistants would arrive with her and make sure all my friends got their wedding invitations. It looks like they stayed.

I head in that direction. Logan spots me first and busts out a laugh when he gets an eyeful of my sweater. "Holy shit," he manages to get out between guffaws. "The best part is, that's exactly how you looked around two o'clock last night."

Yeah, it probably was. "Laugh it up while you can. You'll be getting your turn soon."

His gaze immediately softens and seeks out the girl he's been living with almost a year now. "It can't be soon enough."

A few weeks ago, I might have scoffed at that. I can't now. Instead I just pray like fuck that I get at least a year with Audrey.

I turn to Jeremy, who's wearing a grin as wide as the one on my chest. "Thanks for this," I tell him dryly. "Remind me to pay you back some day."

He laughs. "It'll be worth it. Especially after the boss gets a look."

I hope so. "Where's she at?"

"In the kitchen, last I saw. Let me check with Jess." He switches his red Solo cup to his left hand and quickly texts with his right. "Just a heads-up—she's been in a weird mood ever since this morning."

Shit. I *knew* we should have popped her cherry last

night so she wouldn't spend all day worrying. "Nervous?"

"You think Audrey Motherfuckin' Clarke gets nervous?" Jeremy shoots me a glance that says I must be kidding before shaking his head. "No. Just kind of quiet and distracted ever since she got the call from Bradford. Usually she'd be elated, because she loves winning. But"—his phone buzzes and he reads the screen—"Yeah, she's still in the kitchen."

And I'll head there as soon as he explains what that was about. "What call from Bradford?"

His eyebrows arch upward. "She didn't tell you?"

I shake my head.

"Shit." He grimaces. "Maybe she wanted to surprise you. So forget I said anything."

Not a chance. I narrow my eyes and silently wait.

He looks at my expression and then throws a glance at Logan, as if seeking help from that direction, but the other man's been my friend too long to offer any.

Finally Jeremy relents. "Bradford got a call from the Wyndhams' lawyer. You guys must have scared the shit out of them last night, because they're going to drop the will contest."

Logan breaks into a grin and claps me on the shoulder. "That means you get the inheritance free and clear, yeah? That's damn good news."

"You'd think so," Jeremy says wryly. "But he looks about as thrilled as my boss did."

Not thrilled. More like I'm about to puke. Because

that will contest is the reason for our marriage contract, for our wedding—for everything.

"And she's in the kitchen?" I say stupidly, because I know she is, but my brain doesn't seem to be working.

"Yeah," Jeremy says and points out the direction, as if this isn't his first visit here and I haven't been in this house a million times.

But, shit. Maybe I wouldn't have gone the right way without his help. Because I don't even remember taking the steps that bring me to the kitchen. Instead I'm in a daze and desperately holding on to a single thought: that Audrey brought Jeremy and Jessica along to hand out wedding invitations. If she didn't still plan on marrying me, she wouldn't have bothered.

The haze in my head clears the instant I see her—pale blonde hair up in a sleek ponytail, her lips a lush velvet red, her head thrown back in a laugh. Not in a weird mood at all, as far as I can tell. Instead she's in a small group that includes Jessica, Karen, and Patrick, and appears to be having a good time.

And an even better time when she spots me. Her beautiful face lights up.

Relief fills my chest. I weave through the crush of people until I'm at her side, and drop a soft kiss to her lips. "Sorry I'm late."

"It's okay. Patrick said you probably fell asleep." Her pale eyes are sparkling, and an impish little grin curves her lips. "I heard something about a stag party last night."

"Oh yeah?" I raise a brow and look to Patrick, who's trying to appear innocent.

Then Audrey's gaze skips down to my sweater and her eyes widen before she covers her mouth with her hand, giggling wildly.

"The eyes!" she only manages before dissolving into laughter again.

Patrick shoves a plastic cup full of beer into my hand before tapping his own against it. "Congratulations—you win for ugliest. Your face alone would have done it, but those eye-titties are going to haunt my nightmares for years to come. They're fucking horrifying."

Eye-titties? I glance down. And, yep. Right over my nipples.

I glance at Jessica, who's been silent this whole time. Her shoulders are shaking, tears rolling down her cheeks. Without a word, I make a V of my first two fingers, tap my jiggly nipple-eyes and then point them at her in a *I'm watching you* gesture. Which makes her sputter and snort, but I'm sure as hell never going to underestimate Audrey's Little Helpers again. They know their shit. Because if their goal is to make their boss happy, I'd say they succeeded.

Audrey wipes her eyes, still breathless from laughing. "Oh god. I wanted to win. But I'm outclassed."

Yeah, there's no way she could have ever won 'ugliest' anything. Her sweater is… Fuck, I don't know what it is. Some kind of argyle monstrosity that escaped from the

1970s, maybe. Yet she makes the thing look great simply by wearing it.

"Patrick should win," I say, because his version of an ugly sweater is leaving his shirt unbuttoned and exposing his chest hair. "You've probably got a couple squirrels hibernating in that shit."

"Alas," he mourns, scrubbing his fingers through the auburn thicket over his heart. "The host can't win."

"When we're the hosts, Patrick, we'll make sure you get a prize," Audrey laughs and slips her hand into mine. "I was just telling Karen that she and Patrick should come over to our place for dinner after the honeymoon. I already volunteered you as cook."

After the honeymoon. Thank fuck. "That sounds good, yeah. And, Christ—wait 'til you see this house."

"I've seen it," Patrick replies smugly before glancing at Audrey. "About eight years ago, right?"

She nods. "That's right."

Patrick looks to me again. "While you were playing Sleeping Beauty, we had a little six-degrees-of-separation moment going on here. Because she already knew Logan."

"He designed all my custom furniture," Audrey says.

"And I helped build and install it. So I sure as hell didn't forget a waterfall house that could have made Frank Lloyd Wright weep envious tears. Ah, shit. And here's this fucker"—Patrick snags his arm around the shoulders of the man who joins us—"Audrey, this is my little brother, Mike. He's going to try to ask you all kinds of shit about your business and use it for his classes, but you don't have to pay any attention to him."

Jessica raises her hand in a little wave. "You can come and be friends with me, Mike. I know everything."

"It's true, she does," Audrey says with a laugh. "Are you teaching classes or taking them?"

"Taking them. And I'll accept that offer," Mike adds to Jessica before turning to Audrey again. "But let's be clear here—the person who really needs a little business advice is *this* man."

He points to me and Audrey's smile widens, her brows arching.

"Oh?"

"Yeah. He ever tell you how he's restoring those old cars in my brother's garage? Buys them, fixes them up, sells them."

"He did."

"Did he mention that he never expenses any of that shit off his taxes? Not the parts he buys, not his rent, nothing?"

Both Audrey and Jessica make noises like they were stabbed.

Ah, shit. Dull heat climbs my cheeks and I awkwardly rub the back of my neck. "I'm not good at any of that crap. I just like working on the cars."

"Oh, Caleb." Her gaze full of amusement, Audrey pats my hand. "You're so innocent. But I will guide you on a journey to maximize your profits as you conduct your business."

Not that innocent. "You want me to show you where I conduct that business?"

The way she briefly catches the tip of her tongue between her teeth brings my cock to instant, aching attention. "I would like that very much," she says huskily.

Fuck, yes. With a nod to the others, I lead her through the crowd to the sliding door that opens up to the back of the house. More people are gathered out on the patio but despite the number of friends tossing out greetings and congratulations, I barely slow down. My only hesitation is when I decide whether to take her straight upstairs to my bed or actually show her inside the garage.

But rushing into this might make her nervous. Better to tease and delay until she's so needy that it helps overcome her fear.

The door on the side of the garage is locked, so I don't have to worry that anyone else from the party sneaked in here with the same idea. Her breath shudders as I pull her inside—but I'll draw this out, too. Build the anticipation.

Christ, my anticipation is already really fucking high. Any higher and my cock might poke me in the eye.

The illumination from the nightlight over the workbench barely touches the '59 Corvette that I'm currently restoring, but the dim lighting makes the space seem more intimate, so I don't flip on the halogen bulbs over-head. "There she is."

"Ohhhh," Audrey breathes, moving closer to the car. "I like it very much."

That surprises me. "Do you?"

"Yes." Repainting is one of the last steps, so the color's currently a dull red, but she glides her fingers across the surface of the hood as if it were gleaming. "Do you try to find all original parts?"

"Depends on the car. This one, I'll stick a new engine in there, use new upholstery. But I'll try to get original trim for the body and detailing for the interiors. And sometimes if a buyer gets interested before it's done and wants to pay for what I put into it, that'll change it up."

"Do you already have a buyer lined up for this one?"

"Not yet."

"I'll buy it, then."

I shake my head. "No."

She glances up from the car, her brows furrowing. "Why?"

Because the thought grates on my pride like a rusted gear. "I'm not taking money from you."

"Oh." She bites her bottom lip and averts her gaze. "I guess not, then."

Fuck. The disappointment in her voice is killing me. "You don't even drive," I point out.

"Yes, I do. I really like driving."

That doesn't make any sense. "You have six different

drivers who take you everywhere you go."

"Because I like driving, but I don't like it when other people are on the road with me. All the rules are clearly defined. Yet so many drivers don't even use their blinker! It's so…irritating." Frustration fills her voice, as if even right now, the thought of those non-signalling drivers is pissing her off. "So I *do* drive. And I'll probably drive all the time when robot cars are more common, because they *will* follow the rules."

The image of her zipping around town in this Corvette while surrounded by robot cars is completely fucking adorable. "All right, then," I grin. "But I'm still not taking your money."

She sighs and gives the car another caress before turning away, her gaze slipping around the interior of the garage. "You rent this from Patrick?"

"Yeah."

"You should be deducting at least some of that cost."

"I guess." I don't give a shit about my taxes right now. I don't think she does, either.

She glances at me over her shoulder and her tongue moistens her bottom lip before she asks softly, "And your apartment's upstairs?"

"It is. Though I'll warn you there's not much to see up there. Just about everything is in boxes. Except my bed."

Her breath shudders again at the mention of my bed. Slowly she turns back toward me, and with her every step anticipation pounds harder through my dick.

Until she pauses and glances around the garage again. "You haven't packed up in here?"

My gut tightens. "Not yet, no."

"Oh." That small exclamation is impossible to read. Just *oh*. "Don't you intend to move all this to my garage?"

"I haven't thought about it much."

Which is a damn lie. I've thought about it. Because my stuff upstairs fits into about six boxes. Easy to move and unpack—and pack again if the marriage ends. Even if Patrick rents the apartment out to someone else, I won't be fucked. I'll just find another place. But everything in this garage…that's not so easy to pick up and take somewhere else. Especially if I'll be doing it again before long.

And I've thought about taking it all there, yeah. Thought about how incredible it would be to really settle into her home, to make part of it permanently mine—just like I want to be a permanent part of her life. But I'm not taking my place there for granted.

"If you did, you could save on rent," she says quietly. "You could invest the extra cash back into the business, and eventually make it your primary occupation."

"I could," I say, and maybe she's right—if so, that sounds real damn good—but I'm not going to worry about it tonight. "Come here, baby."

She doesn't hesitate, stepping closer and rising up as if to kiss me. But I've got something to clear up first. Gently I cup her face in my hands.

My voice is gruff as I ask, "What's this about the Wyndhams giving up that will contest?"

Audrey goes utterly still. "You heard?"

"Yeah. But you haven't said anything about it. Why?"

Her throat works. Gaze darting to the side, she tells me, "Because they haven't actually done it yet. It was just their lawyer telling my lawyer that he intended to file a request for dismissal. But it's Saturday. Plus Tuesday is Christmas, so the courts aren't even open, and a lot of people aren't working on Monday, either. So the request for dismissal might not be filed until a few days after the wedding anyway, and then the judge has to rule on it. So if we didn't get married on Monday—"

"The Wyndhams might change their mind?" Scenting blood in the water if Audrey no longer seems to be backing me.

"Yes!" she says, her voice still pitched high. Her words tumble over each other and her eyes don't meet mine. "Plus the marriage contract is valid until the inheritance is distributed to you, regardless of the will contest. That won't be for at least six months—and the Wyndhams might try to bring another challenge to the will before that. So I didn't say anything about it, because nothing really changed."

Christ. If I didn't know better, I'd swear she was lying to me. Everything about her shifty behavior screams that she is.

But Audrey doesn't lie. She claims that she's no good

at it—and if this was an example of her lying, I'd say she was right.

The problem is…everything she just said is true. The courts are open on Monday, but the chances of the will contest being dismissed before the wedding are practically nonexistent. And even without any more challenges to the will, it'll still be a while before I see a penny of my inheritance. Simply being told about the Wyndhams' intentions really doesn't change anything.

Audrey's behavior probably just means that she's nervous as hell. And I need to do everything I can to make this easier for her. So I have no intention of making this about popping her cherry or how it might hurt her, but teasing her with all the pleasure that's yet to come.

"All right, baby," I tell her softly, lowering my mouth to hers. Gently I nip at her lush bottom lip, loving the tiny gasp that escapes her, the way she rises up as if seeking more. "Since nothing's changed, that means I still plan on taking you upstairs and giving you a taste of what our wedding night will be—and every night after that. But tonight, I'm just giving you a little bit. You want that?"

"Yes," she breathes against my lips. "So much."

No nervousness now. Just anticipation and need. And her kiss is sweet and eager, too goddamn eager, because I've got to keep myself on a tight leash and the way she gets so hot so fast threatens to snap that control. She moans as I break away, then shudders as I tip her head back to kiss her jaw, her neck.

Against her ear, I command, "You go around to the front end of the car. I want you bent over that hood with your ass up in the air like I'm about to fuck you good and hard."

Her breath catches, those gorgeous eyes widening. But I don't see fear in them. Only excitement.

She catches my hand and pulls me across the garage with her. And Christ, she's a natural, bracing her elbows on the hood and spreading her feet shoulder-width apart. She paired a knee-length skirt and tall boots with that ugly sweater, making her legs look fucking endless. Normally I might have shoved that skirt up to her waist but the zipper at the back is a temptation I can't resist.

So is her ass. Slowly I pull that zipper down, revealing nothing but pale silky skin and taut round cheeks. No panties. I groan as desire surges into my cock, the throbbing length straining against the front of my jeans like it's lurching for her. "Did you forget your Caleb's-making-me-wet kit?"

"I didn't forget," she says, panting. "I just didn't bother, because I knew I'd be wet all night."

"And knowing that is going to make me hard all night." I slide my hand down the split of her ass, hissing out a breath as my fingers find her already slick and hot and so goddamn ready for my cock. "The first time I have you on our wedding night, I'll be real slow and gentle. But this is how I'll fuck you the second time—from behind, as deep and as rough as you can take it."

She makes a little whimpering sound in her throat and rocks back against my hand. "I want that."

"You'll get it, baby. I won't be able to stop myself from fucking you like that every damn day. But right now, I'm gonna take something else I want."

The rasp of my zipper is loud in the quiet garage. So is the harsh breath she sucks in, her body stiffening.

I mold my palm to her backside, gently massaging as I reassure her, "I'm not taking that yet, Audrey. That's for upstairs. Not bent over a car with your skirt around your knees in a dirty garage, as if this is just a cheap and filthy fuck."

Her tension vanishes as a laugh shakes through her. "A cheap and filthy fuck sounds really hot."

"Hell yeah, it does. But we'll save it for another time. Right now, I just want to wet my dick with all these pussy juices."

And get her used to feeling my bare cock. I grip my shaft and follow the same hot path my fingers took over the curve of her ass to the heaven between her legs, the crown leaving a faint trail of pre-cum over her skin. The dim light doesn't penetrate the shadows between our bodies. I should have flipped on the halogens so I could watch my cock slide through the sultry seam of her cunt. But, fuck. Maybe it's best this way. If I could see what I was doing, my control might burn away even faster. As it is, the sensation of all that scalding wetness brings me right to the edge of coming, pressure building at the base of my spine.

Her body stiffens up again as I drag the broad head through her wet folds, but her horny little moan and the wriggle of her hips tells me that her tension isn't fear. Blood thunders through my veins as the thick tip naturally lodges into the faint well of her entrance. Right where it belongs. With a ragged groan, I force myself to slick my cock downward instead of pushing inside.

"Christ. I knew your pussy would feel like this." I tease her clit with the tip of my dick before dragging it back up through the lips of her pussy, coating my cockhead in her juices. "Hot and drenched, just begging to be filled with my cock, and so goddamn hard to resist. That's why I never took my pants off. I knew as soon as I did, I wouldn't last the night without getting deep into you. I don't know how I'll stop myself at just a little taste when we get upstairs."

"Now." It's a breathless demand. Her hips tilt up, and she lifts up onto her toes until the head of my cock is at her entrance again, as if she's trying to lure me in. "Let's go upstairs now.'

"Not yet, baby. I don't take you upstairs until you come for me." But as incredible as it feels to tease her with my cock, she's not going to come like this.

I drop to my knees. Too hungry for finesse, I bury my face in her cunt, my left hand stroking my cock as her flavor explodes over my tongue. Christ, her pussy. It's so fucking sweet. Almost as sweet as the sound of her ragged little cries and the way her thighs flex and shake as she rocks herself against my mouth. I've made her come with my tongue all week—and made myself come, too, fucking my hand or grinding against the bed while I feast from the delicious heaven of her cunt. Tonight, though, I've got to keep my head, and remember that she needs more. Because I haven't given her much, deciding that the entrance to her pussy was off limits to everything but my mouth until our wedding night. I've drilled my tongue into her every day but haven't let myself take more.

I take it now, teasing that tight entrance with the pad of my thumb, feeling the delicate flesh quiver with every rough lick over her clit. Closing my lips around that swollen nub, I begin to suck at the same time that I gently push inside.

Audrey goes utterly still, then abruptly melts against the car with a loud moan. "Caleb. Oh, Caleb. I like this," she gasps. "I like this so much."

Her pleasure is rocket fuel splashed on the raging fire of my own need. With a harsh groan, I work her clit with my tongue and rub up inside her with my thumb. Fuck, she's so snug. Her slick inner walls hold me in a tight grip, clinging as I thrust in and out. Convulsively the fingers of my left hand squeeze my shaft, but my fist will never feel as good around my cock as this hot little pussy is going to.

Her erratic breaths and jerking hips tell me she's getting close even before she does. And this is always my favorite part, when she begins chanting, "You're making me come, Caleb, you're making me come," as if she thinks I don't know unless she tells me, but it's so fucking hot to hear it from her lips, to hear her go over the edge, to hear her say I'm *making* her do it. "Ah god… ah, you're making me come, I'm going to—"

The choked scream that follows joins the flood of her arousal over my tongue, the pulse of clenching flesh against my lips. All as familiar and as incredible as before. But *inside* her. Christ, inside her. Her pussy clamps down hard, inner muscles constricting and releasing while her body writhes in the throes of her climax. If I'd felt this before, there'd have been no goddamn chance of holding out until the wedding night. Because, fuck. *Fuck.* I need to feel that around my cock.

Mindless lust claws through my gut as I lunge to my feet, my dick throbbing with the violent urge to be inside her, to make her pussy squeeze and suck every thick inch. I need that more than any goddamn thing.

Except for one thing that matters more. Never hurting her.

With the sweetness of her orgasm all over my lips and tongue, I forcibly rein in the animal lust. Just enough to stop myself from fucking her. But Christ help me, I *will* have the nearest thing to it.

Overheated, I rip off my sweater and T-shirt and toss them aside before wrapping my arm around Audrey's waist and hoisting her up against my chest. No longer braced on the floor, her legs fall closed and my bare cock wedges into the narrow channel between the V of her thighs and her pussy. All that hot flesh is still twitching from her orgasm, and the sensation jolts over my shaft like tiny electric shocks.

"Fuck." Teeth gritted, I turn us around and sit back against the fender. "Look at what making you come does to me, baby."

Facing this direction, there's enough illumination coming from the workbench to see my swollen erection jutting up from the clasp of her thighs. Just a few inches and the fat head are visible, flushed a deep purplish-red and slicked with her juices and my pre-cum. Even as she looks, another drop forms at the tip, glistening in the dim light.

Her fingers clench on my forearm. "I do that to you?"

"Yeah, you do. Because my cock only wants one goddamn thing."

"To fuck my pussy raw?"

Ah Christ. Hearing that from her sweet mouth is like another electric shock through my cock, but the breathless, *hopeful* way she says it is what nearly snaps my control again. Snarling, I lift her up until the tip of my dick disappears between her thighs before dropping her back onto my lap, giving my cock a hot ride through the folds of her pussy and over her clit. She cries out, gasping and squirming in my grip.

Against her ear, I growl, "Fuck you raw? When did you start using such dirty talk?"

"I got it from you," she pants. "In my office the first day."

Yeah, that's something I'd say. And I remember some vulgar shit coming out of my mouth in her office and thinking I shouldn't be talking like that. But she remembers my exact words better than I do. "Have you been thinking about it ever since?"

She nods, then gasps when when I lift her again, my cock slipping through those drenched folds, and her body quivers as my shaft glides over her clit. This time I hold her above me, fucking upward in a series of hard thrusts, my hips slapping against her bare ass. A soft cry of pleasure escapes her with every slap until, my chest heaving, I bring her back down.

"I'm not fucking you raw tonight, baby," I say harshly and the disappointed whine she makes is a burning chain pulling on my dick, drawing it up harder, tighter. "But I am going to screw this juicy slit hard and fast. Gotta take the edge off before we go upstairs or I'll lose my head when I'm inside you. So kick off that skirt and put your heels up on the fender. I want a good view of your pussy when I start coming all over it."

What I'm asking of her is awkward as hell, straddling me in a reverse cowgirl with her knees splayed wide and her boot heels precariously braced on the edge of the car. She's completely off balance, forced to lean forward with her back against my chest, so the only thing keeping her from face-planting on the concrete floor is my arm anchored around her waist. But Audrey doesn't even hesitate, and the absolute trust she gives me swells my heart up three sizes bigger.

And my cock, Christ—it's about to burst. Barely holding on, I tell her through clenched teeth, "You reach down and keep my dick nice and snug against your pussy, baby. I want to pump through those beautiful cunt lips and rub up all over your hot little clit."

"That sounds so—" she begins breathlessly but the moment her fingers close over my cock, I can't hold back any longer. With my right forearm locked around her middle and my left hand reaching beneath her sweater for a handful of her soft breast, I haul her straight up into the air before following with a rough jerk of my hips. My shaft tunnels between her sweet pussy and her slick grip, which tightens convulsively around me as I thrust again and again, each time harder and faster than the last. Her tit bounces in my hand, her taut nipple pinched between my fingers. Her ponytail swings like a pendulum before her head lolls back against my shoulder, where she turns her face until her mouth opens against my neck. The hot whisper of her breath is followed by the press of her lips and the swipe of her tongue. Then she's sucking hard on the skin of my throat, moaning brazenly with each thrust, and her unadulterated ecstasy is even more incredible than the feel of her hand or her cunt or anything I've ever known.

Fuck. I need that mouth on mine. Adjusting her upper body to the side, I angle my head to cover her lips in a ravenous kiss. I lick deep into her sweetness and her heat, until she catches my tongue and begins sucking and moaning again.

That's the death of me. Her lush mouth and her unabashed pleasure kill me dead, and an orgasm comes along to bury the remains. I meant to watch my cum splash all over her bare cunt but I can't tear my lips from hers as rapture shoots up the length of my cock in hot spurts. My body jerks and heaves while the ecstasy of her kiss and her moans keep me pumping against her until there's not a drop left.

Her soft, needy whimper when I stop thrusting nearly kills me all over again. Breaking the kiss, I drag in a gusting breath. In my arms, Audrey whimpers once more, rocking her hips, stroking my spent cock—massaging the tip over her clitoris before letting me go and using her fingers, instead.

"Shh, baby," I tell her, getting my hand down there, too, where my cum and her juices have made a slick, sexy mess. "Are you hurting?"

"It aches inside." Frantically she rubs her clit. "It aches so deep."

Because my cock worked her up good but she didn't

come again. I drag her hand away and curl my thick middle finger into her tight channel while my thumb circles her swollen clit. Her inner muscles constrict around me and she cries out, her thighs flexing, the rock of her hips pushing my finger deeper.

"Your pussy's hungry for more, baby." And just begging to be filled up with my cock. My voice raw with need, I ask her, "You ready to go upstairs?"

"Yes." Her breath comes in sobbing little gasps. "Now."

I only slow down to help her step into her skirt and tug up the zipper before taking her into my arms again. Grabbing her ass in both hands, I haul her up against my chest, then get her long legs wrapped around my waist and her arms wreathed around my shoulders. Instantly she begins riding me, grinding her bare pussy against the ridged muscles of my abdomen, chasing the need burning inside her as I head for the garage door. Outside, my sweat-slicked skin steams in the frigid winter air but I barely feel the cold. I carry her up the stairs, kissing her all the way.

Her arms tighten around my shoulders as we pass through my front door. Aside from the one moment when she stiffened up in the garage, she hasn't shown any fear of what's to come. Trusting me to take care of her.

I won't ever betray that sweet trust. She's so damn precious. And knowing that she's giving herself to me here makes my small apartment feel like a palace as I stride through it, a king carrying his heart in his arms. Taking Audrey to my bed for the first time is something I've pictured a thousand damn times, though I always imagined that first time would be our wedding night. This won't have the same end because I'm not fucking her—I probably can't even stay hard if she's hurting—yet everything leading up to it is the same.

Except now I know that I love her. And maybe I always did. Because even when I was imagining our wedding night, stroking my cock to the vision of her, my heart felt so damn full. I just didn't know what I was feeling.

I do now.

As I drag her sweater over her head and worship her rosy nipples until she's restlessly begging for more, I love her. As I adore every inch of creamy skin with my lips and tongue, I love her. As her hands coast down my chest, as she unfastens my jeans and her mouth brings me to aching hardness again, I love her. As I lie down at her side, languorously kissing while my fingers slowly pump inside her, while my thumb strokes her clitoris until she's panting and writhing, I love her.

I love her, and so the hardest thing I've ever done is softly asking, "You still want me to open you up?"

She nods jerkily, whispering, "Yes." Yet the panic she mentioned visibly takes her in its grip, making her tense and shake all over.

My heart aching, I slowly kiss my way down her

stomach, feeling her relax again. A long, lingering taste of her cunt pushes her toward another orgasm. As she hovers on the edge, my thumb stroking her clit, I fit the head of my cock to her untried entrance and press inward.

And don't get anywhere. Her pussy's slick and hot, but the second I got up between her thighs she went rigid. Her legs snapped closed around my waist and she clapped her hands over her face as if to prevent me from seeing her reaction—or simply hiding in the only way she can. But her entire body is telling me how scared she is. Her breasts rise and fall on rapid, wheezing pants.

"Audrey, baby—"

"I'm okay, it's okay, do it," she says all in one panicked breath. "*Doitdoitdoit.*"

Shit. I continue strumming her clit, feeling my own arousal fade. A part of me thinks that I need to shove in, like ripping off a bandage, but her body won't let me and she's so delicate that forcing my cock in would only hurt her more. She's too tense, her flesh resisting, so I slowly increase the pressure until her softness abruptly yields.

Audrey muffles a scream behind her hands.

Instantly I freeze, dread clutching my heart. "Baby?"

She's utterly still and silent now, not even her chest moving.

"Audrey? Breathe, baby. And tell me you're okay."

Her fingers spread and she peeks through them, surprise and confusion shining from her eyes. "It didn't hurt."

Bullshit. "You screamed."

"Because I was so sure it *would* hurt. So I panicked when I felt it going in. But instead it's…" Her hands fall away from her face and she rises up onto her elbows, looking down between us, where the head of my cock is buried inside her. "Really tight. But…it feels good. I like it."

Thank fuck. A huge breath bellows from my lungs and all the blood in my body rushes from my pounding heart to begin pounding at the base of my erection. Her pussy's strangling the thick tip, making her *tight* and *good* into huge fucking understatements.

In a tiny voice she asks, "Am I bleeding?"

The question clears my head. Gently I pull back, then slick my thumb from her clit down to her opening, covertly wiping away the faint red smear from the tip of my cock.

"No, baby." A little blood, but not still bleeding, so it doesn't feel like a lie.

Her smile is blinding and beautiful as she falls back onto her shoulders, her hands cupping her breasts, fingers teasing her erect nipples. Her tongue slides across her pouty bottom lip, her icy eyes alight. "So…is that all I get until our wedding night?"

I laugh and groan, because she has to know there's no damn way that's all she'll get from me. Sitting back, I grip her waist and pull her ass up into my lap, her legs splayed over my hips and her shoulders still on the mattress. She's completely open to me this way—but more importantly, I can easily control how deep I go. Because I'm not going any deeper than I already did. Not tonight.

And that's what I'll keep telling myself.

A little shudder races through her when my thumb returns to her clit, then another when I glide the tip of my erection up and down her wet slit. Arousal roughens my voice as I tell her, "I'm gonna make you come again."

She squirms on my lap, as if seeking my cock. "But I want you inside me."

"I will be." I'm near shaking with the need to feel her squeezing my dick as she comes. Even if it's only an inch. "Your pussy opening is so damn tight. So I'm just going to fuck in and out of your little hole, get it used to taking me in. Because after we're married, I'll be fucking into you real often."

"I can't wait," she pants, her back arching. "I can't wait."

I don't know if she can't wait for me to get inside her again or until we're married, but my answer's the same either way. "I can't wait either, baby."

A ragged moan tears from her throat as I press into her again, watching her delicate entrance stretching to accept the broad crown of my cock. As soon as I'm in, her slick inner walls cling and pull at me, as if trying to draw me deeper. With a tormented groan, I back out, because leaving that sweet heaven is torture but it's so fucking good, too. Her little pussy cinches around me no matter how deep I am, and feeling that erotic grip all over the head of my cock has me gritting my teeth against the need to bury my full length inside her.

"I like this, Caleb." Fingers tugging at her nipples, she moans again through another shallow thrust, biting her lip—then wildly shaking her head. "But it's no good."

"No good?" I rasp out in disbelief. Her pussy's trying to suck me in, her sweet honey dripping down the length of my dick. "This is *no good?*"

It's fucking amazing.

"You have to go deeper," she pants. "Because the tip isn't as fat as the rest. If you really want my pussy to get used to taking you in, you have to open me up with the thickest part."

God help me. I breach her entrance again and can't help but see how right she is, how I'm not fully breaking her in. Because when I really get into her, my heavy shaft will stretch her out more than the crown will.

Her bright gaze is steady on my face. "You promised to open up my tight virgin cunt with your big cock. But you only popped my sweet little cherry. You've got to go deeper to open me up all the way."

Fucking hell. She's figured out how hearing her say dirty shit gets to me, even if she's just throwing my own words back. Blood pounds through my swollen erection, the pulse throbbing at the sensitive tip where her pussy's got me in a chokehold. "You devious little witch."

She laughs breathlessly. "Guilty."

"And so goddamn clever. All right, baby." My voice deepens. "I'll give you a little more."

Because I'm going to open up her pussy real good. Leaning forward, I brace my fist beside her shoulder and she gasps as the movement shoves half of my engorged length into her narrow channel, giving her five thick inches. With my right hand, I get a solid grip on her hip, making sure she can't squirm and buck and take more than I want her to have.

"Like this, baby?"

Her icy eyes are glazed over with pleasure, her nod an erratic jerk of her chin. "I like this, Caleb. So much."

But she's not coming yet, so she doesn't like it enough. Teeth gritted, I withdraw before pumping back in and stopping at the same depth as before, watching ecstasy overtake her expression, her eyelids falling to half mast and her mouth parting on another gasp.

"It's good." She gives a soft cry as I fuck into her again, and her hand comes up to her mouth as if to silence herself before she reaches up and touches my lips, instead. "It's so good."

So goddamn good. I suck her fingers into my mouth, and her entire body arches up, her inner walls twitching around my cock like she's got an electric wire running from her fingers to her cunt. Her pale gaze is locked on mine, and I remember the first time I imagined fucking her. How I believed she'd be still and silent, and thought

I'd have to hammer into her just to crack the ice, to make her pussy melt around me.

But she's not ice. She's a living flame beneath me, hot and bright and so damn beautiful.

She's the most beautiful thing I've ever seen.

"Oh my god. Caleb." Writhing against my grip, she makes a little sobbing noise in the back of her throat. "It's so deep. I'm so full."

With a laughing groan, I drive into her again. "It's going to feel a lot fuller and deeper when you marry me."

Almost dazedly, as if confused by my meaning, she lifts her head. Her eyes widen when she sees how much of my cock she hasn't taken.

"All the way." It's a breathless command. Her fingers slide up to fist in my hair. "Inside me all the way."

Not yet, goddammit. I'm supposed to be opening her up. Teeth clenched, I fuck into her on hard, shallow strokes until there's nothing left of her demand, just soft ragged cries and her cunt cinching tighter and tighter. Almost ready to come. Fuck, I'm barely holding on myself, pressure boiling at the root of my cock. Grunting with every short thrust, I wait until her thighs begin to tremble uncontrollably before giving her what she wants. What I *need*.

And Christ Almighty, there is nothing in the universe as close to heaven as her pussy. The world dims around me as I give her the full length of my cock, until the only light is Audrey, clinging to me with her fists clenched in my hair, her body arched upward in a tight bow, her eyes glazed and unseeing.

So close but still not there. I wedge my hand between us, and the first brush of my fingertips over her clit makes her shudder and exhale a soft, sobbing breath. I'm balls-deep inside her, my body motionless except for my fingers teasing that sensitive bundle of nerves.

"You feel so damn good, baby," I growl against her mouth. "Like your cunt was made to take my cock. Like it was made for me to fuck and fill with cum."

"Oh god. Please."

I know she's begging for me to start thrusting but I shake my head, kissing her again. "I'm not fucking you now. I'm just opening up every fuckable inch of this virgin pussy."

Her inner walls clench around me and she cries out, her feet rubbing up and down the back of my thighs as she desperately tries to find some leverage. "But I *need* it."

So do I. "You want this big cock pumping into you, making you feel good? That's what you'll get every day, after you marry me."

"Please."

Harder, faster, I rub her slippery clit. "You like me this deep?"

"Yes." She squirms beneath me on another sobbing breath. "I love it."

Love. The word flares through me like a wildfire,

setting my soul ablaze.

"Say that again," I demand hoarsely.

"I love it, I love it, I love it."

Her steady chant fills my heart to bursting. It's not the only love I need from her. But it's a damn good start.

I steal another kiss from her lips, then a longer taste as I begin to grind my hips in a tight circle between her trembling thighs, my cock screwing deep within the luscious grip of her body. Her fingernails dig into my shoulders and her strangled cry is muffled by our kiss, but she doesn't break away, her hot tongue slicking over mine as her inner walls begin contracting around my thick length.

It's fucking exquisite. And sheer torture. A harsh groan ripping from my chest, I struggle against the intense rising pressure of my own release as her pussy milks every inch of my cock. Then I grind harder, because I can't stop. I need more time inside her, need to savor every moment that she's climaxing around me.

One more second is all I get before the orgasm snaps through my spine like a whip. I grunt, my head jerking back and my hips jolting forward as if to drive my erection even deeper into her, but there's no deeper. Hot pulses of semen spill into her clenching depths as I come so hard that spots dance around the edges of my vision, and there's only Audrey at the center of it all. At the center of everything. My heart, my soul, my life.

I empty myself into her, all that I have, and I come

for what feels like *years*.

It must be at least next Christmas before I stop. Completely spent, I barely keep myself from collapsing over her and crushing her slender body beneath my heavy bulk. It requires all the strength I have left to roll onto my back and bring her with me, until she's lying atop my heaving chest with my dick still buried inside her quivering cunt. Lifting my head, I meet her lips in a kiss that's all jagged breaths and slick heat, then slowly pull her up higher until her legs are straddling my waist and her mouth is directly over mine. She moans softly as my softening cock slips out of her, and I groan at the wickedly dirty sensation of our combined release dripping from her pussy onto my stomach.

Her mouth curves against mine and, with a slow and deliberate rock of her hips, smears a little more all over my abdomen. So filthy and hot and unexpected—but I *should* expect it by now. She always pays attention to what I like, in bed and out of it.

She's so fucking perfect. So incredible. And not a virgin anymore. I catch her face in my hands, looking up at her with my heart damn near beating through my chest.

"All good?" I ask gruffly.

She nods, then hesitates for a moment before venturing, "And you?"

The uncertainty in that question spins my head around. "Real damn good, baby," I reassure her, then pause as the sound of pounding bass and a few shouts of laughter come faintly through the bedroom wall. "Did you want to go back to the party or…?"

She shakes her head. "I'm tired after coming so many times. Can I nap here?"

I grin, not a bit surprised by that answer. Orgasms often wipe her out. "Yeah, you can."

"Okay." She lays her head on my shoulder, as if settling in, before popping back up again. "Are you staying with me or going back to the party?"

"Staying." Of course I'm staying with her. I slide my palm down her back, urging her to settle again. "I'm working again tomorrow morning. I don't need two late nights in a row."

"Okay," she says again, but doesn't settle. Instead she wriggles around, then sits up and slips her fingers between her legs. "I'm really sticky. I need to—"

"Lie right here while I get a washcloth and clean you up."

"I can—"

"I know." With a quick kiss to her mouth, I roll her over—away from the wet spot. "But I wasn't supposed to get into you that deep tonight, let alone come up inside you. That's my mess making you all sticky, so I'll clean it up."

And if there's any more blood, I can quietly take care of it so she won't panic when she sees it.

Maybe Audrey's already thinking the same, though,

because her gaze seems troubled as she watches me head for the bathroom. When I return with a washcloth in hand, she's scooted up to the far end of the bed with her back against the headboard and hugging her bent knees to her chest.

"Audrey?" Worry clutches my throat. "What's going on?"

Her eyes seem dark and haunted now. "You shouldn't be so sweet to me."

"Why's that?" I kneel on the mattress in front of her, and relief slips through my chest when she doesn't stiffen or pull away from my touch. Gently I part her knees so I can begin cleaning her up. "I like being sweet to you. So tell me why I shouldn't be."

"Because of what I just did to manipulate you."

Manipulate me? My eyebrows shoot upward. "What'd you do?"

Maybe she tossed away her birth control? If so, screw cleaning her up. In ten seconds flat I'll have her on her back and pumped full of more cum.

Her chin quivers. "I already asked for so much. You wanted to wait for our wedding night but I needed this from you, and you gave it."

I meet her gaze and make sure she can hear the truth ringing through every word as I say, "And I was real fucking happy to give it."

"But you didn't want to have sex tonight. You weren't going to fuck me. That's what you said. But I..." Her breath shudders and a sheen of moisture glitters in her eyes. "When it felt good instead of hurting, I wanted you inside me again. So I said you weren't deep enough and that you hadn't done what you promised. And you fucked me. Even though you wanted to wait. Because I pressured you and pressured you for more, but I shouldn't have even asked for it. I should have respected what *you* wanted."

Ah hell. If it weren't for those tears, I might have laughed. Not at Audrey, but at the idea that she took something I didn't want to give.

But it isn't difficult to see where her fear is coming from. She's got power and money like most people only dream of, and she has to be careful how to wield it. That caution has to influence the way she approaches sex, especially with all that's going on in the world right now. Because she's talking about this like she *could* pressure me.

Maybe she could pressure a lot of other people. But those people aren't me. So she's got the context all wrong.

"Three things, baby," I tell her, wiping the cloth up the inside of her thigh as I continue to clean her up. "The first is that you couldn't make me do anything I didn't feel like doing. I'm the same as you that way. You won't go to a party or do shit you don't want to, and I don't do shit that I don't want to. That includes fucking someone. And you weren't manipulating me. I knew damn well what you were playing at and I thought it was adorable and sexy and flattering as hell, knowing you wanted me that bad. But if I hadn't wanted to go along with it, I wouldn't have. The second thing is that the moment I realized you weren't hurting, there was no fucking way I could have resisted getting into you. I've told you that, too. I kept my jeans on for over a week because I knew the second my bare cock got anywhere near your pussy, I was going in deep. Only you saying no or being in pain would have stopped me. But you weren't. So you could have been silent the entire time and I still would have given in to temptation and opened you up all the way. All right?"

Her breath shudders as if in relief when she nods. "And the third thing?"

"That wasn't us having sex. That wasn't us fucking. That wasn't us making love." Which will include all of the above. "That was just me opening you up and doing my damn best to make it sexy for you. But on our wedding night, and every time after that, I'll be doing a hell of a lot more than drilling halfway into your pussy a few times and then busting my nut. But you'll just have to wait to see the difference."

"I will." With her soft fingers, she touches my face, tracing the line of my jaw. "You're such a good man, Caleb."

My heart swells up into my throat. Because if she thinks that, maybe her loving me someday isn't impossible. Catching her hand, I press a kiss to her palm. "I just want to be good for you, Audrey. So that you don't ever regret marrying the bastard who lied to you and hurt you before figuring out what an incredible woman you are. Because by all rights, you should still be angry at me."

"I was never angry. And I won't regret it." A shadow darkens her eyes. "I hope you don't, either."

"Not a chance," I tell her, finishing up with the washcloth and tossing it onto the nightstand. "Still sleepy?"

She nods and slips under the covers, but despite me saying that I won't regret marrying her, the shadow doesn't leave her face.

"Was there something else bothering you, baby?"

She doesn't shake her head. Doesn't answer. She just pillows her cheek on my shoulder.

Because she can't lie well. So she doesn't say anything.

Which means there *is* something else.

My throat is tight as I turn out the light. Holding her close, I try to breathe past the ache in my heart. Maybe my question was too general. There's probably a ton of shit that bothers her, but not anything she wants to share.

But general shit didn't put that shadow in her eyes. Something we were talking about here did. "There's nothing you want to tell me?"

This time I feel the shake of her head, but the subsequent silence rips at my chest. Until she whispers, "I just want to be with you."

And all the pain goes away.

CALEB

I DON'T KNOW WHAT BEGINS WAKING ME UP BUT I know what brings me all the way out: a soft press of lips to mine. Then another.

Audrey, kissing me while she thinks I'm asleep.

I don't even breathe. Eyes closed, I wait about thirty seconds for her to do more. But there's nothing. And she's no longer lying beside me.

Frowning, I sit up. The bedroom's dark. The bathroom light isn't on, so she's not in there. But she's easy to find. As soon as I leave the bedroom, the flashlight from her phone guides me straight to her. The device is lying on top of a box—giving her light to see by as she dresses. Already wearing her sweater, she's standing by the front door and zipping up her skirt. Dismay flashes over her beautiful face when she sees me.

"I'm sorry. I didn't mean to wake you up."

I'm glad she did. Scrubbing my hand over my face, I glance at the clock.

Only one-thirty. The noise from outside tells me the party's still going. I figured it must be morning but only two hours have passed since we went to sleep. "Are you heading back over to Patrick's?"

"Just to get my coat." She balances on one foot while pulling on a boot. "I called for a driver to take me home. She's out there now."

"I could have taken you home, baby."

"You have work in the morning."

"You do, too," I point out.

"Not really. Mia's treating me to a spa day tomorrow. Polishing me up"—she huffs out a breath while pulling on her other boot—"so I can look pretty for the wedding."

"I honest-to-God can't imagine you being any more beautiful than you are right now." The delight that fills her expression vanishes as I add, "You should stay until morning. You'll get more sleep that way. And I'll drive you wherever you need to go before work tomorrow."

She averts her face. Her ponytail's down, and her blonde curtain of hair partially veils her expression. "You never stay the night at my house. So I just… It feels like I should go, too."

Ah fuck. She likes personal interactions to have context and guidelines. And from the very first day, she's been figuring out the rules for an engaged couple, taking many of her cues from me. But some of those rules I didn't mean to establish.

Like this one. My chest is tight as I tell her, "I just didn't trust myself to wait until the wedding if I slept all night in your bed."

"Do you trust yourself now?"

No. But I still want her there. Next to me.

Under me.

Goddammit. "I want to say yes, just so you'll stay. But I'm not going to be an asshole and lie to you." For an instant, she looks utterly devastated and her expression nearly rips my heart out. "I *never* wanted to go."

"But you did anyway."

I can't refute that, so I try a different angle. "Do *you* want to stay? You can if you want to."

She wants to. A wistful expression passes over her face. Then she shakes her head and picks up her phone, using the light to find the front door handle. "That's what I always said. And you always left, anyway."

Shit. I'm such a fucking asshole. "Baby, give me a second to put on pants and I'll walk you over."

"I'll be fine."

"I know you will—" Screw getting dressed, because she's not stopping. Buck naked, I follow her through the door and onto the landing. She stops then, eyes widening as the flashlight beam dances over my cock. Quickly she turns it off, but thanks to the floodlight over the garage door, anyone could still see us up here. Despite the noise coming from the patio, though, I doubt anyone's looking. And I wouldn't give a shit if they did.

All that matters is that she's laughing now. "Caleb, it's snowing out here!"

With an icy wind that's already freezing my balls. Since she's not wearing a coat, I won't keep her long. Just long enough to wrap my arm around her waist and pull her close. "The next time I see you, we'll be at the church."

Her eyes soften. "Yes."

"And the next time I talk to you, I'll be saying 'I do.'"

She makes a happy sound in her throat and rises up on her toes. Her mouth is sweet and warm beneath mine, and the sheer pleasure of kissing her almost makes me forget where I was going with all this. But as soon as she pulls away and says a quiet goodnight, I remember.

Catching her hand, I press a kiss to her palm. "As soon as we're married, we won't be engaged anymore. We'll be husband and wife. And we'll hit the reset button, all right? We'll kiss hello and goodbye, and spend all night together. No gimmicks, no stupid assumptions that'll hurt you, no more waiting for anything. We'll have a clean start to this marriage. Yeah?"

Her eyes seem to glitter extra bright. "A clean start," she whispers. "Okay."

"Good." With another kiss to her cold fingers, I let her go. "I'm going to stay up here until I see you make it into the house. Then text me when you're in the car and when you get home safe."

She bites her lip and nods, her gaze searching my face before she turns and runs down the stairs. Her pale hair seems to glow in the dark as she crosses the lawn.

Even though she's quick, my dick's pretty much an icicle by the time I'm satisfied that she made it through Patrick's front door all right. I head back to bed, but don't think I'll get much sleep. Not with the way my chest is aching. Not with the feeling of something *wrong* pressing down on me, making it so damn hard to breathe.

Not just her being gone—and knowing she only left because I abandoned her every night—though that's enough of a reason. After our wedding, though, that'll be nothing. We'll get that fresh start. New guidelines. Ones that'll make it easy for her to fall in love with me. Just like I fell for her.

Somehow, I need to give her as much as she's given me. Because when it comes to giving, she sure as fuck didn't take her cues from anything I've done. Shit, I've been holding back from day one.

Holding back. While she gives and gives and gives. And never asks for anything in return.

Oh fuck. The pain in my chest deepens as I realize the truth of that.

I held back, refusing to fuck her or to sleep beside

her through the night—holding out for the wedding to make sure she'd marry me, even though she never gave any indication of changing her mind. Not once. Not even after I said all that shit the first night. I was the only one who ever had any doubts.

Yet Audrey never wavered. She didn't only offer me what I asked for in the proposal, either. She opened her beautiful home and said everything there was mine now, too. Not just shared space, but the garage for my very own use, simply because I told her I restored cars on the side. She immediately tried to accomodate me as much as possible and didn't hold anything back. She offered up her home, her body—Christ, even security clearance at her building. All of which involves a hell of a lot of risk for her.

Within one *day*, she did that. Risking so much. Physically, emotionally, financially.

Yet despite being with her all this time, I won't even take the risk of moving an old car and a few tools. And she knew it, too. Right away, she picked up that I didn't intend to move my shit to her garage. And how's she supposed to read that as anything other than me not planning to stay? I want to, but how can she know that when I don't say a damn thing about it?

How the fuck is she supposed to fall in love with me? I'm a selfish asshole who'll take everything she gives but won't offer shit in return.

I haven't even given her my real reason for marrying

her. A clean start? That's a fucking joke. She'll head into the church on Christmas Eve thinking I'm marrying her because of the will contest and a contract based on my proposal. But that's only what brought me to her office that first day. I signed that fucking contract and let her go on thinking that the Wyndhams and the inheritance are why I'm with her. Even though she gave me the truth of her reasons for agreeing to my proposal and they didn't have shit to do with the property; she simply liked me and was attracted to me. Yet I never offered any truth in return.

Then she gave me her trust, the most precious gift I've ever known. Gave it when she revealed what her parents had done. Gave it to me right here in this bed.

I couldn't even give her my trust in return. I never trusted that she'd marry me if I didn't hold back my cock—never trusted her word, though she can't even lie. And I never trusted her with my heart. So I held that back, too.

She's given me so damn much. And I've given her… nothing. A few orgasms, maybe. Nothing she couldn't have gotten from anyone she wanted to.

But I *can* give her more. I need to, if I'm to have any hope of winning her heart. No more holding back. And no waiting until after the wedding to tell her the truth. I'm marrying her because I can't imagine a life without her in it. Because she's my whole fucking world.

Because I love her.

Heart thundering, I sit up and try to remember where I left my phone. A declaration of love isn't the kind of thing that should be texted, but Audrey just left, so she's probably only a few minutes away. I should ask her to come back, for the driver to turn around. Except she might think I'll just try to persuade her to stay the night. So I'll tell her that I'm coming out to her place.

A knock at my front door interrupts my search through the pockets of my jeans. Fuck. It's likely Patrick or someone else from the party who saw Audrey go and who's wondering where the hell I am. But I take it as a sign that I'm supposed to get my ass in gear and to go after her.

The jeans on my floor are the ones I wore while carrying Audrey up the stairs from the garage. The stiff denim looks as if it's stained with ten gallons of jizz and all my other pants are in the washing machine, so I drag the sheet off the bed and wrap it around my waist. Holding the material bunched at my left hip, I unlock the door, ready to tell whoever's on the other side to fuck off for the night.

Except it's Audrey. Looking almost frail in her long cream coat, her eyes shining with tears, her face pale and drawn.

"Audrey?" Shit. Worry clutching my heart, I cup her cold cheek in my hand, my gaze desperately searching her from head to toe. "What's the matter?"

"I have to tell you… I need to—" She abruptly stops.

Her throat works. Her expression is shadowed, just like it was in bed earlier. When she wouldn't talk about what was bothering her. "Can I come in for a minute?"

"You don't even need to ask." But I need to get out of the damn way. I back up, giving her room to walk through the doorway. "Are you okay?"

She doesn't answer that, which means she's not. Instead she presses her back against the wall just beside the door, her hands balled in her coat pockets and her shoulders hunched. "It's about the clean start. I have to confess something first. So it can really be clean."

"All right," I say, then add, "Let me get you a glass of water first, baby."

Because every word she just said doesn't worry me as much as how they sounded. Raw and hoarse, like she's got broken glass ripping up her throat. I'm across the room when her next words bring me to an abrupt halt.

"I lied to you."

I swing around to face her again. "When? About what?"

"Tonight." It's barely a whisper. "And about why I didn't tell you the will contest was being dismissed."

"Yeah, I picked up on that," I tell her, because she really is the worst liar in the world. She was so damn shifty, I knew there was something. Except I still can't see what she was lying about. "What part of that wasn't true?"

"It was all true. It just wasn't my reason for not telling

you.”

"Then what was your reason?"

Her beautiful face is a picture of misery as she hunches deeper into her coat. "So you would still think that you needed to marry me to defeat the Wyndhams. I didn't want you to find out that you'd basically already won before the wedding, because I was afraid you might cancel it. So I lied. But I should have given you the choice instead of trying to deceive you. That's not how we should start a marriage—and you didn't lie to me earlier because you said it would make you an asshole. So I'm an asshole for lying. And I understand if you're angry with me," she adds in a tiny, wavering voice. "Or if you don't want to marry me anymore."

"I'm not angry, baby." Far from angry. So much relief balloons inside my chest that I'm lightheaded with it.

Relief…and hope. She lied so that I'd marry her? That's the best goddamn thing I've ever heard. Because it sounds a hell of a lot like what I was doing—so desperate for her to marry me, I concealed the truth behind my reasons.

But I'm not holding back anymore. So in a rough voice, I admit, "Though I have my own confession before we make a clean start. And I think we should tear up that marriage contract."

She seems to stop breathing. "You do?"

"I do." Now it's my throat that feels real fucking raw. "Because I don't want to get married for the reasons I gave you in that proposal. I want something that means more. Not just spite and money—or even sex."

Though we'll still have plenty of that.

"Something more?" Anguished yearning fills her expression as her shadowed gaze searches my face. "You mean…love?"

"Yes, Audrey." My heart feels as if it's about to explode, because all that yearning I see in her—that's exactly what I feel. And for the first time, I wonder if she's a lot closer to falling for me than I believed. I wonder if she already has. My voice is ragged with all the threadbare hope I've pieced together when I tell her, "I want to marry for love."

Her eyes become shimmering pools, and she pulls in a quick, shuddering breath. "Okay. But even without a contract, I'll still pay for the lawyers if you need me to."

"All right," I agree and start back across the room, intent on kissing her and holding her—because if she's still talking about lawyers, maybe she doesn't feel safe enough yet to admit her love. So I'll keep telling her about mine.

I'll tell her over and over again.

But on my first step closer, a choking noise erupts from her throat. Blindly she reaches for the door handle, and on a high-pitched and thready, "I'll tell Jessica to cancel the wedding," she flings open the door and is gone.

Completely stunned, I stare after her. Because I

just…? And she seemed to…? But now she's racing down the stairs. Running away from me. And cancelling the wedding.

Over my dead fucking body.

"Audrey!" I roar her name and head after her. "We are *not* cancelling any goddamn thing! Do you hear me?"

She had to. Everyone just heard that. I charge out the front door to a chorus of cheers and shouts of encouragement from the patio. And she's not anywhere in sight. Fuck.

"Did Audrey come that way?" I call down to them.

"No, man!" is the response, along with a "The toga party was last year!"

She's not there. Panic begins to claw at my gut. Icy concrete burns my feet as I head down the stairs. I head past the garage, my gaze sweeping the yard and the sidewalk—and landing on the black car parked a little ways down the street. Audrey's driver.

Quickly I cross the lawn, every step crunching through three inches of snow. The woman in the front seat is playing with her phone. She sees me and quickly gets out to open the door, but when I glance into the back seat, Audrey's not there.

I look to the driver. "Did she go into the house?"

"I didn't see her come down." She grimaces and gestures to her phone as if explain why she wasn't looking in that direction, then eyes my sheet. "Do you want me to go in and—"

"No. Just wait here. But if she shows up without me, don't leave. At least not until I've had a chance to talk to her."

She arches a narrowed look at me. "Mr. Moore. You're a very nice man, but if she tells me to go, I'm going."

"Please." My voice hoarsens. "Just wait for me. I told her I love her, and she ran away, and I don't know why."

Her lips purse. After a long second, she gives a tight nod.

"You're an angel. Do you know if her assistants are still here?"

She shakes her head. "I took them both home an hour ago."

But maybe Audrey doesn't know that. Maybe she went into the house looking for them so that Jessica can cancel the wedding.

Or maybe she was emotionally overwhelmed and raced for the nearest dark room.

I start for the house before the obvious answer hits me. The garage. Because she disappeared so damn fast. But the door is at the bottom of the stairs. And I didn't lock it when I carried her out of there earlier.

Hiking up the sheet, I head back across the snow, panic easing its grip on my gut. This is simply the same thing she did after the tree lighting ceremony. She got overwhelmed and looked for a quiet place to settle down. There's no fireworks this time, just all that guilt she's been suffering over her lie—on top of whatever worry she's been feeling since this morning after Bradford's call, and the fear that she might be hurt tonight when I took her virginity. Plus this crowded party, then having sex for the first time, and barely any sleep yet. That sounds like a hell of a day.

And maybe it was. But I'm completely fucking wrong.

I open the garage door, expecting to find her in the darkest corner with her back against the wall, eyes closed. The dim light over the workbench is still on, but I don't see her.

Instead I hear her. Hear her loud, wrenching sobs. My throat locks up and my chest clenches tight. Audrey told me what this is. It's the reason I opened her up tonight instead of our wedding night. Because being overwhelmed isn't the only reason she might run away and hide.

She's *hurting*. And I can't fool myself into thinking that it's a splinter or that she twisted her ankle on the way down the stairs. She ran away from *me*.

Something I said or did is making her cry like that.

"Audrey?" Getting her name out through the sudden lump in my throat is like pushing a boulder through a keyhole. It just doesn't fucking go.

The anguished sounds she's making claw up the inside of my chest as if my heart is a trapped, feral animal desperate to get free and go to her. I find her on the opposite side of the Corvette. She's sitting with her back against the wheel and her knees drawn up, her face buried in the wadded ball of my ugly sweater. The heavy knit barely muffles the uncontrollable sobs heaving from her chest, or the agony that fills each one.

"Audrey? Oh god, baby. Please." Seeing her like this wrecks me. Eyes burning, I crouch beside her, reaching out to touch her knee and gently let her know I'm here. "Whatever it is—"

Her body stiffens and she jerks her leg away, then curls tighter in on herself, still sobbing into the sweater. As if protecting herself from me.

As if she can't bear my touch.

Reeling from the pain, I fall back while the whole world darkens and shatters apart within my chest. Just a few minutes ago, I thought I had everything. But I have nothing. Nothing at all, except an endless well of desolation within the wasteland that just opened up inside me.

Yet my pain doesn't matter. Only she does.

With every movement aching in my joints like I'm a dying old man, I settle in beside her, my back against the passenger door—and careful to keep a few inches between us.

"I'll be here with you, baby," I tell her in a voice crushed by the devastation of not being able to touch her. "You aren't alone. I'll stay until you stop hurting."

She must be able to hear me, because that only makes her cry harder. Each great gasping sob has to be ripping up her throat and lungs, but I know she can't stop them.

And I don't know how to help her.

My vision blurring, I tip back my head and stare blindly out at nothing—trying to remember what I said. What might have done this.

What did I say? That I had a confession to make. That I wanted to tear up the marriage contract.

Ah fuck. The contract that—to Audrey—represented the beginning of our marriage. Not the ceremony, but when she signed our marital agreement. To her, me saying we should tear it up must have been the same as asking for a divorce. And I said it right after she worried that I'd be angry with her for lying…and she was afraid I wouldn't want to marry her anymore. But I should have been clearer.

"We don't need to tear up the marriage contract, Audrey. I only meant that I didn't want the Wyndhams' lawsuit to be the reason for our marriage. But we can keep it if you want to." Because the contract doesn't stipulate that we *have* to get divorced after I receive my inheritance. One of us would have to initiate the proceedings. And I sure as hell won't. If Audrey loves me… she wouldn't have reason to, either. "We'll do whatever you want, baby. The contract, the wedding—anything you need, I'll give it. Because I can't fucking bear to see you like this."

My reassurance appears to ease her pain. She doesn't stop crying, but her sobs don't seem so violent now. Or maybe she's so physically exhausted that they're dying out.

Or…she's trying to stop for my sake. Because I said I can't bear it.

Shit. I need to be more careful about what I say. About *how* I say it. And I'm not going to assume anything about her reactions unless she actually tells me how she's feeling.

I'll just wait for her. I would wait forever, but only another ten minutes pass before her sobs ease into hiccuping gasps.

She lifts her face from the sweater but doesn't look at me. Only straight ahead, her eyes swollen and her face ravaged by her tears. They're still spilling down her cheeks when she shakily whispers, "I swore that I'd never ask for more than you want to give."

Because she doesn't want to be like her mother. But she never could be. She would never *need* to be. There's no limit to what I'd give her. Not now. I'm done holding back.

"Anything you want, Audrey, just ask. I'll give it."

"Oh, Caleb. You're always so sweet to me." Her eyes close, more tears sliding from beneath her lashes. "It's not right for me to ask this. But…can I have a week?"

"A week?" To reconsider the marriage? Something else? I won't make any assumptions here, either. "Just tell me what for, baby."

"You want to marry for love. So I understand why you don't want to marry me now that the will contest is done with. But if I can just have one more week with you—"

She glances over as I begin shaking my head—not saying no, but in sheer disbelief at what I'm hearing. She thought I didn't want to marry *her* for love? This isn't about the contract, but because she *still* thinks I don't love her? I can barely take it in.

But in that gesture of stunned incredulity, she sees rejection. Her wavering voice shatters.

"A day, then? Just one last…one *last*—" Anguish crumples her soft mouth. Curling forward, she covers her face with the sweater, and the rest emerges on jagged shards of breath. "Just one…more day…with you. *Please.*"

That final plea is a keening cry, her body wracked by agonized sobs that seem to rip her apart inside. Each one shreds my heart. In a million fucking years, it never would have occurred to me that she would hear me say that I want to marry for love and not understand that I'd fallen for her.

But how could she know? I held back everything, never showed her or told her that I wanted anything more personal from her than sex.

"Audrey. Baby." Voice thick, I kneel in front of her. My shaking hands hover so close to touching but I can't yet, I can't. I have to fix this first. I wasn't direct enough before. I will be now. "You can have a day. You can have a week. You can have forever. I want to marry for love, which means I want to marry *you*. I love you, baby. I'm so deep in love with you, I'll never get out. And I'll never want to."

She goes utterly still and quiet except for the uncontrollable shuddering of her breath.

Each word choked by emotion, I tell her again, "I want to marry you because I love you. But I'll love you if you don't marry me. I'll love you no matter what you do. But I *do* want you to marry me. Not for spite, not for the inheritance—but for love."

She lifts her head, her teary gaze searching my face. Her throat works, and her voice is only a faint rasp when she says, "I'm not marrying you because I love you."

"No?" I don't believe it for a second. Not after this. "I think you do love me."

"Of course I do." A deep hiccuping shudder moves through her. She wipes her tear-streaked face with the back of her hand, and I give her the edge of my sheet to use as a tissue. "But it's not why I'm marrying you."

Of course I do. My heart swells up so fucking big. "Why, then?"

"Because you asked me to marry you," she says simply. "That has always been my reason. I would have pursued you regardless, but that's only dating. The reason I'm marrying you is because you brought me a proposal— which became a marriage contract."

The one I wanted to rip up. "And we'll let that contract stand. It doesn't matter. But what we clearly need is another proposal."

Her mouth curves into a watery smile. "Do we?"

"Yeah." And I'm already kneeling in front of her. Gently, I take her hand—and she doesn't stiffen or pull away. Instead her fingers intertwine with mine, and my voice is raw with emotion when I begin. "I want you to marry me, Audrey Clarke. I want you to love me and let me love you for the rest of our lives. Will you?"

Sheer joy glitters in her eyes. "Yes."

All the shattered pieces of my world slide back together. Everything empty fills again, then overflows. My hands shake with the force of my emotions as I bring her fingers to my lips and press a kiss to her engagement ring, then the backs of her fingers, one by one, before tugging her forward.

She rocks up onto her knees, so we're face to face—but although I intended to kiss her, I'm stopped by her warm hand cupping my jaw. She looks up at me, amazement shining from her beautiful eyes.

Wonder fills her voice. "You're the only person who has ever loved me."

Oh, baby. Heart aching, I capture her mouth. All the love I feel burns through every brush of our lips, every slide of our tongues. Suddenly it's so much clearer why she never suspected that I would marry *her* for love. She truly believes that nobody does.

But I can't let her go on believing it. Resting my forehead against hers, I tell her gruffly, "I'm not the only one. Jeremy and Jessica love you. Reverend Foster loves you. Mia loves you. And these are just the friends of yours that I've met. I bet there are plenty more."

Doubt clouds her expression, but hope lifts her tone. "You think they do?"

"I know they do." I cup her face in my hands. "I suppose no one really goes around saying it. Especially employees to their employers. Or adult male mentor figures to teenaged girls. It's too easy to be misunderstood as something sexual or romantic."

"Yes," she agrees softly.

"I'll say it to you. So much you'll get tired of hearing it."

Her mouth curves. "That won't ever happen."

"And I won't ever get tired of saying it. Hell, every time I kiss you, I'll be saying it." I demonstrate with another taste of her lips. "And you love your friends, too?"

"Of course."

Always 'of course.' As if loving is so natural for her. But usually being blunt and open is natural for her, too. "Yet you never said anything to them? Or to me, either. That's not like you."

"I didn't want anyone to feel obligated to reciprocate my feelings. Especially since no one is going to…" She trails off, as if once again grappling with the idea that there *are* people who love her. In a small voice she says, "You *really* think they do?"

"Yeah, baby. Maybe they're not in love with you like I am. But they love you." And I'd bet my left nut there's more than a few unlucky bastards out there who are in love with her, too. "Because you're so damn lovable. As soon as they get to know you, my friends will love you, too. So will our kids."

"Our children?" Pained yearning darkens her eyes. "You think they'll be able to?"

Not wondering if they'll be able to love. Wondering if they'll be able to love *her*.

Her parasite of a mother and shit stain of a father have a hell of a lot to answer for. Because of them, the most incredible woman in the world has spent most of her life believing she wasn't loved. That she *couldn't* be loved.

Yet Audrey still spent so much of that time quietly giving her love to others. That has nothing to do with her parents and everything to do with who Audrey is.

My throat tight, I nod. "I'm sure they will, baby. Our children are going to love you as much as I do."

New, happy tears glisten in her eyes and a beautiful smile curves her lips. "They will love you even more… my big, sweet, sexy marshmallow."

"Full of gooey stuff just for you." I grin when she delicately snorts out a laugh. "You want to go upstairs and practice making those kids?"

Because I don't want to hold back anymore.

Though temptation lights her face, she shakes her head. "I want to, but…I'm really tired. And a little bit sore."

I'll rein it in, then—and send her home, so she can sleep in tomorrow morning rather than wake up when I go to work. "You've had a hell of a day, baby. I'll walk you to the car."

And the next time I see her, she'll be walking down the aisle toward me. Almost thirty-six hours of sheer torture while I'm waiting to make her mine.

At the car, the driver flashes me a discreet thumbs-up while she opens the door—then she tactfully slips into the front seat, leaving me standing alone on the curb with Audrey, still only wearing my sheet. With concern, Audrey glances down at my bare feet but I stop her before she can say a word.

"I'll be quick," I reassure her, tipping her chin up until she meets my eyes. "I want to be sure there's nothing else in the way of our clean start. Is there anything we still need to say?"

"Just one thing," she tells me, reaching up to cradle my face in her hands. "I love you, Caleb Moore."

A tangle of sweet emotion knots my in throat. *Just one thing.* But it's the only thing that matters. And it's all that needs to be said. So I kiss her once more, then let her go.

The next time I kiss her, she'll be my wife.

AUDREY

HERE IS WHAT HAPPENED THE FIRST TIME: I walked through the elevator doors, and the sight of Caleb Moore standing in the wrong place threw me so off-kilter that I didn't even dare to look at his face. He unbalanced *everything*.

Here is what happens now: I walk through the church doors, and Caleb Moore's fascinating face is the only thing I let myself see. Because everything else in the church is off-kilter, the symmetry just a little bit off. Not the pews on either side of the aisle that are filled with our friends and the people who care about us, not the decorations or the architecture of the church itself. But up ahead, Reverend Foster waits at the altar and

Caleb stands to the right side, his dark eyes locked on mine. Yet on the left side, there's nothing. Just an empty space that is so, so *wrong*.

Until Caleb holds out his hand. When I take my place beside him, the whole world rights itself again.

But it's not the same world it used to be. This world seems…unreal. As if it's a dream. And I've felt like this for almost two days now.

This is a world where people love me. So nothing is familiar—not even myself. Because this woman that people love…I'm not used to being her. The past two days I've had the strangest sense of being disconnected from my own body, as if all this love that surrounds me belongs to someone else. Yet I don't think Caleb's wrong about how my friends feel. I simply had to open my eyes to the possibility that it was true, and when I see my friends' deep and genuine happiness for me, I think that it must be. So every minute spent with Mia, Jeremy, and Jessica while preparing for the wedding ceremony has been filled with the amazement of this discovery, which continually seems new and surprising. Perhaps one day it will finally sink in.

But knowing that Caleb loves me…I don't think the wonder and amazement will ever fade. It might always feel like a dream.

At least everything feels real as he takes my hand. He's absolutely beautiful in the formal morning suit that he opted for over a tuxedo, each piece perfectly tailored to his tall, muscular form. And the way he *looks* at me with so much awe, so much desire, so much love burning in his eyes…

"Audrey, baby," Caleb murmurs, lightly squeezing my fingers, his brown eyes full of laughter now. "Come back to me."

Whoops. I hyperfocused on his fascinating face. But who wouldn't, if Caleb looked at them like that?

Filled with sheer joy, I grin up at him. "My rubber band didn't go with this dress. What did I miss?"

"Only the sermon," Reverend Foster says dryly. "But you rarely listen to those anyway. I'll email it to you."

Perfect. "So are we married now?"

"Almost." Caleb's fingers tighten on mine, his voice deepening. "We still have to say the vows."

The vows. They are why I prefer a marriage contract to this ceremony. I can't easily tell whether people are speaking the truth, or if they mean something other than what they are saying. But a contract with terms that are explicitly spelled out allows less room for ambiguity or misunderstanding. So signing that agreement felt more binding than words spoken in ways I might not fully perceive.

But that was only until Caleb spoke them to me.

No ambiguity lurks beneath the raw emotion thickening his voice as he promises to honor and cherish me. There's no way to misunderstand the depth of the devotion in his warm gaze as he vows to forsake all others.

And the truth of every word lies naked upon his beautiful face when he swears to love me as long as we both shall live.

Even if he hadn't said the words on Saturday night, I'd have known he loved me today. I couldn't have made any other possible interpretation when his vows are written so clearly in his every word, his every look, his every touch.

The unadulterated force of his love fills my own heart achingly full as I repeat the vows—and he knows so well that I can't lie. That I mean every word I say. On this day, I would have revealed myself to him, too.

But there's nothing left to hide when Caleb cradles my face in his big hands. When he reverently kisses my lips.

When he becomes mine, and he makes me his.

I don't know what to call the emotion that crashes over me then, but I'm dizzy with it as Caleb takes my hand and leads me down the aisle. A car is waiting outside to take us to our reception at the Clement Hotel, which is only a two-minute drive from the church—yet I intend to make the most of every second alone with him.

Caleb must have the same intention. His strong arms haul me into his lap and he hungrily feasts from my mouth, then he groans when his callused palms slide up the bare skin of my back.

"Fucking hell, baby. Wedding dresses aren't supposed

to be this goddamn hot. You know what all your naked skin did to me when you turned around at the end?"

I'm sitting on what it did to him. Smiling against his lips, I say, "I wore it because I want to dance with you again."

And my dress is a floor-length white silk version of the backless red dress that I wore to the mayor's cocktail party last week—and our reception is in the same ballroom. All I want to feel is Caleb holding me close again, his hand against my bare skin.

"We'll dance, baby. Just hope that I don't end up losing my head and fucking you in front of everyone."

I won't hope too hard. I slip my fingers down the length of his wedding tie, then trace the edge of his dark green waistcoat, a color perfect for a Christmas wedding. "I like your suit. It's just like you—a little old-fashioned and a lot sexy."

"You can thank Jeremy for picking it out. Shit, we're almost there," he swears as the car begins to slow, kissing me again. "How flexible is your schedule today? Can we skip out of this thing early?"

"Oh, Caleb," I tell him softly, because he's still so innocent in so many ways. "As of this afternoon, you are Mister Audrey Motherfuckin' Clarke—which means we can skip out whenever we want. I'd like some cake before we go, though."

His eyes narrow. "You know your assistants' nickname for you?"

"It's *my* nickname for me. I told Jeremy and Jessica what it was when I hired them, so there weren't any misunderstandings about exactly who I am."

"So you give yourself a badass name, yet I get stuck with the same 'marshmallow' that I had as a kid?"

"Are either of those names wrong?" I dare him to say they are.

He laughs, shaking his head. "No, baby. Except for the part where I'm soft."

"I can tell," I murmur huskily. His thick erection is a steely length beneath me—a length that will soon be inside me. My inner muscles clench with anticipation. "I love you…my husband."

A possessive gleam lights his eyes. "I love you, my wife."

That dizzying emotion sweeps over me again, a whirlwind that lifts me off my feet until I'm flying, strangely disconnected again from this woman who is *so* loved. Yet at the same time, I'm right here with him—holding his hand as we make our way to the ballroom. Aside from the staff catering the event, we're the first to arrive, so I lead him through the maze of dinner tables to the center of the room. Turning me to face him, his hand possessively slides down my naked back before he pulls me close.

Someone must have alerted the string quartet, because we've only swayed together for a few moments when a sweet melody begins playing. Yet the only rhythm I feel is the one beating in his chest, where my hand rests over his heart. The only music I hear is the devotion in Caleb's deep voice when he murmurs "I love you" against my lips.

More guests arrive and we continue dancing. Jeremy and Jessica didn't plan a reception that would force me to stand in a line, greeting people and shaking their hands. And it's Christmas Eve, when attending a long social event might be more stressful than fun, especially for those with holiday preparations or family at home, so no one has to wait for dinner or cake or pictures or speeches. The buffet and bar are open, one of the cakes is sliced, the dancing has already begun—and if all they want to do before leaving is pick up the gift bag I've provided for each guest, they are more than welcome to.

I wouldn't know they were here, anyway. There's only Caleb, holding me so close while sheer emotion sends me spinning and soaring, looking down at myself in his arms.

But there *are* speeches, of course. And friends to laugh with—and a cake to cut.

Nothing ever tasted sweeter than Caleb's kiss after I feed him that first bite. Nothing ever made me hungrier than the look in his eyes when I lick lemon buttercream from my thumb—until he takes my hand and licks the frosting from the tip of my second finger. I'm so much hungrier then.

So is he. His gaze is utterly ravenous as I rise up onto

my toes and murmur against his mouth—"My panties are *so* wet."

Primitive need flares across his expression before he kisses me—a kiss that clearly takes all of his strength to pull away from. His voice is a soft growl as he says, "We'll take the rest of your cake to go."

Jessica's already prepared for this. I barely get out the request for a to-go slice before she hands over a bag containing a square bakery box, my purse, and phone. "The top tier. Plus everything else you'll need that isn't already married to you. I'll call and let them know you're on your way up."

Emotion swells up through my chest, so big and bright. "Thank you. And I love you," I tell her even as Caleb takes my hand and begins pulling me toward the exit. "Jeremy, too. You're both wonderful and I'm so happy to work with you. Tell him I said so."

"I will." Her dark eyes glisten and her smooth, buttery voice has scratches in it. "We love you, too, boss."

Then I'm flying again, dizzy with so much love—while laughing and almost running to keep up with Caleb's long strides. But we're going the wrong way.

I tug on his hand. "The elevator's in that direction."

"And the lobby's in this direction." His eyes are a fevered gleam. "It's a four-hour drive to your lodge. I can't wait that long, so I'm getting us a room."

Laughing, I tug him toward the elevator again. "I already thought of that. Everything's ready to go."

He instantly changes direction. I look into the bag for the key card that'll give access to the top levels, and practically hear his teeth grit in frustration when other hotel guests board the elevator at the same time. An older couple glances at our clothes and offers their congratulations, and I suspect that if not for their presence, we'd have consummated our marriage in the elevator.

As it is, Caleb doesn't even notice my call button selection until the car has emptied. "Which floor is 'RF'?"

"The roof," I say, pulling him forward as the doors open. "Because I don't want to spend four hours driving to the lodge, either."

ONLY THIRTY MINUTES PASS BEFORE THE HELICOPTER touches down in front of my cabin, the blades whipping up a small blizzard of powdery snow. Waiting for us is the small team of personnel who came up earlier today with our luggage and to prepare the house for our arrival. They're flying out as soon as we fly in—so I'll have an entire week utterly alone with Caleb.

With my *husband*. A word that means so much more than I imagined, now that we've spoken our vows.

Leaving the helicopter, Caleb doesn't let my feet touch the ground, cradling me in his arms as he carries me to the front door. His silent laughter shakes through his chest when he looks up at the cabin. Warm light spills through the windows on the upper and lower levels, welcoming us in. "It's never what I expect."

With my arms linked around his shoulders, I ask him, "What isn't?"

"This place. I was expecting a ski resort. Not a cozy log cabin."

"Do you want a ski resort?"

"No, baby." His voice deepens as he continues up the porch steps. "I just want you."

He's all I want, too. His warm lips fasten over mine as he carries me over the threshold, kicking the front door closed behind him.

"The bed's in the loft," I tell him between soft, panting kisses.

That's where he finally sets my feet down, though his mouth never leaves mine. Standing in front of a crackling fireplace, he slips my coat from my shoulders while I tug at his tie, his collar. My dress slithers to the floor in a puddle of white silk. A moment later he releases the jeweled comb from my hair, and the long strands tumble out of their elegant twist to curl over my bare shoulders.

Almost naked already, but I'm still working on his shirt buttons. I laugh against his lips. "You have the easier job."

"I'll finish it. Just keep kissing me," he commands gruffly, and I do. Cupping his beloved face in my hands, I rise up onto my toes and keep going, higher and higher, spinning but this time I don't get so far out of myself, as if the dizzying emotion is finally sinking in and settling beneath my skin—but it's light, *so* light, and so big that I still feel as if I might float away if I wasn't holding onto him.

"Audrey." A pained groan rumbles from his chest. "What is it? Are you hurt?"

Because tears are slipping down my cheeks. "No. I feel...I don't know."

"Happy or sad?"

"Happy. So happy." But I've been happy and this isn't the same. "More than happy. More than *everything*."

"I know, baby." Strong fingers cradling my jaw, he gently kisses my lips. "It's the same for me. Ever since you said you loved me. And this whole day. I thought it was so damn perfect—first marrying you in front of everyone, and then celebrating with our friends. Everything was pretty fucking amazing. I didn't think I could be happier. But it was just...like the spiked punch at the wedding. Because when I'm alone with you, it's like drinking straight from the bottle. It's so much stronger."

Pure, undiluted emotion. So powerful that we're dizzy and drunk on it.

"So much stronger," I agree on a whisper, then rise onto my toes again.

His mouth claims mine only for an instant before he groans and backs away. "Just give me one second. One second to look at you like this, so I can always remember it."

Standing in the firelight, wearing only my panties.

His gaze devours me, but I'm just as entranced by the sight of him. While kissing, he managed to get everything off except for his dark trousers, and those are unbuttoned with the suspenders hanging loose from his hips. The aggressive bulge of his cock tents the fine wool. His ridged stomach contracts with every ragged heave of breath, his broad chest and powerful shoulders stacked with muscle. He's so big, so tall…and all mine.

And I never want to forget this, either—the way he looks now. The way he looks *at* me, his face flushed with arousal and his heavy-lidded eyes inflamed with desire. Nothing has ever been sexier than the way he slowly drags his lower lip between his teeth when his focus drifts downward, as if already anticipating the taste of my nipples…and lower. As his gaze pauses on my panty-covered pussy, I can't stop my thighs from squeezing together or my whimper of need, because his reaction is everything. Hunger and tension seem to battle within him, a war between his need to look and his need to touch, his big hands clenching and unclenching at his sides, his muscles like corded steel.

Hoarsely he says, "I just can't believe you're mine, Audrey. I'm the luckiest bastard in the world."

I laugh, my heart swollen so full. "At least one of us needs to believe this is real."

His fiery gaze meets mine again. "What's not real to you?"

"That I can be loved like this," I confess shakily. "I

feel like it all must be happening to someone else."

Instantly the war that waged within him seems to cease. As if his battling desires no longer pull him in opposite directions, and everything within him abruptly focuses on…me.

Without another word, Caleb comes for me, crossing the distance in a single powerful stride. His left hand wraps around the nape of my neck and he pulls me into a devastating kiss, shattering my senses with every deep, hot lick between my lips. As if he means to consume me alive, to drown me with pleasure.

As if he means to destroy any doubts about who this is happening to.

My trembling legs barely support my weight when he abandons my lips. Desperately I cling to his shoulders as he bends me back over the iron band of the forearm he wraps around my waist, lifting my breasts to his mouth. With a growl, Caleb lowers his head to feast. Like a man possessed, he lavishes his attention on my nipples, suckling and licking the taut peaks, the force of his hunger almost painful but too sweet to run away from.

Far too sweet. Like the exquisite ache building inside me, the ache that isn't a hurt but just need, need, *need*. Frenetic desire that transforms my clinging hands to fists that clench in his short hair to tug and demand. That changes the breathless chanting of his name to a desperate plea, begging for him inside me.

But Caleb has no mercy, dropping instead to his knees. No longer demanding, the grip I have on his hair becomes my strongest anchor against my husband's sensual storm. Strong fingers hook into the waistband of my panties. His dark eyes lock with mine as his warm breath penetrates drenched silk.

In a rough voice, he says, "Let me tell you what's happening to you, Audrey. I'm making love to you on our wedding night. Not someone else. Because I'm so in love with you."

"I know. I *do*." My body begins to shake as he slowly drags my panties down over my hips. "I love you, too. So much."

So much I can hardly bear it. Or this. The electrifying pleasure of his mouth, the long hot lick through my saturated folds. The fervid hunger in his groan. The commanding pressure of his fingers digging into my backside as he holds me still for the relentless teasing of his tongue.

My legs nearly give out when he sucks on my clit, but I want, need, so much more. "No more waiting, Caleb. I need you inside me."

With a groan, he buries his face against my belly, rolling his forehead from side to side as if in denial. His mouth glistens with my arousal when he looks up at me, his voice harsh with strain. "I'm not holding back with you, baby. This isn't waiting. This is the first part of doing."

Making love to me. "We've got the rest of our lives to spend on foreplay."

"Yeah, we do." Pleasure darkens his eyes, either at the thought or because his fingers just took over for his mouth, his thumb circling my slippery clit. I curl forward on a gasp, bracing my hands on his shoulders as a thick finger pushes past my entrance, gently thrusting. "But your cunt is so damn delicious—and I want this night to be good for you. I want it to be perfect."

It will be. It already is. It's been perfect since the moment we spoke our vows. But that perfection isn't because of pleasure or an orgasm.

"And I want to finish what we began in the church today," I manage to get out, then my brain almost melts, my back arching as he adds a second finger, stretching my inner walls and making me feel so full. The rest emerges on a rush before I completely lose my mind and come. "I want to consummate our vows, to make you a part of me, and hold you so deep inside that you're the only thing I know. I want to give myself to you and make you mine when I do. I want to take my husband. And I want my husband to take his wife."

"*My wife.*" Feral possession tightens his expression. In a powerful movement, he surges to his feet—and I cry out in surprise as he lifts me with him, his right hand gripping my bottom and his left hand cupping my pussy, two fingers still scissoring within me. "Wrap your gorgeous legs around me, wife."

And my arms, linking tight around his neck, holding on as I cling to him with my legs around his waist. The iron bar of his forearm across the small of my back pins my torso to his broad chest. A soft whimper escapes my throat as he withdraws his fingers from my liquid heat.

"You'll give yourself to me right here." His biceps bulge and flex as his hand works beneath me, tearing open the remaining fastenings on his trousers. "Take me in easy, let your little pussy get used to having this big cock again. Then I'll carry you over to that bed and claim what's mine."

Oh god, yes. Wildly I kiss him, tasting my arousal on his lips. With a grunt, he hefts me higher. The blunt head of his erection parts my intimate folds, hard and hot as it prods my entrance, and I automatically glance down to see though there's not an inch of space between us.

"Look at me, Audrey." He rasps out the command and my focus snaps back up to meet his burning gaze. "Look at me while you fill yourself up with my cock. And know that I'm completely yours whether you take me or not."

I know he is. Devotion and love shine from his eyes as fiercely as when he spoke his wedding vows. "Now?" I whisper breathlessly against his lips.

Jaw clenched, he nods. Waiting for me to take him, his every muscle like high tensile steel as he aligns me over his rigid length. Straining not with the effort of holding me, but the effort of holding himself under control as I relax the tension in my thighs.

Gravity does the rest. Pressure builds at my entrance, then my own weight forces my drenched flesh to give way to the solid thickness of his cock. Only a few inches, but we both groan at the incredible sensation of my inner muscles stretching to accommodate his heavy shaft. We're face-to-face, Caleb's head slightly bowed and his forehead pressed to mine, his gusting breaths a ragged storm against my parted lips. His supportive arm around my back prevents me from falling but also denies me any further assistance from gravity, and his erection is so thick and hard and so good inside me that my legs begin trembling, my muscles quivering uncontrollably. Simply clinging to him is suddenly all that I can do.

"Help me," I beg, desperate to take all of him. "I can't—"

Jagged lightning flashes behind my eyes as Caleb's hips surge upward, driving his cock deep. *So deep.* Filling me completely, and the stunning pleasure of his possession sears my nerve endings with white-hot ecstasy. My head falls back on a loud, helpless moan.

Instantly strong fingers tangle in my hair, bringing my face close to his again. Caleb's features are a taut mask of arousal, his teeth gritted. "You've given yourself to me? Sealed your vows?"

"Yes," I gasp against his lips, my overfilled sheath still adjusting to the unyielding hardness wedged so far inside me. "You're mine now, Caleb Moore."

His eyes blaze. "I've always been yours," he grinds out. "And it's time to make you mine."

His mouth captures mine in a scorching kiss as he strides toward the bed. The movement stirs his pulsating length within my body's tight clasp, each step sending jolts of ecstasy streaking through my sensitized flesh. But even as I tighten my arms around his neck, trying to rise up and ride him, he wrenches me upward, off of his cock. My disappointed whine is cut short when he gently lowers me onto the mattress.

But he doesn't follow me down as I expect. He remains standing by the bed, his huge erection bobbing and gleaming with my juices. The shaft and crown are flushed a purplish red, as if angry it's no longer inside me.

So is my pussy. My inner muscles furiously clamp down on the nothing that fills me now. Moaning, I clench my thighs together to ease the ache. "Caleb?"

"Just give me another second, baby. I want to look at what's mine." Tension pales his lips as he wraps his fingers around his slick cock and begins to pump. "Our vows didn't include a promise to obey. But I want you to obey me now and spread those long legs."

The command sweeps through me on a wave of sheer need. Delicious heat spills deep within me, expanding outward from my center. My body feels utterly heavy, weighed down by the desire flooding through my limbs, pressing me into the bed as if Caleb was already over me, his cock plunging deep.

I need that. My pulse pounding in my ears, obediently I part my thighs, spreading them wide. My breaths come in sharp gasps as his hungry gaze settles on my exposed pussy. He groans, his knuckles whitening as his grip on his cock tightens.

"You're so damn beautiful, Audrey." The mattress dips as he climbs on, and my heart seems to sway and swell with the movement, everything within me rolling toward him though my body stays in place. Sweat glistens over his skin as he draws nearer, his hands shaking when they begin trailing up my legs. The aggressive jut of his erection between his heavy thighs draws my gaze to the pearls of cum dripping from the smooth tip.

Yet despite his turgid arousal and obvious need, he barely touches me. His palms skim from my ankles to my calves in the lightest of caresses, his fingers trembling.

Sheer wonder fills me at the sight. "Are you nervous?"

"No. And yes." His throat works, and his voice is hoarse as he continues, "I've got a handle on the sex part. But I've also got my whole life, my whole future right here before me. So I need to be careful with it, because you're so fucking precious."

And he's so incredibly sweet. Tender emotion melts through all the liquid desire swirling within me. "I'll always feel safe with you, because I know you'll be careful whether you're gentle or rough. And if you *are* rough, Caleb, I won't shatter."

"I know," he says gruffly. "You're so strong and resilient, baby. And so generous, so loving. You're too damn good for a selfish asshole like me—but I'm taking you anyway."

Abruptly he drags me closer, friction warming my back as I slide across the bedspread. His fingers curl under my thighs and he raises them higher, higher, then rocks forward until he's braced over me with my knees hooked over his elbows and his swollen cock parting the soaked lips of my pussy.

Everything about the position is forceful, commanding—and every part of him is hard, from his corded muscles to his thick erection to the demanding fingers that tilt my chin up to meet the claim of his mouth.

But his kiss is so gentle, and his voice a low murmur against my lips. "Will you take me, Audrey?"

"I will, Caleb," I vow, clasping his face in my hands. "Today. Tomorrow. Forever."

His warm mouth seeks mine again and his kiss deepens, capturing my moan of pleasure as my body yields to his sweet, inexorable possession. The taut strain of my inner walls echoes the adjustment taking place even deeper inside, as Caleb becomes a part of me. Truly making me his wife. Giving me his heart and his life. It's so big, so much. Almost too much too take. But I do.

I always will.

Holding him tight, I take him all. When his

enormous cock is seated deep within my pussy, filling me completely, he pauses for only a moment to hoarsely groan, "I love you, baby," before he begins to move.

He loves me. And I'm no longer outside of myself, looking down—as if his every long, slow thrust forces me back into the flesh that he's worshipping with his lips, with his hands, with his body. No longer disconnected, but exquisitely and gloriously contained within my own skin, this woman who's crying out as he fills me again and again, relentlessly loving me, making me his.

So endless. So delicious. I didn't know it would be like this. The luscious burn, the frenzied need—none of that is new, yet it's so much more than it was before. Not just lust and pleasure, but joy and astonishment as my hands cling so tight to his shoulders, as my hips twist and writhe beneath his, the ecstasy within me stretching tighter and tighter. As if with every thick, devastating stroke of his cock he's driving more of this heart-swelling emotion into me, until I'm almost bursting.

But when the orgasm hits, it's not an explosion that frees all that trapped emotion. Instead a cresting wave crashes through me again and again, drowning my senses in the euphoric wonder of Caleb loving me. Desperately I gasp for air, arching as my body convulses. He abruptly stills inside me, groaning my name against my lips as my inner muscles constrict, and his ragged exhalation gives me the breath I need to survive the deluge of his own release, the hot pulse of his cock that sends me under again, coming helplessly as he pumps me full of his seed.

Then he kisses me and kisses me, before rolling over onto his back and taking me with him. I sprawl bonelessly over his chest. For a long moment I can't do anything but catch my breath, luxuriating in the feel of his hard body against me, within me.

Until gently he withdraws, sweeping his hand down my back, murmuring that he loves me. At that, I kiss him again. He's not even inside me now, but I'm closer to him than I've ever been, as if he's burrowed beneath my skin. As if all the love he fucked into me is still there.

Lifting my head, I search his gaze—and see the same joyous wonder and blissful contentment that I'm feeling. My hand trembles as I trace his lips. "You told me our wedding night wouldn't be the same as our first time, but I didn't realize how much different it would be."

A rough laugh escapes him and he shakes his head before kissing my fingertips. "I just meant that I'd last longer than a few pumps. I didn't know it would feel like *this*."

It was different for him, too? "It hasn't before?"

"No, baby." His voice is like gravel. "Never. Not even close."

"I like that very much," I tell him softly, with emotion clogging my throat and my heart so, so full. "So this is what it feels like to be loved?"

A rough groan rumbles from his chest. "Whatever this feels like, baby, it's because you *are* loved. I love you so damn much." His palm gently cups my cheek. "But how does it feel?"

Sudden tears sting my eyes. "Happy," I tell him with a tremulous smile. "But not like the happy that I'm used to. It's more than laughing or smiling. I could have all the money in the world and not buy this. It's as if I've been given everything, simply because you love me."

His throat works, and he nods. "That's what you loving me feels like. But as if I have no money at all, yet still have everything. That's what you've given to me," he says thickly, then threads his fingers through my hair and captures my mouth in a sweetly sensual kiss. Because our wedding night isn't over yet.

And we both have so much more to give, our wedding night might never end.

CALEB

ARRIED TO AUDREY, I SUSPECT EVERY DAY will be just like Christmas. But the day after our wedding actually *is* Christmas, and I wake up not long after sunrise to a warm cabin and a cold bed, with my wife's sweet scent clinging to my skin. I drag a pair of flannel pajama pants out of the dresser, because her employees didn't just bring our luggage yesterday but also unpacked everything. The wrapped presents that I stashed in my duffel bag are already under the tree—along with a pile of other gifts that I hope are wedding presents and not from Audrey to me.

She already gave me her heart. I don't need anything else. Just her.

I hit the bathroom and head down the stairs from the loft, my steps slowing as I take in the view through the enormous windows. Holy shit. Last night it was too dark when we arrived to see anything except snow and more snow, but her cabin sits at the end of a small, ice-covered pond, with jagged white mountain peaks rising in every direction. It's utterly fucking stunning.

But I shouldn't be surprised that she built her cozy getaway in a place like this. Of course she did.

And the majestic beauty surrounding us is absolutely nothing compared to the sight that greets me downstairs. With her back to me, Audrey sits on a stool in front of the breakfast bar that separates the kitchen from the living room, her head bent over a sheet of paper. Her pale hair is stacked up in a messy bun, her feet encased in fuzzy green-and-red striped socks…and she's wearing the white dress shirt that I got married in. The long sleeves are rolled up to her elbows, and the hem almost hits her knees.

She's the sexiest, most beautiful thing I've ever seen.

My cock thickens as my gaze devours her. Then she absently flips up the collar and turns her face into the fabric, as if trying to inhale my scent, and my heart cinches up tight in my chest.

I can give her more of me than that.

She doesn't seem aware of my approach before my arms circle her waist from behind, yet she doesn't stiffen in surprise. Instead she sighs with pleasure and tilts her head to the side when I nuzzle her bare neck.

"Good morning, wife."

"Good morning, husband," she replies with a smile, reaching back to clasp her hand around the nape of my neck. "I missed you."

"I missed you, too." Less than five hours ago, I fell asleep beside her. But I began missing her the moment I woke up. "Are you always up this early, or is it because it's Christmas morning?"

"Both." There's a smile in her voice. "I made you coffee. But you might have to make it again, because it was a while ago."

Made for me, because she doesn't drink coffee. Touched by her thoughtfulness, I tilt her head back so I can tease her mouth open for a taste between her lips. And she's sweet.

So sweet. And tart. Just like lemon buttercream.

I nibble at her bottom lip. "You had cake for breakfast?"

"Yes." She grins against my mouth. "It's Christmas."

I have something just as creamy and tangy in mind for my breakfast, but I'll fuel up with food and caffeine first. Audrey appears engrossed in whatever it is she's doing, anyway—and she must have been at it for a while, because the coffee's stone cold.

Sticking a full mug into the microwave, I check out the array of yellow sticky notes arranged into neat columns on the counter near her elbow. In front of her is a sheet of paper overlain with a grid, and with other sticky notes tacked onto the squares. Whatever this project is, she's giving it her full concentration. Lower lip trapped between her teeth, her eyebrows knitted together, she sticks another note into an empty square.

"What is that, baby?"

"My schedule."

"I thought you weren't working this week." It's fine if she has to, but I'm pretty damn sure she didn't want to.

"I'm not working. This is our honeymoon schedule."

Aside from the day we leave, we don't have a schedule. At least, we didn't have one yesterday. The calendars on our phones were empty. "Don't you usually wing it when you're out here?"

That's what she told me before. Whether summer or winter, she makes certain her time at the lodge is completely unstructured.

"That was before we had sex. Now I want to make sure we can have as much as possible and in every position. So the idea of making a schedule for it got into my head."

A sex schedule? Grinning, I look closer and make out what she's written on some of those stickies. *Cowgirl. Doggy. Sixty-nine.*

My god, I love this woman.

She picks up an *Against the wall* and chews her bottom lip while considering the open blocks of time. "How many hours of sleep do you usually need?"

"Usually around six hours." *Blow job*. Another *Doggy*.

Obviously she has great faith in my stamina. Teasing her, I add, "Maybe six and a quarter, if I'm really worn out."

"Quarter?" Dismay tightens her expression as she stares down at the grid. Then she begins pulling off the stickies, putting them back into the array by her elbow.

"Hold up. What are you doing, baby?"

"I only broke it down into thirty minute blocks." An almost desperate frustration fills her voice as she gestures to a short stack of paper at the end of the counter. "I have to redo it again. Can you get me a new sheet from the desk?"

Redo it…which she's already done at least a dozen times. I pick up that stack of paper and find a collection of partially finished grids—each of them abandoned when she made a tiny squiggle in a straight line or drew a slightly uneven row.

My beautiful, brilliant Audrey. I hope to hell that I'm doing the right thing when I gently catch her hands, stopping her. "How about this? I'll take care of the sex schedule. I'll make sure we hit all the possible positions, and I can guarantee you that we'll be fucking as often as we can."

Hope fills her eyes. "Will you?"

"Yeah, baby," I reassure her, bringing each of her hands to my lips and pressing a soft kiss to the center of her left palm, then the right. "Just pass that paper over here, and I'll make sure it's done."

"Okay. Thank you so much." As she pushes the

schedule across the counter, she blows out a breath that puffs her cheeks, and there's sheer relief in that shuddering exhalation. "I put everything on stickies so it's all easy to move around and update. But…don't let me look at it."

"I won't." I glance down to see what she's already stuck onto today's column. Not all sex.

Breakfast.

Open Christmas presents.

Make love by tree (Caleb's choice of position).

Suck cock in shower.

Ride cock in bed.

Nap.

Ice skating.

That pulls a chuckle from me. I'm a little surprised that isn't a *Screwing while skating*—maybe a little disappointed, too, because I wouldn't mind trying. My dick's rock hard after reading this list, but I'm fascinated by it, too. Sex is another area where Audrey has taken many of her cues from me, letting me lead. Yet this is a captivating glimpse into what she's fantasized about.

I glance up from the schedule. "We can skate on the pond?"

She nods, stacking up the array of sticky notes into a neat pile. "Usually. If the ice isn't thick enough, we can switch skating out for another activity."

Maybe for one of today's other items. She's got a good ol' *Long, hard fuck* before *Christmas dinner*, followed by yet another *Doggy*. Probably because she came so damn hard when I took her from behind last night—and that wasn't even a proper pounding. She wasn't on her elbows and knees with her ass in the air. Instead I pulled her back against my chest, held her close while I pumped into her long and slow. The entire night was long and slow. Rather than fucking her hard and rough, I wallowed in the sweetness of her, the heat of her, and the sheer luxury of her wet velvet cunt.

My attention stops on the last item for today, sudden wariness clutching at my chest. "What's this? *Mechanic & Ice Queen*?"

I called her that once. Hurt her with that once. And can't imagine why the hell it's on the schedule now.

"Oh." An impish little grin curves her mouth. "That's when I say, 'Don't touch my soft, delicate skin with your rough, dirty hands!' and then you punish me with your long, thick cock."

Holy fuck. The microwave dings, but I don't reach for my coffee. I don't make any movement at all, because if I go anywhere, it'll be across this counter and straight between her thighs.

But before I touch her, I need to clarify something. "Am I punishing you because you don't want it, or am I punishing you for *saying* you don't want it when you really do?"

"For saying I don't want it." From beneath her lashes, she casts me a hot and glittering look. "Like the time I pretended that I didn't want you to kiss me goodnight. Maybe you pushed me into the back seat of the car and told me to open my mouth and then made me lick your cock with my lying tongue."

A groan rips from me. Because fuck, yes. "All right. This sticky note is going to the top of today's schedule."

Before we open presents. Because the first thing I'm doing this Christmas is making her hot little fantasy come true.

A fantasy that takes a warped perception I had of her, one that hurt her and ate me up with guilt, and turns that pain into something that'll give us both pleasure. Whether she did that consciously or not, I have no idea. Maybe it just originated because Audrey pictured that first night going differently, and thought I might like it, too.

If so, she's not wrong about that. That image of Audrey as the ice queen was the first one in my head. It was the first Audrey I ever fantasized fucking. I know better now, but the thought of making the ice queen melt for me, making her admit how much she wants me, is still hot as hell.

I head around the counter but she continues stacking those sticky notes—maybe oblivious to me, maybe just pretending to be. But the startled gasp when I spin her stool around isn't pretend, and neither is the rounding of her eyes when she gets a look at the size of the erection tenting my pajamas, forceful enough to pull the waistband away from my stomach.

Excitement gleams in her wide, laughing smile. She obviously tries her best to sound outraged, but it comes out breathless with anticipation. "What do you think you're doing, you cretin?"

Crowding in close, I cage her between my arms and the breakfast bar behind her. My voice deepens to a hardened growl. "You got what you wanted, Audrey. You married me to get your hands on my property. You thought this was going to be all business, but it's not. Because now I'm going to take what *I* want—and get my dirty hands all over you."

"No!" she gasps eagerly, swaying toward me. "I don't want you to touch me with your dirty hands!"

Oh shit. Laughter shakes through me, and I cup my hand around the back of her neck to pull her close, pressing my forehead to hers. "You're so bad at this, baby."

She's giggling. "I know. But it's fun. Is it still sexy?"

"There's not a damn thing you do that isn't sexy." Such as the way her breath catches when I grab hold of that messy bun and tug her head back. Or her soft, needy whimper when I skim my lips up the length of her exposed throat, then say harshly into her ear, "But I know your secret, Audrey Motherfuckin' Clarke. People see an ice queen when they look at you, but the truth is that you're burning up inside. I bet if I touched your little pussy right now, you'd be wet enough to drown me in it."

"Oh, Caleb. You're *so* good at this," she moans.

Because I don't need to pretend anything. I just need to want her, be desperate to have her. Which comes real damn easy. "Does that mean you want me to touch your pussy, baby? I think you do."

"You're wrong!" Her hand flattens on my bare chest and weakly shoves. "You think that just because you're so handsome and tall and strong, I'll get all hot for you? You think that just because…you're so…" Her fingertips begin tracing the ridge of my pectoral, her hungry gaze following the same path, the tip of her tongue touching the bow of her upper lip. "…so muscular and gorgeous and have such a big dick, I'll ever let you get anywhere near my…my…my diamond-encrusted pussy with it?"

She glances up at me when she spits out the *diamond-encrusted*, her icy eyes dancing with laughter.

This is the best Christmas ever. "I think your tight, rich-girl pussy wants my big, dirty cock real bad. Tell me you don't."

Abruptly her laughter transforms into the cold, withering stare that should shrivel me up but instead squeezes burning drops of pre-cum from the tip of my cock. Despite that look, her face is flushed with arousal, each panting breath lifting her breasts within that over-size shirt.

"You think you can steal the clothes off my back and get away with it?" With a snarl, I rip the buttons halfway down the front, spreading the sides open to reveal her soft little tits and fat rosy nipples. Gasping, Audrey tries to cover herself but I catch her wrists and look my fill. "Your pretty nipples are hard as diamonds, too. You're telling me I'm not turning you on?"

"I… No—" Biting her lip, she looks up at me imploringly and whispers, "What should I say?"

Because it's so hard for her to lie. And I'm guessing we've gone further than any script she prepared during her fantasies. "Just keep saying no when you mean yes, baby. Just keep telling me that you don't want me to touch you." She's so incapable of pretending that it'll be clear if her 'no' is ever real. "Maybe you'll claim it's just the cold—"

"It's cold in here!" she exclaims with a cheeky grin. "And you tore my shirt open!"

"So I'll have to warm you up." I let go of her wrists to knead her breasts in my big hands, to gently pinch her nipples. Lips compressed into a thin line to muffle her moans, she begins squirming on the stool, and I can fucking *hear* the way her pussy juices are sliding all over the seat. Groaning, I bend my head to suckle one pouty bud, then the other. Her fingers thread into my hair and she holds me to her breast, writhing and whimpering *no no no, I don't want you to touch me like this.*

She's so goddamn hot and horny. Teeth gritted, I raise my face to hers again, reaching down to stroke my aching cock. "I'm gonna fuck your little pussy, baby—"

"No!" *Yes.*

"Yeah, I am. Gonna get in real deep and fill you with my cum." I wedge my hips between her trembling thighs. "And I don't want you to fight me or try to get away."

"Okay," she agrees breathily.

Well…shit. "Hold up, baby. Timeout."

Though the only timeout is from playing this game, because my dick's throbbing with the need to be inside her and she'll probably go off like a rocket the moment I touch her clit. Her eyes are glazed with arousal when she looks up at me, and I cup her cheek, waiting until she focuses.

"No matter what I say, I actually mean that I want everything," I tell her softly. And I probably should have laid this out for her before. She likes rules and guidelines. "The same way that your 'yes' is 'yes' and your 'no' is 'yes.' If I say I want something, I want it. And if I say I *don't* want you to do something, I'm really saying I want you to do it."

Her lush mouth curves. "All right."

"And while we're at it, you don't need to come up with lies. If you want something, just say 'please don't' in front of it. If there's something I'm doing that you want me to continue doing, you tell me to stop—and I'll keep going. But I'll know if you really mean it, okay?"

Because she can't act worth a damn.

"Okay," she whispers huskily, then her tongue darts out to moisten her lips. "Please don't make me suck your big cock until you come."

Christ help me. My balls tighten as lust surges through my stiffened length, and my gut clenches with sheer need. But the desire isn't what feels like a punch to my chest, isn't the thing that staggers me. Instead it's the realization that this whole scenario she started is about punishing her with my cock—about what I'm doing to her—and yet within that scenario, Audrey's fantasy is pleasuring *me*. It's not just about fucking, though there's that, too. Instead it's similar to my fantasies, which aren't only about getting my nut off. They're usually about making her come over and over again, until she's so wrecked by orgasms that she's helpless to everything but her need for me.

If that's where she wants me, I'm not too far off. Except me being helpless to my need isn't going to leave me lying there, boneless and quivering, coming endlessly. Me being helpless to my need means losing all control.

But I'll hold on a bit longer, play this through.

I catch her chin in an unyielding grip, my thumb rolling past her soft bottom lip to meet the pearly barrier of her teeth. "Are you afraid of sucking my cock, baby? I bet you are. Because you know you'll love it. You'll love wrapping your lips around my shaft, love drinking down all my hot cum."

Eyes wide, she tries to shake her head, then flicks out her tongue to tease my thumb. "What about this, instead?"

Her lips close around the tip and she begins to suck.

Oh, fuck. It feels so damn good. Better than any thumb has a right to feel.

"That's good practice, baby. But it's not enough." Roughly I drag my waistband down, freeing the pulsating rod of my cock. "On your knees, Audrey."

Her breath shudders. She sinks down in front of me and hungrily stares at my erection.

The sight of her kneeling there already has me on the edge of coming. "You went down real easy, baby. I guess you really do want it."

"I don't want it. Please don't make me do this," she pleads, her gaze enraptured as I stroke the meaty length in my fist, as beads of pre-cum slide down the smooth head. "It's too big for me to take it all in my mouth."

There's no lie in that. "Yet you sure are looking at this cock like you're starving for it. Or maybe you think that if you make me come, I won't have anything left in me to fuck you with."

For an instant she hesitates, glancing up at me. Not certain if me coming now will end this.

I give her a mean smile. "You won't get so lucky, baby. I'll be hard again in minutes. But I'd love for you to try." If she does make me come, it'll take off the edge enough that I can punish her with my cock for as long as she needs. "I know you're hungry for it. Aren't you?"

Mouth pressed tight, she offers me another withering glare.

I laugh. "Maybe your icy stare frightens away other

men, but that look just makes my dick even harder. Now open up." My hand wrapped around the base of my cock, I tap the sticky tip against her mouth in a vulgar little kiss. "Suck me dry, and maybe it'll save you from having to take this big cock into your cunt, where I'll do so many goddamn filthy things to you with it."

"I don't want your cock in my pussy *or* in my mouth! But I suppose…if this might save me…" Tentatively she extends her tongue, watching me with a ravenous gaze as her breath whispers over the wet tip of my cock, followed by a slow, hesitant lick.

"That's right, baby." It's low and hoarse. "That feels real good. But if you want me to come, you better start sucking instead of licking."

With a moan, she takes the head into the wet heaven of her mouth and begins working that thick knob, bobbing her head. Teeth gritted against the urge to thrust, I watch her hungrily devour my cock. The fat tip fills her mouth up, stretching her lips, but I know she can take a few inches of my shaft before she starts choking. She did last night.

"Take me deeper," I demand roughly. "Or do I have to force you to take it?"

She breaks away, gasping, "Please don't."

Ruthlessly, I grab that messy bun again. She whimpers as I shove my swollen erection past her parted lips, her tongue massaging the underside of my shaft as I push deeper, stopping when I know I've hit her limit.

My eyes damn near roll back in my head when she starts moaning and sucking, her slender hands coming up to stroke what she can't get into her mouth, and there's not a goddamn thing here that's pretend. Audrey's doing everything she can to make me come, as if it's a personal challenge now—and my wife likes to win.

She's going to. A tortured groan reverberates through my chest when I can focus again, because she's looking straight into my eyes, watching everything she's doing to me. And the sounds she's making, holy hell. Moaning thirstily, then gasping and gulping for breath before slurping her way down my cock again. She's a fuckable fantasy come to life, kneeling before me with her plush lips wrapped around my dick and her gorgeous hair a disheveled wreck from me pulling on it this way and that. The torn white shirt hangs off her right shoulder, exposing her breasts, which gently bounce in rhythm to the movement of her head.

"Look at your nipples, baby," I rasp out, barely hanging on to this role I'm supposed to be playing. Barely hanging on to anything. Not control, not sanity. Nothing except her hair. "They're even stiffer and redder than when I was sucking on them. I bet your pussy's just aching for me to fuck it. Because no matter what you claim, you love this."

Even as her sultry moan hums along my shaft, she gives me that withering stare again. And it's too fucking much. Her hot mouth around my cock, ice shooting from her beautiful eyes.

My fingers convulsively clench in her hair and I hold her in place for the cum barreling down my pulsing length and spilling onto her tongue. Then her throat starts working as she swallows, each undulation of her tongue pulling me deeper, drawing out my orgasm. I'm lightheaded when it ends, as if I emptied more than my seed into her mouth. As if my whole goddamn soul went with it.

"Fuck." I stagger back a step, so drained that for a second I wonder whether my erection really will have trouble recovering. Then I get a look at the way Audrey's triumphantly licking her lips as she elegantly rises to her feet, and my cock starts twitching to life again. It'll need a couple of minutes. But I'll keep good and busy until then.

Especially after she tosses at me, "You got what you wanted! Please don't ever touch me again."

I pitch my voice dangerously low. "You still don't want me to touch you? Still won't admit how hot your pussy gets?"

"No," she says, raising her chin haughtily. "Because it doesn't. Now excuse me while I go and wash the taste of you out of my mouth."

Christ, she's so damn adorable, pretending to flounce away on a path that takes her right past me. But her eyes are bright and sparkling, and delighted laughter fills her scream when I snag my left arm around her waist and drag her full-length against me. Her soft breasts flatten against my chest before she pushes against my shoulders, leveraging her upper body backward but getting nowhere thanks to the iron grip I have on her waist.

Her body goes utterly still the instant she feels the fingers of my right hand trailing up her thigh. "Oh no," she gasps and widens her stance eagerly, offering easy access. "Please don't touch my pussy! I'm so soft and delicate there. And your hands are so rough and dirty!"

"I'll do as I damn well please. So you better not close your legs and try to keep me out."

"I better not…? Oh." Her thighs snap together and she crows, "You're too late!"

Her face is flushed with lust and laughter, and she looks so pleased with herself. God, this woman. I want to give her everything.

But especially give her what she wants. Gruffly I tell her, "You think I don't know why you're keeping me out? Because your pussy will expose what a liar you are. It's soaked, isn't it?"

"No," she moans, moving restlessly as my fingers continue toward the tight V of her clenched thighs.

"Then I suppose it won't matter if I rub your little clit, either? Does it feel good when I touch you like this?"

With the blunt pad of my middle finger, I tease the slick nub at the apex of her sex. Her breath stutters, her lips parting, her eyelids fluttering.

"Does it feel good, baby?"

"Stop it," she whispers helplessly and I circle her clit faster and harder, her hands clenching on my arms. "I don't like it."

"Your pussy likes it. You've got it closed up tight but my finger's already wetter than when I started. Should I try to get in deeper and see how drenched it is?"

"No." It comes out as a thin, needy cry. "Don't."

I do. And holy fuck, she's so goddamn hot and wet as I work my thick finger farther into her slit and press into her narrow channel. She's moaning *no please no* the whole time, her head rolling from side to side, her thigh muscles letting up on the pressure locking her legs together and her hips lifting as if to push me in deeper.

"Fuck, you're so tight," I growl as her inner walls clamp down on my invading finger. "Do you still have a cherry in here, baby? Did I marry a virgin?"

Eyes glazed with pleasure, she shakes her head.

"So you let someone else touch this delicate pussy? Maybe some rich businessman with soft hands?"

Those icy eyes clear and she snaps, "No!"

That was a real *no*. She doesn't like me going in that direction.

I don't like it much, either. "Someone like me, then? A mechanic with dirty, callused hands and a big cock? Did you let him break in your virgin cunt and pump a load of cum inside you?"

"Yes," she says breathily, softening again. "Because I love him. He's so sweet and wonderful to me."

That sweet and wonderful bastard has two thick fingers screwing into her pussy, his thumb is rubbing her hot little clit, and he's fucking dying for a taste of both. Snarling, I tell her, "You can forget about that asshole. You've got me for a husband now, and it's my cock you crave. I'm the only one you want."

"No," she cries out softly, her hips starting to twitch erratically.

"You're lying to me," I grit out between clenched teeth. "And if you lie to me, I'll have to punish you for it. Do you know what happens to good little rich girls who lie? They get a rough, nasty fuck."

Her cunt constricts around my fingers. "Oh my god. No, *please*."

So wet. So hot. "You're going to come, aren't you? You say you don't want my touch but you're about to come all over my hand."

She shakes her head wildly, moaning, "No, no, no. Stop making me come, stop making me come—"

Then looks completely bewildered when I do. With confusion in her eyes she stares up at me, biting her lip against the desperate frustration still twisting through her hips, a frantic whine sounding low in her throat.

I suck her juices off my fingers, hungry for a deeper taste, but this is already a little mean. She's right on the edge, hurting. She loves my mouth, but giving her anything except the hard fuck I just promised would be cruel.

Loosening my hold on her, I stroke my erection with the wetness still coating my palm. "After all that lying, you think I'll let you come on anything but my cock? And you better not try to get away, baby, or your punishment will be a lot worse when I catch you."

It takes a second for my meaning to sink in, and another second before she's got her legs steady enough to make a break for it. Then she shoves at me, and this time I let her push me back a step. Free of my grip, she races toward the Christmas tree, jumping on top of an oversized leather ottoman as she goes—just like she jumped on her bed one time, I remember. Claiming the high ground. Turning, she checks to see how close I am. Indecision wars on her beautiful face for an instant. Because my Audrey loves to win. But she also wants to be caught. And I'm real damn curious about how long she'll try to evade me.

Only about two seconds. Because as I approach the ottoman, she leaps off in the other direction, speeds around a couch, then abruptly flings herself facedown over the cushioned arm, her butt in the air and her fuzzy socks flailing.

"Oh no!" she wails. "I tripped! Now you'll catch me and punish me!"

And she fucking kills me. In every way, she kills me. I've never seen anything so damn adorable or funny or sweet, and I might have fallen to the floor laughing if that long shirt hadn't also slid up over her ass, and if her awkward position wasn't teasing me with a glimpse of wet, pink pussy. So instead of laughing, instead of falling, my aching cock drags me into place behind her. She's hanging over the couch's arm with her elbows braced on a seat cushion, her blonde hair falling out of her bun in a wild, curling tangle. Her ass is positioned perfectly, tilted up at just the right angle for a hard fuck into her cunt, and her feet don't touch the floor. Which means she won't be able to get any leverage once I've put weight on her.

Her quivering body goes utterly still as I press the thick head of my cock to her small opening. "Oh please no," she whispers, her voice full of need. "I don't want you to—"

Fill her. So deep. She cries out as one powerful thrust takes me home. And that's where I stay for an endless moment, wrapped in a paradise of snug, wet heat. Fuck. Teeth gritted, I grind into her before drawing back, her slick inner walls clutching tight and trying to suck me in.

"Oh my god," Audrey gasps. She's come up on her hands, holding herself up straight-armed and with her spine bowed in a deep arch. "Please don't do that again."

"I intend to do it a thousand fucking times." I give her a shallow thrust before pulling almost all the way out, then take her hips in a firm hold. "Don't struggle."

Immediately she begins to wriggle her ass, fighting my grip, and a groan rips from my chest as all that motion works her swollen channel up and down my shaft. I shove in to the hilt, and she falls forward with a little scream, then buries her moan in the cushion.

I grind into her again, deep and slow. "Christ, you're so fucking wet. You love my big cock stretching your hot little pussy, don't you?"

"I don't love it," is her muffled cry. "I don't."

"There you go lying again. So you know what happens now, baby?" I tell her hoarsely. "I'm going to fuck your pussy raw."

Her cunt clamps down on my cock so fucking hard that stars burst behind my eyes. Suddenly she goes wild, coming up on her hands again, fighting against my grip, begging, "No, no, no please *please* don't fuck me like you want me more than anything."

Like I want her more than anything. And I remember the hopeful way she said this before. Fucking her pussy raw. But it was never about the fucking. It was about someone wanting her. The ice queen who isn't icy at all, but who simply doesn't show emotion in a typical way. This fantasy isn't about her pretending to be cold and not wanting me, then being fucked as punishment. It's about someone seeing through the ice to the flame within, about someone wanting that inner flame so desperately that they'd do anything to have her.

Just like I would.

It's with only a bare thread of control left that I curl my fingers around the front of her throat and bend over to growl into her ear, "I *do* want you that much, Audrey Motherfuckin' Clarke. More than any other goddamn thing in the world. You understand?"

Her breath coming in sobbing pants, she nods. "Yes, Caleb. *Please.*"

"Anything you need, baby." A rough lick of my tongue up the side of her neck makes her shiver uncontrollably, then I release her. She falls forward onto the cushion again while I dig my fingers into her hips and unleash the beast that's been clawing me up from the second I met her. Rabid lust that sinks its teeth deeper into me with every savage thrust. Her pussy seizes up on the fourth stroke, her scream muffled by the cushion, her sock-covered heels drumming my lower back. Every time before, I stopped and held myself deep inside her while she orgasmed, savored the convulsions of her sweet flesh over every inch of my cock, but now I fuck my way through her clenching sheath with bone-rattling jerks of my hips.

I need to feel her come again. Ruthlessly I grip her quivering thigh and push her left leg forward, with her knee pressed against the back of the couch and giving me a better angle to ram deep, the thick curve of my erection powering over the spot in the front wall of her cunt that gets her off every damn time. Audrey cries out, her hips hitching up and down, her pussy nearly strangling my shaft. Grunting, I fuck her harder.

Blistering heat roils the length of my spine, sparks

firing at the base of my cock as the wet sounds of our fucking and the unadulterated pleasure of her moans echo through the room. There are words mixed in, gasps of *love you* and *please* and *like that oh god just like that.* Then her head jerks forward, her back arches and she comes all at once, a liquid rush of clenching heat that threatens to drag me along into oblivion.

But I'm not done. My arm beneath her waist, I haul her up and swing her over toward the oversized ottoman. Her body hangs like a rag doll's, head lolling, her pussy still holding my cock in its voluptuous grip. She moans a little protest as I pull out and lay her back on the smooth leather, but the orgasm wiped her out and she doesn't have much protest left. Not much of anything left, but I want so goddamn much from her.

She moans as my mouth closes over her clit. Because she's not coming again just on my cock, I damn well know that. But I'm not fucking her raw unless she's along for the ride with me.

And she's so sensitive, so hot, it barely takes any time to get her going again. Barely any time before I'm shoving her knees up to her shoulders and thrusting deep, her pussy soft and slick, clutching my thick length in its hot, greedy grip.

She pushes her fingers into my hair and pulls me down for a kiss, a tangle of breath and tongues and teeth that becomes impossible to keep as I begin to thrust. But she holds me close and I tell her every filthy thought

I've ever had about her, spill in words every drop of cum that my fist ever produced while I was imagining her face, her pussy, her lips, her sweetness, her kiss. I confess every dirty thing I want to do to her now and in the future, every reverent thing, hard and slow and fast and easy, all of it so damn perfect because I want her so bad and because she'll be with me.

And this time when the orgasm rolls through her, lifting her body beneath mine with her head tilted back on a silent scream, I go over with her, pumping into her clenching depths until there's nothing left.

Nothing except for another kiss, and the years that stretch ahead of us. I claim her lips a final time, a slow and sweet taste of my beautiful wife, before pulling away. We're a sweaty tangle of legs and arms, with the remains of her shirt still buttoned around her waist. Her head is at the edge of the ottoman, her ass at the opposite edge, a puddle of cum and juices beneath her—and we aren't where we started out. The ottoman was sitting in the center of the living room but I fucked it across the floor, and we're parked now in front of the Christmas tree.

Probably for the best, since Audrey is blissed out and boneless. As often as I'll be fucking her, I'll need to add more naps to the schedule.

But there's something else on the schedule next. After finding my pajama pants, I use her ruined shirt to mop up her inner thighs and the leather beneath her. All she's wearing now is one fuzzy sock—I find the other beneath the couch and slip it over her ridiculously dainty foot. Then I spread her legs, because I want to kiss her but don't want that dreamy smile on her lips to disappear. And it's an utterly decadent treat to kiss my wife's creamy pussy beside the Christmas tree, to kiss her slow and deep, and to know her soft sighs of pleasure are just for me.

That dreamy smile is still there when I finish, her eyes glittering with joy and love as she looks down at me. "Merry Christmas, Caleb," she says softly.

"Merry Christmas, baby." I rise up over her, swiftly kiss her lips. "Ready to open presents?"

Anticipation lights her face and she nods. "Let me grab a robe and—"

"No need." I turn toward the tree and root through the stacks of gifts. The clumsily wrapped ones are mine, so they're easy to find. "I've got this for you."

She's sitting up on the ottoman now, naked except for those socks and with her legs crisscrossed. Eagerly she takes the gift, her "Thank you," full of warmth and surprise as she turns the floppy rectangle over in her hands. "What is it?"

"Open it."

And no lie, I'm a little nervous as she does, because what the fuck do you get a woman like Audrey? If something makes her happy, she buys it. And she could easily buy something like what I'm giving her—she might have a thousand of them in her closet already—but I'm hoping this one will be a little more special.

Her lips part as she carefully peels back the edge of the wrapping paper. "Oh. Oh, *Caleb*. Is this the red flannel you always wear?"

"Yeah, baby." Just a regular old flannel that's been worn and washed many times over. But she told me once it looked so soft, and I've caught her petting it a few times.

She brings it to her face and inhales, her eyes closing. "It smells like you, too." All at once she's unfolding it, slipping her arms into the sleeves. Her eyes are shining with tears as she looks at me. "Thank you so much. I love your gift. It's the best thing I've ever received. You're so sweet and wonderful to me."

"It's just a shirt, baby," I tell her, all fucking choked up, because I know she truly means all that and I didn't really expect more than maybe a pleased smile and for her to wear it right away. But she shakes her head, so I shut up and hold out my second gift. "Here's the other thing."

Just a small box, so I'm guessing she thinks that it's jewelry. And it is a ring, I suppose. Not for her to wear, though.

With a soft gasp, she pulls out the key ring. "Is this…?"

"To the Corvette? Yeah."

"But you said—"

"I told you I wasn't going to take money for it. And

it might be a while before you can actually drive it any-where, because I've still got a lot of work to do before it's ready. But maybe there'll be more robot cars around by then, anyway."

With a laugh, she rocks forward and kisses me. "I love it. Thank you. And this just gives me even more reason to invest in self-driving car technology. Now it's my turn!"

Clambering off the ottoman, she snags a thin present wrapped in gold paper. "The first!"

I take it, eyeing the other gifts. "Are these all…?"

"Wedding gifts." Smiling, she plops down on the leather again. "We can open them over the course of the week instead of today."

"Sounds good." I tear open the gold paper—and find a manila envelope. "What's this?"

"Open it." She looks almost nervous, worrying her bottom lip between her teeth as I open the envelope. "I know you don't like me to spend money on you, and this isn't *really* spending money, but something I wanted to set up for you, so that you can spend *your* money."

"Baby…" I don't even know what to fucking say. It's paperwork to establish a charity—The Nicole Moore Foundation.

"Because I know you intend to give your inheritance away," she continues softly. "And you can still do that—a one-time donation to whatever charity you like. Or I can help you establish this. Then you put your inheritance into it and let me take care of the investments, and over the years you can give away that same amount many, many times over, and all in your mother's name."

Oh fuck. My eyes are suddenly stinging, my throat clogged with emotion. I swallow hard, putting the paperwork aside and clasping her face in my hands. "I love you so fucking much, Audrey," I tell her hoarsely. "And, yeah. We'll do that."

She smiles, so bright and beautiful. "I'm so glad. We'll establish the Phoenix House and use that money for so many wonderful things, Caleb. You'll see."

"I believe it." I've never believed in anything like I believe in her. "Thank you, baby."

She kisses me, then pulls back—this time with the impish smile that I know and love so well, the one that says she's about to do something fun. "And one other thing."

"I'm ready." Barely. My emotions are a ragged mess after that last gift.

In her fuzzy socks and flannel shirt, she scoots around the tree and hauls out a gold-wrapped slab—then nearly staggers under the weight. I lunge forward to steady her.

"Oh wow," she exclaims, laughing and gratefully handing it over to me. "I didn't realize it would be so heavy."

She's not kidding, though it's more awkward than heavy. When I saw it under the tree, it looked like a painting or something similar—like a big wrapped canvas. But it's got the heft of solid wood.

Her eyes are sparkling and she claps her hands together, watching as I set it down and start tearing at the wrapping, exposing a smooth slab of oak beneath. "I asked Patrick to make it for me."

That explains the wood. Though I still can't figure out what the hell…? Letters are carved into the face of it and—

"Oh shit." A laugh busts out of me before I even reveal the entire thing.

It's a sign. A giant business sign, with WYNDHAM TRASH in huge letters.

"I already own a recycling center if you want it!" Audrey exclaims, bouncing up and down in her excitement. "We just have to change the name!"

She really would, too. Laughing, I pull her close and kiss her hard. "No need for that, baby. This sign is enough."

"You like it?"

"Fucking love it." I look it over again, my heart so swollen it feels about ready to burst through my chest.

What I'm *not* feeling…is anger, or resentment, or any of the shit that's eaten me up for so long. I still hate the Wyndhams. That won't ever go away, I bet. But any desire to do anything more to them is gone. Over with. I've barely thought about them since meeting Audrey, and all the poison that was left in me disappeared after the night at their mansion. So going forward, I don't want to give them any more room in my head or in my heart. Not even enough room for spite.

But this sign is pretty fucking amazing. Too amazing to go to waste. "What I'll do is hang it up in your garage—*our* garage," I tell her. Because that's where my other business will be, restoring cars. "And seeing this sign up on the wall will make me laugh every time I look at it."

"Me, too," she grins, then suddenly bites her lip again, clutching her fist to her chest. "I feel so full right now. It almost hurts, how full."

"I know, baby. I do, too." I cup her face in my hands, searching her beautiful eyes. "You know what it is?"

"How much I love you," she whispers.

"That, too." With my thumbs, I gently caress her cheeks. "But it's also the new world we're building together, right here between us. It's a hell of a lot to take in."

She nods solemnly. "Like your cock is."

A laugh shakes through me. "Yeah, baby. But you managed that."

"I did." Her smile is wide and she reaches up, her fingers tracing my lips—tracing my smile, I realize. "I have a proposal for you, Caleb Moore."

"Do you?"

"Mmm-hmmm. What do you say to the thought of trying to make our new world even bigger? Because I'm not quite ready for it yet…but maybe in a year or so, I can toss my birth control and—"

My mouth interrupts the rest. And I'm kissing her too hard to say it right away.

But my answer is yes.

CALEB

FIVE YEARS LATER

T WAS THE NIGHT BEFORE CHRISTMAS, WHEN ALL *through the house*

Not a creature was stirring, not even a mouse;
The stockings were hung by the chimney with care,
In hopes that St. Nicholas soon would be there;
The children were nestled all snug in their beds;
While visions of sugar-plums danced in their heads…"
Our children are snuggled in bed, too—with Audrey between them as she reads from the oversized book on her lap. By the look of it, they're almost out. Three-year-old William's chubby cheek is half-smushed against

Audrey's shoulder, his head slowly dipping forward, and a line of drool darkens the silk sleeve of Audrey's dress. On her other side is Nicole, his older sister by all of six minutes, and whose thick brown lashes are drifting downward even as I watch from the bedroom doorway.

Audrey glances up, never pausing in her gentle recitation, but giving me a clear signal with her eyes: *Get out of here before they see you standing there and get excited all over again.*

I grin and blow her a kiss, but get the hell out of there as commanded. Our kids are little miracles, but bedtime is always a challenge. Most nights, that doesn't matter so much. If they keep us awake half the night, we adjust our schedules. But this is Christmas Eve, and I want to spend my anniversary night with my wife.

While waiting for her, I busy myself bringing presents up from the garage, where we've been hiding them from the kids. It's the first Christmas that we haven't spent at the lodge, though we're heading up to the cabin right after Christmas. But the kids took part in a preschool play today—with William dressed up as a lamb and Nicole pretending to be a rabbit—and we wouldn't have missed it for the whole fucking world. Neither had lines, but they were dedicated to their roles. We've had a rabbit and a lamb running around the house for a month.

I'm not surprised that when Audrey makes her way downstairs, the silk dress she wore to the play has been exchanged for her long flannel shirt—my old shirt that she makes me wear now and again so it smells like me—and fuzzy socks.

Pride fills her voice. "They're already better actors than me!" she announces.

I laugh and pull her close, wrapping my arms around her. "You won't be so glad about that when they're fifteen and trying to convince us that they really, *really* are only going to the library to study."

She blinks. "You think they'll be lying? I was always in a library at fifteen."

"Yes, but we've already agreed that they take after me." Nuzzling her pale hair, I begin to sway with her. It's Christmas Eve, the anniversary of our wedding, and I'm going to dance with my wife. "How many times did you have to read that poem to them?"

"Five."

And even though they fell asleep near the beginning of the fifth time, she would have finished it before leaving them. Audrey couldn't not finish. "You're such a good mom, baby."

"Do you really think so?" There's a slight catch in her voice.

"I know so, Audrey. Our kids are as lucky as I was—we all have amazing mothers."

Her breath shudders and she buries her face in my chest. I hold her close, letting her work through whatever emotion is hitting her so hard—though I can guess. Her own parents did a real fucking number on her, and although she's mostly dealt with it all, now and again an insecurity creeps up on her.

But she's the best damn mother. And has been from the beginning. Knowing how she fears pain, I suggested that we could adopt instead of getting her pregnant—but Audrey decided that she wanted to do it. So she did. And we had a whole lot of discussions with her doctors about pain management before and after, yet sheer panic still hit her a couple of times leading up to the birth.

That's why we stopped after the twins. Not because she didn't want to go through it again. I'm the one who can't.

But two is a good number. Just like zero would have been. Just like a thousand could be. As long as she's with me, the world we've made together will always be exactly the right size.

And she's changed my world in ways that I hadn't expected. Like quitting my job at the auto shop not long before the kids were born. Partially to spend more time with them—we both cut down our working hours, but I cut mine way back—and partially because Audrey's more of an inspiration than she knows. Living with her, seeing the way she approaches work and pursues what makes her happy, made me realize how fucking stupid working at my job was. Because I enjoyed it, but I didn't love it. And I'm not in a situation where I needed that job just to eat or put a roof over my head. So I saved up what I didn't spend on rent that first year, and put it all back into my remodeling business. Which is still small and still slow, but between my work and my kids and my wife, I spend every minute doing what I love doing, and being with the people I love being with. Not everyone is this lucky. Hell, very few people are this lucky. So I won't squander what I've been given.

And I've been given everything.

After a few minutes, Audrey softens against me. "I love you, Caleb."

"I love you, too, baby." I press a kiss to her silky hair. "You're all right?"

She nods. "Yes," she whispers. "You?"

I truly couldn't be better. "Hell yes. The kids are asleep, I'm holding the most incredible woman in the world in my arms—all because five years ago, she married me. And because in about five more minutes, I intend to be deep inside her pussy."

"In five minutes?" There's a smile in her voice—and a husky edge that tells me five minutes might be too long.

"I want to finish dancing with you first." I bend my head to tease her lips. "Why? Are your panties wet?"

"No," she says.

She's not lying. But her panties are always wet when I'm dancing with her. Which means one thing—and that one thing sends a surge of lust the length of my erection, hardening the thick flesh to steel.

"You're not wearing any panties, are you?"

Her head tilts back and she gives me an impish little

grin. "Nope."

Fuck. Well, there's only one solution for it. Hauling her up against my chest, I get her long legs wrapped around me, and we both groan as I slide deep, deep. Five years, and the wonder and pleasure of being this close to her never lessens. Instead it simply grows. Just like my love for her does. Five years ago, I gave her all the love I had. But she keeps filling my heart up with more love to give.

So I kiss her while she holds me tight inside her, and we keep dancing. Because tomorrow might be Christmas, but Audrey's in my arms, making love to me—so I've already got the greatest gift a man could ever receive.

❊ END ❊

HAPPY HOLIDAYS!

I hope you loved The Wedding Night Before Christmas! If you're looking for more contemporary holiday romances with discreet covers, don't miss my two-in-one special edition of Secret Santa & All He Wants For Christmas.

If you enjoy a bit of suspense in your holiday reads, keep an eye out for Only One Bed, coming in Winter 2022.

And for all you fantasy romance lovers out there, don't miss The Midwinter Bride, available now with a new discreet cover.

You can find more information and links at my website: katiwilde.com.

Until next year!

—Kati

FIND KATI

Website: katiwilde.com

Twitter: @katiwilde

Facebook: authorkatiwilde

Instagram: authorkatiwilde

WANT TO KNOW WHEN KATI HAS A NEW RELEASE?

Check out any of the sites above, or sign up for Kati's spam-free email newsletter at:

katiwilde.com/newsletter

www.ingramcontent.com/pod-product-compliance
Lightning Source LLC
Chambersburg PA
CBHW021803110726
47902CB00006B/1632